D0048938

Lurlene McDaniel

The End of Forever

TWO NOVELS
Somewhere Between Life and Death
Time to Let Go

Published by Laurel-Leaf
an imprint of Random House Children's Books
a division of Random House, Inc.
New York

This edition contains the complete and unabridged texts of the
original editions. This omnibus was originally published in
separate volumes under the titles *Somewhere Between Life and
Death,* copyright © 1990 by Lurlene McDaniel, and *Time to Let Go,*
copyright © 1990 by Lurlene McDaniel.

www.randomhouse.com/teens
Educators and librarians, for a variety of teaching tools,
visit us at www.randomhouse.com/teachers

RL: 5.2
ISBN: 978-0-375-84170-5
July 2007
Printed in the United States of America
10 9 8 7 6 5 4 3 2

CONTENTS

Somewhere Between
Life and Death

This book is dedicated to the memory of Kaitlyn Arquette, September 18, 1970–July 17, 1989—a flower whose season was all too brief—and to her family, who will treasure her memory forever.

. . .

I would like to express my thanks to Erlanger Medical Center, Chattanooga, Tennessee, and to Dr. Reggie McLelland of Covenant College.

. . .

To every thing there is a season, and a time to every purpose under heaven: A time to be born, and a time to die . . .   —ECCLESIASTES 3:1–2 (KJV)

Chapter One

~~~

"Where's Amy?"

"Late. As usual." Erin Bennett didn't even try to hide her annoyance.

Her best friend, Shara Perez, heaved a sigh and sprawled across a bench in the deserted studio. "Honestly, Erin, your sister's gonna be late to her own funeral."

"Not so," Erin muttered, adjusting her leotard and stretching her right leg over her head. "*I'll* be in charge of taking her to her funeral, so I know she'll be on time for that."

Shara giggled. "Now what do you suppose Freud would say about that? Maybe you really wish you were an only child, like me."

Erin rolled her eyes, hating to admit that she'd often wished that very thing. And with only fifteen months between her and her sister, Erin realized that she'd never had the luxury of being the one-and-only. "I just think Amy's being a pain," she said. "She knows how much this dance number means to me."

"Come on, Erin. You know Amy's not like that. She never forgets anything on *purpose*."

Erin began to pirouette across the polished dance

floor in wide, sweeping circles. She forced herself to concentrate on her form instead of her anger toward her kid sister. She'd have thought that being a sophomore at Briarwood School for Young Women this year would have matured Amy. Instead, Erin found herself constantly making excuses for her, covering for her tardiness and irresponsible attitude. It was embarrassing, but Erin couldn't seem to stop. Amy always managed to rope her in and get her own way, while still being sweet, outgoing, and likable.

As a junior and the president of the Terpsicord Dance Troupe at Briarwood, Erin felt she had a reputation to maintain among her peers. Amy's lack of seriousness really annoyed her, but she didn't know what to do about it.

The door to the dance studio flew open. "Am I late?" Amy called as she skidded across the oak floor.

Erin stopped spinning, caught her breath, and walked over to where Amy stood, all big blue-eyed innocence. "Three-fifteen, Amy. I said 'Be here by three-fifteen because we have to knock off by four today.' Shara made it on time. I made it on time. But you? Well, as usual we're both standing around waiting for Amy. And you're so late that we're not going to get any serious rehearsing done today. The recital's in March—only four weeks from now." Erin knew she was wasting valuable time, but she was determined not to let Amy off too easily.

"Only four weeks? Yikes! Time's slipping by all right, but just wait till you see what I've got."

"This had better be good, Amy. Ms. Thornton is

counting on the three of us to make this number the high point of the show. I'm beginning to wish I'd never asked you to do the dramatic readings."

"Oh, come on. When I'm a famous actress, you'll look back on this and laugh. Here, take a look at this." She handed Erin a large leather-bound book. "Won't it be perfect on the podium for me to read from? I won't have to use that dorky library book. I can just tuck copies of the readings inside. It'll look so much more elegant, don't you think?"

Erin eyed the old leather-embossed volume, struggling inwardly to stay angry. She had to admit that Amy was right. The book would be so much nicer and would really contribute to the overall effect. "Where'd you get it?"

"It's Travis's grandmother's."

Travis. The name alone made Erin's pulse skip a beat. "Did he loan it to you just for the recital?" She stroked the rich leather cover imagining that Travis had held it.

"Sure."

Erin felt her resolve weakening. Her sister was irrepressible, and no one could stay mad at her for long. That's probably why she attracted friends so easily—as well as the undivided attention of Berkshire Prep's cutest senior, Travis Sinclair.

"It's a nice touch," Erin admitted. Amy grinned and bobbed on the balls of her feet. "But I really need you to be on time," she added sternly, not wanting Amy to think she was off the hook entirely.

"So what are we waiting for? Let's get started."

Erin signaled Shara, who started the music on a cassette player and began to sing. Soon she was immersed in the dance, and once she was lost in her art, nothing else existed. Not even her aggravation with Amy.

"Erin! Come help me get dinner on the table," Mrs. Bennett called.

Erin wandered into the kitchen. "I thought it was Amy's turn to help with dinner tonight," she said. "Where is Amy, anyway?"

"She's working on a history paper that's due tomorrow, and I'm running behind." Her mother rattled pots and pans. "Honestly, I don't know why I ever thought owning my own boutique was a good idea. Customers are so scarce that I should just shut down the place until spring comes."

"Doing a paper! What about *my* homework?"

"Your father and I have the faculty party tonight at Briarwood. I didn't think I'd *ever* get out of the store. Thank goodness Inez could stay until nine and close the place up." She paused from her task of measuring water for rice and pinned Erin with a glance. "You *are* working this Saturday, aren't you? I'm counting on you to hold the fort all day since neither Inez nor I can come in."

Erin almost exploded. "But it's Amy's turn to work. I promised Ms. Thornton I'd help the freshmen dancers for the Terpsicord recital. And speaking of the dance recital, Amy was late again today for our rehearsal. We're never going to get it together for the show if she can't show up on time for practices."

"You've got plenty of time before the show," Mrs. Bennett said. "Besides, I think I gave Amy permission to go do something with the Drama Club on Saturday. Some car wash, I think."

"But it's her turn to work! Just like it's her turn to do dinner."

"Amy's filled in for you plenty of times, Erin. All last week in fact, while you took those extra dance classes."

"But I traded with her two weeks ago so that I'd have last week free."

"Erin, I really don't have time to quibble over how you and Amy keep scorecards over chores. I need help *now*. You know how your father hates to be late. And don't forget, if he wasn't on the faculty at Briarwood, we'd never be able to afford to send you girls there."

Erin held her breath and counted to ten. She didn't have to be reminded that she wasn't in the same league as the rest of the school body, which included Tampa's richest and most socially elite families. Nor was it easy having her sister *and* father at the same school with her. Erin was grateful that he taught computer science, which wasn't a part of her liberal-arts curriculum, so their paths had never crossed in the classroom. Perhaps that was another reason why Amy irked her. It never seemed to bother *her* that they were different from the other girls.

"Erin?" Mrs. Bennett said. "Are you going to stand there staring into space all evening?"

Erin started. "All right, I'll help tonight," she grumbled. "But it really *is* Amy's turn, and I swear this is the last time I get roped into doing *her* chores. You let Amy get away with murder."

"Don't be so dramatic." Mrs. Bennett paused from chopping vegetables. "You know how it is with Amy. Sometimes it seems as if we let her get away with too much; but Erin, you've always been the dependable one. I can always count on you."

"Thanks," Erin muttered, not feeling at all as if she'd been complimented.

Later, sitting at the dinner table, Amy entertained them all with stories about her day at school, and Erin found it impossible to stay mad. Amy *did* have a dramatic streak, and she smiled at Amy's accurate imitation of Miss Hutton's high-pitched nasal voice. "'Miss Bennett,'" Amy mimicked, telling a story on herself. "'If we are going to read Edna St. Vincent Millay aloud, it would behoove us to have read her poetry silently first, now wouldn't it?'"

Mr. Bennett chuckled deeply. "That's exactly how she sounds at faculty meetings too."

"You two are awful," Mrs. Bennett said. "She's just a lonely woman whose whole life is wrapped up in that school and you kids."

"She does donate a lot of her time to charity work," Amy said. "And I'm not knocking her; I just think she's funny."

Erin half listened to the rest of the dinner conversation. She wished she could make her parents laugh the way Amy could. Why couldn't she be less serious about school, her dancing, her whole life? Why did she always feel so out of sync? She looked across the table at Amy. How could two such different people come from the same family? How could two such different individuals coexist in the same house until the day Erin would leave for college?

Erin began to count the days until she would be on her own and free of her pain-in-the-neck, easygoing sister, Amy.

Chapter Two

Later, when their parents had gone out and Erin was alone in her bedroom doing homework, Amy knocked on her door. "I'm busy," Erin announced.

"But I'm lonely."

"How can you be lonely with your radio going full blast? And didn't you just get off the phone?"

Amy cracked open the door and poked her head inside. "I had to tell Travis you were driving me in tomorrow for that—ugh—seven A.M. rehearsal."

"Don't you dare complain! If you were on time for afternoon rehearsals, this one wouldn't be necessary."

Amy stepped into Erin's room. "Don't gripe at me."

"Do you know I work out every morning before school starts?" Erin put her hands on her hips and stood in Amy's path. "Just think, I've stretched and danced for an hour before you even get to your homeroom."

"That's why you're a dancer and I'm into acting. Plays happen at night. Then you go home and sleep until noon."

Erin felt exasperated enough to shake Amy. "You're impossible. Now would you please leave? Unlike some people, I didn't get my work done earlier."

8

"Are you still mad about that?"

"And about working at the boutique Saturday—"

"Half a day," Amy interrupted. "That's all I'm asking, just one teensy, weensy half a day. The afternoon half. I'll do the morning because I know you're supposed to help Ms. Thornton—"

"No way," Erin was adamant.

Amy dropped dramatically to her knees and clasped her hands. "Oh please, *please*? I'll be your best friend."

Erin stepped around her, out the door, and headed down the hall. "Buzz off. I won't do it."

Amy started after her on her knees, her arms pumping at her sides. Erin refused to watch, because Amy looked so ridiculous, she was afraid she'd laugh and give in to her. "I mean it, Amy, leave me alone." Erin ducked inside Amy's bedroom to escape and stopped short.

Amy almost rammed into the back of her. "What's the matter?"

"Good grief, Amy. It looks like a survival camp in here." Erin stared in dismay at the upheaval. The bed was unmade, clothes hung from chairs and half-open drawers, even the bedside lamp. Papers and books were scattered about the floor.

"My goodness," Amy said mildly. "Maybe thieves broke in."

"How can you *live* like this?"

Amy flounced on her bed, sending pillows and clothes flying. "One of us is neat and orderly, and one of us isn't." She smiled innocently.

"It's nothing to brag about, you know."

Amy jumped off the bed and hauled Erin next to her in front of the mirror. "Look at us, Erin. You're tall, blond, and graceful, and I'm—well—short, round, and fully packed." She patted her hips.

Erin tried not to smile. "What's your point?"

"We're different, that's all. You got the looks, talent, and brains, and I got"— Amy tousled her shoulder-length curly dark hair—"dandruff."

Against her will Erin laughed. "All right, you win. You sure can wear a person down, Amy. I'll go in for you on Saturday. But this is positively, absolutely the last time I bail you out because you've overcommitted."

Amy smiled broadly and gave Erin a quick hug. Then she took a frizzy red clown's wig off her dresser and put it on her head. On her nose she stuck a fat, round red bulb. "What do you think?"

"You look like Bozo."

"Good. I told Miss Hutton I'd do a gig for the Children's Home at Easter."

"I thought you didn't like her."

"She's okay, but don't tell anybody I said so. I like doing crazy things like this and making people laugh. I know it's silly, and it's not half as important as your dancing, but it's me."

"Amy, my dancing is no more important than your acting. You'll be a great actress someday—*if* you ever get serious about life."

Amy gasped in horror. "Oh, I hope I *never* get serious. What would people think?"

"I've got to get back to my homework," Erin said, shaking her head in exasperation.

"Wait a minute." Still wearing the wig and nose, Amy dashed to her desk and picked up a packet of snapshots. "Did I show you these yet? They're the photos Travis and I took on Christmas Day at his house."

Erin tried to keep her expression blank as she sorted through them, but in truth she was tied in knots. Why did she have to be so attracted to him?

Amy leaned over her elbow. "That's the one of him kissing me under the mistletoe. His little brother took it, and I thought Travis was going to kill him."

Erin's heart ached, and she quickly handed the photos back to Amy. "They're nice."

"I don't know why Travis is interested in *me*," Amy mused. "I mean he's only the hottest thing at Berkshire Prep. I think every girl at Briarwood is in love with him."

"Not everyone," Erin said, looking away as she said it.

"Well, of course I didn't mean you. But a lot of them are. Cindy Pitzer for instance." Amy made a face. "She's been telling people she really likes him and that she's going after him."

"I wouldn't worry about it," Erin said. "*You're* the one he's dating."

"True," Amy said with a bright smile. She tossed the photos onto her dresser and turned toward Erin. "Oh, by the way, a couple of Travis's friends have asked me about you. If you ever want to double with us—"

"No," Erin interrupted sharply, too sharply, and Amy gave her a surprised look. "I mean, thanks but no thanks. Between school and dance classes, I haven't got time for dating. You know how much I want to go to Florida State, and the competition's stiff."

"But that's two years away."

"I have to concentrate on one thing at a time."

"Well, if you change your mind . . ."

"You'll be the first to know." Despite Amy's protests Erin returned to her room, but she found she couldn't get back into studying. She thought about Saturday and her promise to work for her sister. Why had she let Amy talk her into it? Why did she always give in to Amy's pleas? "Because she's just *Amy*," Erin explained to the empty room.

With a sense of vengeance, she quickly set her alarm clock for five-thirty, relishing the thought of dragging her sister out of bed for the early rehearsal. At least Amy would be on time for *something*.

On Saturday morning Erin poked through the racks of clothes in her mother's boutique while eyeing the clock. She'd been on duty an hour, and not one customer had stepped through the door. Outside the day looked bleak and blustery, and the parking lot for the small shopping center was nearly deserted. The cool, cloudy day meant there would be few who wanted their cars washed, so the Drama Club's fundraiser would probably be a flop. "Serves Amy right," she muttered.

Erin spied a bright red jumpsuit and impulsively

snatched it off the rack and dashed into a dressing room. She emerged and stood at the three-way mirror. The outfit made her look years older, more sophisticated. "Wow," she mumbled, hardly recognizing herself. She wondered if Travis would think she looked pretty. She closed her eyes and imagined that he was standing next to her.

"Not bad, Erin. You look terrific."

The voice startled Erin. Her eyes flew open wide. In the mirror she saw Travis Sinclair, and he was looking over her shoulder, straight into the glass, straight into her eyes.

Chapter Three

~~~

"Travis! I—uh—I didn't hear you come in."

"I know. I'm sorry if I scared you." He glanced around the deserted shop. "Where's Amy? She told me she was working today."

"She took off for the afternoon because of the Drama Club car wash."

Travis snapped his fingers. "Oh yeah, now I remember. She did tell me about it, along with a million other things. You know how Amy is—fastest mouth in the West." He grinned, and Erin's heart beat faster.

"The car wash is at the gas station near Briarwood."

"That's right. I guess I should drive by and get them to wash mine. Not that it needs washing, but if I don't take it, Amy will never get off my case."

Despite what Travis had said, Erin could tell by his tone how fond he was of her sister.

He picked a blouse off a rack and held it up. "Actually, Erin . . . there is something I wanted to ask you."

In spite of herself Erin felt her mouth go dry. "What's that?"

"Amy's birthday. It's two weeks away, and I'm kind of out of ideas for a present. Any suggestions?"

14

Erin sagged, suddenly aware of how tense she'd become. "What makes you think she gives her wish list to me?"

"I was just thinking that since you're her sister, you could help me pick something special, that's all. I don't care what it costs, just as long as Amy likes it."

"There's nothing you couldn't pick out that she wouldn't like, Travis, but I did see her going through this stuff last week. She found a sweater she was crazy about. Now, let's see . . . which one was it?" Actually, there hadn't been one, but Erin wanted an excuse to be with him.

Travis stood next to Erin, watching her hands push through the rack of clothing. "Hope you can find it," he mumbled.

"Ah, here it is." She held up a bright blue sweater for his inspection, grateful that she was familiar with Amy's tastes.

"Uh—it's real nice." He fingered it. "Soft too."

"It's got angora in it."

"What's that?"

"Rabbit fur."

"You sure she liked it?"

"Positive. But don't tell her I helped you pick it out. It would be better if she thinks you chose it on your own."

Travis nodded. "Fair enough. Can you gift wrap it?"

Erin rang up the sale and showed him an assortment of wrapping paper. "Which do you like best?"

Travis knit his brows and pondered. Erin noticed

15

how his wavy dark hair complemented his olive complexion and that his eyelashes were long and thick. "This one," he said. She fumbled with the paper, begging her hands to obey her will. He lounged against the counter as she worked.

"Amy talks about you a lot, Erin," Travis said. "All about what a great dancer you are."

"She exaggerates—she just wants to get out of those early-morning rehearsals."

"I guess you know her tricks," he said. "She really does think you're a terrific sister, Erin. You should hire her as a press agent for your dancing career."

"I'm going to college first," she told him, creating a large pink bow from a spool of satin ribbon. "Then I'll go after a professional dancing career. Once I get too old to dance professionally, I can still get a good job teaching dance like Ms. Thornton."

Travis shook his head. "You and Amy sure are different. You have the rest of your life all planned out, and Amy barely makes it from day to day. She just figures that things will work out her way."

"She's not serious enough. You know—single-minded. She can't say no to anybody if they ask her for a favor. So she spreads herself too thin." Suddenly Erin realized that what she was saying might be taken as criticism.

"That's one of the things I like about her," Travis countered. "She's not like other girls. She's never too busy to listen if you want to talk. And nothing's too crazy for her to try."

Erin thought of the clown wig and nose. She

didn't know many girls who'd have the guts to do that kind of spontaneous acting. She knew she wouldn't. Erin sighed, forced a big smile, and held out the neatly wrapped package. "All done."

"Hey, that looks good. Think she'll know I didn't wrap it?"

"I'll never tell," Erin said. When he took the gift, their hands brushed. She drew back quickly as static electricity snapped between them.

"I could say this was a shocking experience," Travis said.

"Don't," Erin said with a groan.

He crossed to the door and turned. "Thanks, Erin, for the help with the gift and the talk. You may be more like Amy than you think."

In an effort to hide her embarrassment, Erin rolled her eyes. "Please don't tell me that. I don't think the world's ready for two Amys." She watched him drive off, and her heart filled with yearning. More than ever she knew she cared about Travis Sinclair. And more than ever she realized that there was nothing she could do about it. Absolutely nothing.

Later at home Erin tried to do her homework, but fireworks from the den kept interrupting her concentration. She couldn't hear much, just the low rumble of her father's voice and an occasional outburst from Amy such as, "Daddy! You can't mean that!" and "That's not fair. I've already made plans," and "It's a stupid old paper!"

She heard doors slamming, Amy's feet running

up the hall, and another door slamming. Whatever ultimatum their father had delivered, Amy certainly hadn't talked him out of it. Erin felt a perverse sense of satisfaction and guilt. She warred with herself. "It's nothing she doesn't deserve. This whole house revolves around Amy. I'll just let her stew about it tonight and ask her about it in the morning."

But guilt won out. Erin sneaked down the hall to Amy's room and tapped on the door. "Can I come in?"

"Sure."

Amy was sniffing and hanging up the phone when Erin entered. The room was in its usual state of disaster. She eased onto the bed. "Bad, huh?"

"The worst." Amy twisted a tissue around her finger. "Daddy's grounded me for the entire weekend. And he says that if I don't finish my history paper by Monday, he won't let me take my driver's test on my birthday next Friday. He'll make me wait a whole month!" Her eyes filled with fresh tears. "Travis and I were supposed to go to a concert tomorrow night, and I just called and told him I couldn't go."

"Oh, Ames," Erin said, using her sister's nickname, "that's a drag."

"It sure is." Amy blew her nose. "Travis really wants to go, and I'm afraid if I don't go with him and Cindy Pitzer finds out, she might try to get him to take her. I couldn't stand the thought of him asking anyone else—especially Cindy." Amy wiped her eyes with her shirtsleeve. "So I came up with an alternate plan."

"Don't ask me to write your paper," Erin warned.

"And I won't cover for you if you try to sneak out your window either."

"I hadn't thought of that. . . ."

"Well don't think about it."

"No, I already talked about it with Travis, and he says it's okay with him if it's okay with you."

"What's okay?"

"I don't want him to go with another girl. And I don't want him to go alone since his buddies all have dates. So I need for him to go with somebody I can trust." Amy turned tear-stained, innocent blue eyes on Erin. "I told him *you'd* go with him."

The whole time Erin was getting ready for the concert, she kept telling herself that she'd done her best to talk Amy out of the idea. Yet deep in her heart, she knew she was glad she was going, and that she was more excited about it than anything she'd done in ages.

"You look super," Amy told her as Erin put the finishing touches on her makeup.

"Thanks."

"I'm jealous," Amy admitted in a small voice.

"Now, just a minute. This whole thing was your idea."

Amy scuffed her foot on the carpet in Erin's bedroom. "I know. But it still matters that you're going instead of me."

Erin kept applying mascara, forcing herself not to catch Amy's eye in the mirror. She was afraid that if

19

she did, Amy would see the truth there. "It's too late to change plans."

"I know." Amy sidled her another look. "I didn't expect you to look so pretty either."

Erin stopped the mascara wand in midair and turned from her vanity table. "Why, Amy? I've worn this outfit a hundred times before."

"Maybe so, but somehow tonight you look different . . . better . . . sort of *glowing*."

Erin felt her cheeks redden. "Don't be silly. I'm excited about the concert, that's all. How's the paper coming?"

Amy grimaced. "Fine, if you like researching the Crimean War. Too bad it's not out on video. I could watch it on the VCR and then write about it."

"Oh, Ames, you're impossible. Maybe when you're set to storm Broadway, someone will have written a play about it that you can star in. Then won't you be glad you read all about it?"

They both laughed. In the distance the doorbell sounded. "That's Travis," Amy said, jumping to her feet and rushing to the door. "Let me prepare him for the shock of someone actually ready to go out on time."

"Take your time. I won't hurry."

"Thanks, Erin. I really do mean it. I want you both to have a ball."

Alone, Erin began to feel guilty. "It's what Amy wants," she told her mirror image. "Travis likes Amy, and he's just taking me because he wants to see the concert." She was positive of those two things. But she made certain that her wheat-colored hair was perfectly combed and that she used an extra spritz of her best perfume before she left the room.

The concert music was too loud and the civic center smoky, and by the time Erin and Travis got back to the Bennett's house, Erin had a splitting headache. They had barely gotten in the door when Amy started firing questions at them. "How was it? Was it loud—I mean *really* loud? And who else did you see there? Don't spare any details."

Travis gave her a hug and a smile, the first genuine smile Erin had seen on his face that evening. "Awesome," he told Amy.

Erin felt slighted. He hadn't acted as if he'd had an awesome time. Amy pulled him into the living room, where a bowl of fresh popcorn and cans of soda waited on the coffee table. "Sit down and start talking."

Erin followed hesitantly, suddenly feeling like an extra with no lines to read. A lump formed in her throat, and she tried to wash it down. She heard Amy and Travis talking, saw their heads close together and their hands touching. Without a word she turned and went to her room.

Chapter Four

"You've got to get them all out in one breath, or your wish won't come true," Mrs. Bennett reminded Amy as she set the birthday cake on the dining-room table.

"No problem there," Travis said. "We all know that she's full of hot air."

Erin laughed along with her mother and father as Amy punched his arm. "There're *only* sixteen candles," she said. "This'll be a cinch."

Mr. Bennett flipped off the light switch, and the fire from the candles reflected off Amy's face. Erin saw how radiant her sister looked. She felt ashamed of how she'd acted on the night of the concert, keeping to herself once Travis had gone home and not wanting to talk much about the night.

"What flavor's the cake?" Travis asked.

"Devil's food with white boiled icing," Mrs. Bennett said. "It's Amy's favorite."

"Devil's food? I should have guessed." Everyone laughed again.

Amy filled her lungs and puffed out her cheeks. Mr. Bennett snapped a photo just as she blew on the candles, and in seconds all that remained were spirals of smoke. Amy stood and took a bow. "And you doubted I could get them all in one puff." She held out her hands. "Okay. No one eats until I get my presents."

"Not fair," Mr. Bennett called.

"Life isn't fair," Amy said with a grin.

"Well, I want my cake, so I'm not holding out," Travis said, and forked over the box Erin had so carefully wrapped weeks before.

Erin watched as Amy tore into the paper. So much like Amy, she thought. Erin would have carefully removed the tape from each end and neatly folded the paper back. Amy held up the blue sweater and squealed. "It's gorgeous! I've never seen anything so pretty. Thanks a million."

Travis offered Erin a questioning glance, but she only shrugged her shoulders as if to say, "Isn't that just like Amy to act as if it's the first time she's laid eyes on it?"

Her parents gave Amy a generous gift certificate for clothes and a professional makeup kit. "To hold all that clown stuff," Mrs. Bennett explained.

"It's fabulous," Amy said. "Now I'll look like a real pro!" She hugged them both, then turned toward Erin. "Well?" she asked.

"Well what?"

"Well where's my present from you?"

"*Moi?*" Erin asked flapping her eyelashes. "Didn't I get you a gift for your last birthday?"

Amy danced up and down. "Give me my present, or I won't show up for the recital next Saturday night."

Erin rolled her eyes and leaned toward Travis. "A trained seal could read the part."

"Could not!" Amy protested.

"And be on time for the rehearsals."

Amy made a face. "I'll never be late again. Promise."

"Never?"

Amy crossed her heart, then leaned into Travis's other side. "It's my party, and I'll lie if I want to." They all groaned over her pun.

Erin handed over a shoe-sized box, which Amy shook. "It rattles," she said, shredding the paper. She lifted out a shiny key chain. A key and a small rectangular box dangled from one end, and a large solid-brass letter A from the other.

"Let me explain," Erin said, taking the chain from Amy's hand. "First, the key is to my car, which I will let you borrow."

"You mean you're going to let me use *your* car? Thanks, Erin. Thanks a lot."

"On very rare occasions," Erin emphasized.

Amy turned to her father. "Does this mean I won't be getting my Porsche this year?"

"The dealer was back-ordered, so we thought we'd hold off for a while," he told her with a straight face.

She swung around to face Erin, who continued. "This," she pointed to the small box on the chain, "is something that you need in order to keep track of the keys." Erin crossed to the far side of the room and put the keys on the edge of the buffet. "Now whistle," she told Amy.

Her sister obliged, and the box let out a high-pitched whine. "If you ever misplace your keys, Amy—of course we all realize that will never happen." The others joined in with shouts of, "Never!" and "Not Amy."

"If you can't find them, all you have to do is whistle," Erin interrupted.

Amy clapped gleefully. "I love it! Oh Erin, it's super." She bolted out of the dining room, and in a minute they heard her whistle and the box whine.

Mrs. Bennett offered Erin an approving nod. "Looks like you've found the perfect gift. And it's nice of you to share your car."

Erin couldn't help but feel pleased with her choice. Travis caught her eye, and the approval she saw there caused her pulse to quicken. Mr. Bennett yelled out, "Amy, where are you? Are you going to cut this cake, or are we supposed to take chunks out of it with our bare hands?"

"I'll do it," she said. "But I get the part with the most icing."

Mr. Bennett handed the camera to Travis. "Can you get a shot of us together? I intend to have plenty of pictures to embarrass Amy with when she's a refined old lady."

Travis looked through the viewfinder and aimed. "Squeeze in tighter." The Bennetts bunched around Amy, who hunched low and peeked from behind the cake with a silly grin. "You've got frosting on your nose, Amy," he said. "I'll wait while you wipe it off."

Erin muttered, "All we ever do around here is wait on Amy."

Amy crossed her eyes, and Travis snapped the shutter.

On Friday after school Erin found Shara in one of the music rooms, practicing her songs for the upcoming recital. Shara's haunting, lyrical voice sent goose bumps up Erin's arms. "I thought I'd better get some extra practice time in," Shara said, signaling Erin into the tiny, soundproof room.

Erin wished Amy would take her part in the recital half as seriously. "No hurry," Erin told her. "I'll wait." She sat in a metal chair.

"I'm glad you're sleeping over tonight. With my mom visiting her sister and Dad working late at the hospital, I dreaded the thought of being home alone." Shara said. "After dinner we can go to a movie at the mall and then maybe do some cruising."

"Cruising at the mall? Only nerds hang around the mall on Friday night."

"Now don't be negative. You never know."

"*I* know," Erin said.

"Just remember, Erin, Spring Fling comes up after Easter, and I for one intend to go this year. That requires meeting somebody to ask."

To Shara it was all so simple, but Erin found it far more complicated. She didn't want to attend the big Briarwood extravaganza with just anybody. She wanted to go with a guy who mattered to her. Unfortunately, the only guy who mattered was off-limits. "What about you and Kenny? You were seeing a lot of him before Christmas."

"Kenny's old news. He was nice enough, but sort of dull, if you know what I mean."

"And you don't want to go with a bunch of girls like we did last year? I'm hurt."

Shara made a face. "No thanks. I want to buy something ridiculously expensive and watch some guy's eyeballs pop out when I walk through the door."

"If that's all you want, wear your birthday suit."

"If all I wear is my birthday suit, he'll run off screaming," Shara grumbled. "Don't you want to go? You're a dancer, after all."

"There's no similarity between that kind of dancing and the modern and jazz that I like to do."

"But picture yourself slow-dancing with someone tall, dark, and sexy." Shara did a few spins around the cramped room. "Then later, in the moonlight . . ."

It was all too easy for Erin to picture. "Sorry, Shara. I can't imagine meeting Mr. Right at the mall."

"You have no imagination." Erin smiled. The problem was, she had too much imagination. "I'll bet Amy is taking Travis," Shara said.

"She's already on me to help her pick out something at the boutique. Her taste in formal wear is as crazy as she is, and so far she can't settle on anything."

"Knowing Amy, she'll turn up in her clown makeup," Shara said.

"Knowing Amy, she'll be so late that everyone will have gone home by the time she gets there."

Shara chuckled and picked up her books. "Come on, let's go. If we hurry, we can grab a bite at my house, then go to the early show. That'll leave us about an hour to hang around before the mall closes."

Hadn't Shara heard a word Erin had said? But rather than argue, Erin grabbed her things and left with her friend. "Don't forget, we have rehearsal tomorrow morning," she told Shara.

The blond-haired girl groaned. "You're a regular slave driver, Erin."

"The recital's next Saturday night, and we're going to be best in the show."

"Is Amy supposed to meet us at the studio? She'll be late."

"Not tomorrow," Erin said with a smug grin. "I set her alarm ahead an hour. I figure that should put her there right on time."

"You sneaky devil," Shara said with a laugh.

Erin tapped her forehead with her finger. "There's more than one way to outwit my sister's internal clock. You just have to use your brain and be creative. Like it or not, time is where people exist between living and dying. Even Amy Sue Bennett has to punch a time clock, just like the rest of us mere mortals."

"That's deep," Shara said with mock seriousness.

"That's reality," Erin countered, giving her friend a playful shove. "So get a move on it before time runs out on us and the mall closes."

28

Chapter Five

~

It rained the night of the recital, and Erin was afraid attendance would be down, so she kept peeking from behind the massive red curtain to watch the audience file down the aisles. By the time the program started, there were no empty seats in the theater.

Her number was last on the program, and as the curtain lifted for her performance, she sensed hundreds of eyes on her, making her adrenaline pump. Earlier she'd felt as if she were tied in knots, but now, in the hushed atmosphere of the darkened theater, she was charged—completely calm, yet full of power for the dance.

Amy, dressed all in black, stood behind a Lucite podium at the far left corner of the stage. The elegant leather book lay open to her place. The music started and Shara sang. Erin arched her back, poised on pointe upstage, then walked on a diagonal to center stage. With perfect timing Shara's song crescendoed, and Amy read from Psalm 139.

"Oh Lord, thou has searched me and known me. . . ." Erin began a controlled series of *balances*. "I will praise thee, for I am fearfully and wonderfully made. . . . My substance was not hid from thee,

29

when I was made in secret." As Amy read excerpts, Erin spun faster—her back erect, her arms forming a circle in front of her. The words became her music now. She leapt, executing a perfect spin in the air, landed, and dipped backward until her long hair brushed the floor as Amy read: "And lead me in the way everlasting." She lost all sense of time until the last strains of the music faded and she posed dramatically in the center of the stage, with only the spotlight surrounding her.

Applause erupted, pulling her back to reality. She rose and blinked as the houselights came up, and smiling, she grasped Amy's and Shara's hands and bowed. Once the curtain closed, the three girls collapsed into hugs and squeals of relief. After weeks of work it was over. Erin could scarcely believe it. The other performers converged from the wings offering congratulations.

Ms. Thornton swept through the ranks saying, "Wonderful performance, ladies, really outstanding. Every one of you was spectacular. Now if your parents start coming backstage, don't let them hang around too long. After all, we have a party to throw."

They scurried toward the dressing rooms, where Erin plopped on a metal chair in front of the vanity mirror and reached for her cold cream. The girl next to her, a sophomore, said, "You were sensational, Erin."

There was no mistaking the admiration on the girl's face. "Thanks," Erin told her.

"Aren't we a super team?" Amy asked as she

dragged a chair over and positioned it between Erin and the other girl. "Pass your cold cream, please."

Slightly annoyed, Erin asked, "I thought you brought your own. Where's that fancy kit Mom and Dad bought you for your birthday?"

Amy shrugged and smeared the cream on her face. "I guess I was in such a hurry to be on time, I left it on my bed."

Erin rolled her eyes. "Oh, Amy . . ."

"But I remembered my regular makeup." She grinned and slathered on more of the greasy cream. "How long's this party supposed to last?"

"All evening. Why?"

"'Cause I told Travis to pick me up at eleven."

"You're going out? It's raining like crazy outside. Does Mom know?"

"Mom gave me permission."

"Oh," Erin said, annoyed. Amy was just barely sixteen, and already their mother was changing the curfew rules for her.

"We're going to the latest Freddy Krueger flick. It doesn't start until midnight." Amy looked absolutely comical sitting talking with her sister while her stage makeup ran in streaks down her face.

One of the girls pointed at Amy and started laughing. "Take a look in the mirror, Amy," she said. Another dancer said to Erin, "Amy's such a riot. It must be a blast living with her."

"It's just nonstop laughs around our house," Erin said, smiling stiffly. She faced the mirror and studied her exotic makeup. The eye shadow made her look older, more glamorous. *No matter what I do or say, the spotlight always turns to Amy*, she thought. *Maybe if I leave on this makeup, I'll become somebody more exciting than Erin Bennett*.

Amy reached in front of Erin for a box of tissues. "Listen, if Ms. Thornton misses me, will you cover for me?"

Erin suddenly remembered the award Ms. Thornton had planned to give Amy. It would serve her right if she left before she got it. She started to hint that it might be best if Amy didn't run off with Travis before the party was over but then peevishly decided against it. "Sure, Amy. I'll cover."

"Thanks. You're a true sister." Amy removed the last of the cold cream and stared hard at the mirror. "Good grief, where'd my face disappear to?" She made a production of looking under the long vanity table, beneath jars, and through some of the tabletop clutter while the other girls laughed and kidded her. Finally she retrieved her purse and pulled out a makeup pouch. "Here it is! I found it!"

"Stop being such a show-off," Erin said crossly.

"Gosh, Erin, I'm sorry. Am I embarrassing you?" Amy asked sincerely.

Erin felt her face flush. Some of the other girls had heard, and she knew she must have come across as a prima donna. "Of course not."

"I'd never do that on purpose, you know."

The dressing-room door opened, and Ms. Thornton peered inside. "Let's get a move on ladies. Everything's set up on stage, and it's already ten o'clock."

The room burst into activity, and soon Erin found herself alone. She still hadn't even begun to remove her stage makeup and dress for the party. She sighed and stood, glanced around at the jumble of duffel bags and clothes, and wondered where hers was buried. She hated being late. Her irritation with Amy returned. It had been the news about her sister's date with Travis that had started it all.

In the mirror she eyed her costume. The gold bangle earrings and the beautiful scarf tied around her hips made her remember the day she'd been alone with him in the boutique and he'd told her she looked pretty. Now the scarf looked limp and sad, and the jewelry seemed tarnished. Why couldn't she be the one with the date? She was older than Amy. Why couldn't Travis Sinclair be interested in her?

"Stop it," she demanded of her reflection. "Just stop wishing for the impossible." Erin found her duffel bag, quickly removed the elaborate makeup with cold cream, reapplied her everyday makeup, and changed into jeans and a sweater.

The stage was bathed in fuchsia and gold lights, and a sheet cake sat on a table decorated with balloons and banners. Ms. Thornton had thought of everything. Shara wove through a group of girls and came up to Erin, handing her a piece of cake on a napkin. "What kept you? I changed in the other dressing room."

"Amy got to chattering, and before you knew it, everybody was ready but me."

Shara toasted Erin with her cake. "We were a hit, weren't we?"

Erin gave a lackluster shrug. "I guess so."

"What's bugging you?"

"Nothing."

Shara arched an eyebrow. "Amy?" She asked, intuitively.

"She's such a pain sometimes."

"So what's Amy done this time? She did a terrific job on the readings for your dance."

"I know," Erin shrugged, frustrated because she could never put into words how she really felt about Amy. Unable to think of anything, she took a bite out of her cake.

"Having a good time?" Ms. Thornton asked as she walked over to where they stood.

"Super," Erin and Shara said in unison.

"I really think your number was outstanding, Erin," Ms. Thornton said. Shara excused herself, and Ms. Thornton continued. "You just keep growing and maturing as a dancer."

"Thank you," was all Erin could manage. Her instructor's opinion meant more to her than anybody's.

Ms. Thornton studied Erin thoughtfully, then said, "In fact, I'd like to recommend you to the Wolftrap Dance Academy in Washington. The director is always looking for the brightest and the best. I'm sure I could get you in on scholarship this summer. Of course, Allen will want you to turn professional and go to New York." A knowing smile crossed Ms. Thornton's face. "But I know you're geared for college, and after you get your degree, you can still pursue a professional career if you want."

A dance scholarship with Wolftrap! Erin didn't know what to say. Ms. Thornton put her hand on Erin's shoulder. "We'll discuss it in more detail later, but I'd like you to start thinking about it now."

Before Erin could utter a word, one of the girls came over. "Ms. Thornton, we're out of sodas."

"Already? I thought I bought plenty."

The girl shrugged. "I guess we were really thirsty."

Ms. Thornton puckered her brow and spoke almost to herself. "Well, I'll just have to run to the store."

"I'll go," Erin offered.

"I don't know. . . ."

"I don't mind. My car's right outside."

Ms. Thornton glanced around at the stage full of girls before turning again to Erin. "If you're sure you don't mind. Here, let me give you some money."

Erin tagged after the teacher, who retrieved her purse and handed her some cash. "Buy a whole case. That should hold us for the rest of the party."

"I'll be back in a flash." The news about the scholarship had lifted her spirits so much that Erin felt she could have flown to the store.

"Don't forget your raincoat," Ms. Thornton called before Erin could open the backstage door.

"Oh yeah." She dashed to the dressing room,

found her coat, and was again almost out the door when Amy stopped her.

"Where are you going?"

"To the store. We're out of sodas."

Amy grabbed Erin's arm. "Oh let me go! Please. I've had my license for a whole week, and I still haven't had a chance to use the car."

Erin paused. "But I told Ms. Thornton I'd go."

"She won't mind if I go instead. You said I could drive your car as part of my birthday present."

"How about if we go together?"

"Ugh!" Amy made a face. "I want to drive by myself this time. Pretty please? I'll be your best friend."

Erin thought about the cold, damp March weather and about her car heater that was on the fritz. And about how much she'd love to corner Shara and tell her about the Wolftrap Academy and the dance scholarship. "If I let you go for me, don't mess around. Get the sodas and come right back. Okay?"

"Don't worry. I'm meeting Travis, remember?" Erin remembered. "I'll be back in a jiffy."

Amy started out the door, and a blast of damp wind hit them both, making Erin shiver. "Where's your coat?"

"I think I left it in the dressing room."

"You'll get soaked. Here take mine. And here's money for the sodas. Get a whole case!" She yelled as Amy jumped over puddles and dodged raindrops.

She watched as Amy struggled with the car's stubborn door before climbing inside and starting the engine. In the glow of the mercury lamppost, the car looked hard and colorless. Amy waved and turned toward the street, the headlights' sweeping arc cutting through the darkness and the pouring rain. Not knowing why, Erin stood at the door and watched until the taillights had disappeared completely into the night.

Chapter Six

~~~

"What're you doing here by the door?" Shara's question interrupted Erin's vigilance over the parking lot.

"Just watching Amy. She went to the store to get more sodas." Erin stepped inside, and the heavy door snapped shut.

"You look like it's bothering you."

"Ms. Thornton asked me to go, and I let Amy badger me into going instead."

"So?"

Erin shrugged. "Nothing, I guess." She looked at Shara and suddenly remembered what Ms. Thornton had said about the Wolftrap Academy. "Hey, guess what? Ms. Thornton really liked my dance, and she's going to recommend me to the director at Wolftrap."

Shara's eyes grew wider as Erin told her. "That's excellent. Would your parents let you go to Washington for the summer?"

"They'd better! I figure if I work really hard between now and June, I can convince them that this is really important to me. I mean, this is the chance of a lifetime. Wolftrap was started by people who were trained by Martha Graham." Erin said the name of the modern-dance pioneer reverently. "Can you imagine? *Me* working with teachers like *that*."

Shara seemed sufficiently impressed. "I guess it'd be like me getting a recording contract. You're lucky you have someone like Ms. Thornton helping you."

Erin knew that was true, and she was determined to fulfill Ms. Thornton's faith in her.

"Hey Erin! Shara!" Donna Gaines called. "Come on out here. Ms. Thornton's gonna show us the tape of the show."

The girls hurried back to the main stage, where everyone was sitting on the floor, eyes glued to a TV that had been propped on the table beside the half-eaten cake. Ms. Thornton asked, "Back with the sodas, Erin?"

"I—um—I let Amy go get them for us."

The rest of the dance troupe moaned. Someone said, "Amy! Good grief, the party'll be over before we see her again."

"Yeah," someone else added. "Amy has two speeds—slow and no-show."

Laughter rippled through the group. Erin felt as if she should say something in her sister's defense, but nothing came to mind. After all, it was true.

"Settle down, ladies," Ms. Thornton directed. "She'll be here eventually. Let's start the tape."

Erin dropped to the floor next to Shara and drew her knees against her chest, watching the screen intently. The sound quality was tinny, but the images were clear and sharp. One after the other the dance numbers proceeded across the screen. The girls pointed at themselves, with several groaning over mistakes. By the time her number started, Erin's palms were sweating. She wanted so much for it to be good.

On the tape she heard Amy's voice and vaguely wondered why it was taking her sister so long to return. Erin concentrated on her movements, evaluating them critically. Her leaps were high, but she decided she needed more arch to her back. She made a mental note to work on flexibility. Could she ever be ready for a place like Wolftrap?

Applause sounded as the tape ran out and electronic snow splattered over the screen. Everyone began to stand and stretch, and Erin pulled herself up too.

"Is that someone pounding on the backstage door?" Ms. Thornton asked.

"Maybe it's Amy," somebody suggested. "Her timing's perfect. The party's over."

"I'll get it," Erin called, rushing for the door, determined to throttle her sister for blowing such a simple mission. She jerked open the door and looked right into Travis Sinclair's face.

"Where's Amy?" he asked. Erin realized that Travis was mad. "She said she'd be waiting right here by the door. I knocked real quiet, but she didn't open it, so I had to beat on it."

"Gosh, Travis, is it eleven o'clock already?"

"Eleven-fifteen. Hey, Erin, it's wet and cold out here. Do you think I could come in?"

Flustered, Erin held open the door, and a dripping Travis stepped inside. "This was supposed to be a subtle exit," he grumbled. "Now it looks like half the world's in on it."

Erin turned to see the Terpsicord girls as well as Ms. Thornton emerging from the backstage shadows. Ms. Thornton asked, "What's going on?"

Erin felt her cheeks grow hot. How did Amy always manage to put her on the spot? "Um—this is Travis Sinclair. He was supposed to pick Amy up and take her—er—home," she finished lamely, hating herself for lying.

Ms. Thornton looked doubtful. "I was about to give out some awards for our work here tonight," she said.

Travis shifted, jamming his hands into the pockets of his trench coat. "I could wait here by the door."

Ms. Thornton glanced at her watch. "It's late, Erin. What time did Amy leave anyway?"

"Ten-thirty."

"Even Amy should have been back by now."

A small shiver of fear shot up Erin's spine. "I can't imagine what's keeping her. Maybe she had car trouble. I mean, my car's old, and sometimes it gets cranky."

"We could drive around and look for her," Travis suggested.

Several girls offered to take their cars and look also. "No," Ms. Thornton said. "You all stay put. Erin, you and Travis go. But be back here in thirty minutes whether you find her or not."

Erin agreed and ran behind Travis through a pelt-

41

ing rain to where his car was parked. Her teeth were chattering, and Travis, fiddling with the heater buttons, asked, "Which way did she head?"

Erin pointed, and he drove out of the lot and down a dark, deserted road. Erin chewed her bottom lip, peering through the side window. It was hard to see through the film of rain, so she kept rubbing the palm of her hand over the glass, even though it didn't help. "I should have never let her go in my place," she said miserably.

"Don't worry. Knowing Amy, she ran out of gas and is sitting in some diner munching out."

Erin was touched by his attempt to comfort her, but she knew that she'd had a full tank of gas. The rhythmic slap of the wipers matched Erin's heartbeat. *Steady*, she told herself. *Everything's fine.* "I don't see any cars broken down along the road," Travis said after he'd driven several miles. "What store do you think she might have gone to for the drinks?"

"I don't know. There's a bunch of minimarts on this street and two grocery stores farther north."

"Then we'll stop at all of them and ask if anyone's seen her." Travis made a U-turn and headed back toward Briarwood. "We'll start at the one closest to the school and work our way down." Erin clutched her coat—Amy's coat—closer to her body. "Are you cold?" Travis asked, turning up the heater.

She was shivering, but she was sweating too. "Thanks," she mumbled.

They stopped at each brightly lit store and described Amy, and each time the sales help shook their heads. In one of the larger grocery stores, Travis talked to the store manager while Erin canvased each checkout girl. The answer was always the same: "Sorry, haven't seen her."

After having no better luck at the second of the big supermarkets, Travis sat in the car brooding and staring out at the falling rain. "We'd better keep going," Erin told him.

He turned to face her in the bucket seat. "We're ten miles from the school, Erin. She wouldn't have come this far."

Erin grew agitated. "You don't know that for sure. It's too soon to give up."

"I'm not giving up. It's just that she must have gone somewhere else."

"But where?" By now Erin was really scared, because even Amy wasn't this irresponsible. They sat in silence. The rain beat on the metal roof, and Erin felt a headache coming on.

"Maybe she went home," Travis ventured.

Instantly Erin brightened. "I'll bet you're right. She probably wanted to change clothes before going to the movie. Let's go check my house."

Travis started the engine, and Erin caught sight of the digital clock on the dashboard. "Ms. Thornton!" she cried. "We promised her we'd be back in half an hour."

"Is there a phone at the theater?"

"Yes."

"Then we'll go back and call your house from there."

"The more I think about it, I'll bet that's just what happened," Erin insisted. "Honestly, my sister can be *so* thoughtless sometimes. I know you like her 'free spirit,' Travis, but you've got to admit that sometimes she's her own worst enemy."

They returned to the back parking lot of the theater, and Erin jumped out before Travis had turned off the engine. She raced through the rain, stepping into puddles and feeling the water sop through her sneakers and thick socks. She forgot to turn up her coat collar, and cold water ran down her neck. She pounded on the stage door, and it opened immediately.

"Did you find her?" Ms. Thornton asked.

Travis came through the door, and it banged hard behind him. "No luck," he said. "We hit every store for miles, but no one remembered seeing her."

"We thought that she might have gone home for some reason," Erin said, her voice sounding breathy. "I thought I'd call my house from here."

"Of course." Ms. Thornton led the way to a small office and flipped on the light.

The glare stung Erin's eyes, and the room seemed to take on a surrealistic glow. She picked up the telephone receiver and punched her number. "Where'd everybody go?" she asked, counting the rings.

"I sent the girls home, but I promised to start the phone chain once we heard something." The phone chain was Ms. Thornton's method of dispensing information to the dance troupe. She called one person, who called another, and so on down the line until everyone got the message.

By the tenth ring Erin realized no one was going to answer. A hard, heavy sensation lodged in her stomach. "No one's home," she said.

"Had your parents planned to go out?"

"No." Erin's voice had become a whisper. She hung up the phone. "Something's wrong, Ms. Thornton."

Ms. Thornton put her arm around Erin's shoulder. "Let's not jump to any conclusions. There're lots of possible explanations—" She was interrupted by the sound of someone banging on the back door.

The three of them ran toward it, but Travis got there first and yanked on the handle. A blast of wind and rain blew in with a short, plump woman.

Erin blinked. "Inez!" she cried, recognizing her mother's sales assistant from the boutique. "What are you doing here?"

Inez wrung her hands and grabbed Erin by the forearms. She was crying. "Erin, there's been an accident."

"Mom and Dad?" Erin almost gagged.

"They're at County's emergency room. It's Amy, Erin. Amy's been in a terrible wreck."

Chapter Seven

Erin would remember the ride to the hospital with Travis as a series of dreamlike impressions—rain falling, the red gold aura of mercury vapor lamps flashing past the windows, the stuffy heat in the car, the silence between her and Travis, the thudding of her heart. None of it seemed real. Yet when Travis turned the car into the entrance marked Emergency Only, Erin recoiled. The building loomed tall and forbidding, not at all friendly. Somewhere inside Amy lay, hurt and maybe in pain, and that frightened Erin even more.

The emergency waiting room was a zoo, with too many people crammed into too small an area. Babies cried, and people who looked very sick slumped in wheelchairs. Erin searched for her parents. "Where are they?" she asked.

"Maybe we should ask someone," Travis suggested.

"I'd rather look for them myself," she told him, darting up a hallway like a mouse caught in a maze. The smell of alcohol and disinfectant was making her nauseous. Nurses passed her, too busy to stop, so Erin ventured up another corridor, where she saw her mother and father huddled outside a closed door.

She ran toward them. Her father's face was the color of chalk, and her mother's mascara made dark smudged rings beneath her eyes. Erin threw herself into her mother's arms. "What happened? How's Amy?"

"No one's sure what happened," Mrs. Bennett's voice sounded tight and very controlled. "The police said that she lost control of the car, it hit a tree, and her head hit the steering wheel. Evidently she didn't have her seat belt on."

"Amy hates the shoulder strap," Erin mumbled. "Have the doctors told you anything? How long has she been in there?"

"Maybe an hour. The ER doctor came out once and said that since it's a head injury, they've called in a neurologist. We're waiting for him to tell us something now."

"But she's all right, isn't she? I mean they're probably just stitching up cuts or something, right?"

"All they told us is that it's a head injury," Mrs. Bennett said again. She let go of Erin and stared at her full in the face. "What was she doing driving in the rain at night anyway?"

Erin's voice began to quaver, and she clenched her fists to control her shaking. "She went out for sodas for the party. We ran out."

"What's the matter with Ms. Thornton? Why would she send Amy? She's only had her license for a week. I always considered Thornton to be a responsible person."

Erin squeezed her mother's arm to stop her angry

tirade. "I—it wasn't her fault. I was supposed to go, but Amy begged me to let her go instead." Erin dropped her gaze to the floor, where shiny tiles marched in neat, clean green-and-white formations. The pattern began to blur as tears filled her eyes. "I—I let her take my car."

Mrs. Bennett grabbed Erin's shoulders and shook her. "Erin! How could you have been so thoughtless? You know Amy's not an experienced driver."

"I know. . . . I'm sorry. . . ."

"I've always counted on you, Erin, to have common sense. I would expect Amy to be careless, but *you!*"

Her mother's face was livid, and Erin shrank back toward the wall as her father stepped over and put his arm around her. "Stop it, Marian. It's not Erin's fault. It was an accident."

Erin huddled against her father's side, watching her mother's eyes blaze and her lips compress into a line. Mrs. Bennett turned and walked away down the corridor. "D—daddy . . ." Erin buried her face in her father's coat. It smelled of rain and pipe tobacco.

"It's all right, Princess," he said soothingly. "She's upset. She doesn't really blame you." He stroked Erin's hair absently. "We were getting ready to watch the eleven o'clock news when the cop came and told us. He gave us a police escort down here."

"Inez came to the theater to tell me."

"We figured it would be better than having the police come tell you. And even if I could have reached you by phone, I didn't want you to hear it that way."

He glanced both ways down the hall. "Where is Inez anyway?"

"I guess she's out front with Travis. I rode here with him. Maybe I should tell them something."

"Go on. I'll talk to your mother."

The waiting room was even more crowded now. It was warm too, heavy with the distinct odor of pain and sickness.

"Erin, what's happening?" Travis asked. She felt her knees buckle, and he guided her to a chair that was miraculously vacant.

"We don't know much yet. Amy lost control of the car, and it hit a tree. A specialist is in with her because it's a head injury."

Travis knelt beside her, and Inez hovered at her elbow. Erin twisted her hands in her lap. They felt like blocks of ice. "She's hurt real bad, Travis. I can feel it."

"Maybe not. Maybe she just needs stitches, or some bones are broken. It takes time for them to check her over and figure it all out. I came here with a broken arm once, and it took forever for them to check me over and send me to X-ray and everything."

"This hospital has a good reputation," Inez interjected in a soft Spanish-accented voice. "The trauma unit was featured in the newspaper last month. You know, they have a heliport on the roof, and they fly in patients from all over Florida because the best doctors work right here."

"I hope she isn't hurting," Erin whispered.

"Don't worry, they give you a shot for pain," Travis said.

"Amy hates shots. When we were little, I always had to go first, and if I cried, nothing could make Amy take her shot. One time it took two nurses and Mom to help hold her down. After that I didn't cry again." The memory was so vivid that Erin could suddenly smell the isopropyl alcohol and hear Amy shrieking. "Maybe I should go back to Mom and Dad."

"You'll let us know when you hear from the doctor, won't you?" Travis asked.

"Yes." Erin saw fear in the darkness of his eyes. "As soon as I know anything." She hurried out of the waiting area and returned to her parents.

"I didn't mean to blame you, Erin," Mrs. Bennett said the minute Erin appeared.

"I know, Mom." But truthfully Erin felt guilty. She never should have let Amy talk her out of going to the store, or she should have at least gone with her.

Mrs. Bennett leaned against the wall. Mr. Bennett asked his wife, "Would you like some coffee?"

"No, I'd like a cigarette."

Erin knew that her mother had stopped smoking three years ago. "There's a soda machine in the other corridor," she said, trying to take her mother's mind off the nerveracking wait. "I could get you something cold."

"No. Thanks," she added as an afterthought. "What's taking so long?"

Erin was wondering the same thing. Her stomach felt queasy, and her head was throbbing. Down the hall doors swung open, and a tall man in a white medical coat emerged. Erin tensed. She knew he was coming for them.

"I'm Dr. DuPree, your daughter's neurologist," the man said when he approached. Introductions were made, but then the doctor's attitude turned crisp and professional. "Your daughter has suffered a massive head trauma."

"Amy," Erin blurted, not sure why she wanted him to know. "My sister's name is Amy."

Through black-rimmed glasses his blue eyes studied her kindly. "Amy is stable now. We've got her on a ventilator—that's a machine that breathes for her."

Erin's heart squeezed as if fingers had grabbed it. "Why?"

"We've done a CAT scan. That's a special X-ray of her brain," he explained. "Right now there's a great deal of swelling, and we can't determine the extent of her head injury. But she can't breathe on her own."

Erin's mother gave a little gasp, and Dr. DuPree turned his attention to Erin's parents. "I believe in being completely honest with my patients and their families. I won't lie to you, but I won't give you false hope either. Amy's condition is very serious. I'm having her moved up to Neuro-ICU, where she'll be monitored around the clock. We'll run another CAT scan in a couple of days."

He used such phrases as "severe contusion" and "intracranial pressure" and "diuretics to reduce fluid," but the words slid around in Erin's mind. The only

51

thing that made any sense was when Dr. DuPree said, "She's stable, but comatose."

For a moment no one spoke; then both her parents began to talk at once, questions upon questions, which Dr. DuPree answered. Erin backed away, picturing Amy in a hospital bed surrounded by strangers. "I want to see my sister," she demanded, interrupting the dialogue between Dr. DuPree and her parents. "I want to stay with Amy."

Dr. DuPree took one of her hands. His palm was warm, and she noticed that his fingers were long and immaculate. "There's a waiting room next to Neuro-ICU for families of critical patients. All of you can stay there tonight."

Erin's dad said he'd talk to Inez and Travis, then meet them upstairs. Her mother kept firing questions at the doctor during the ride up the elevator to the seventh floor. Erin steeled her body and emotions with her dancer's iron discipline.

Hospitals and doctors help people, she told herself as she approached the solid door of the Neuro-ICU area. *Amy will be out of here in no time.* She stared at the door, while behind her Dr. DuPree and her mother waited for her to push it open.

"People come out of comas don't they, Dr. DuPree?" she asked. Erin shoved open the door, not waiting for his reply, because deep down she was too terrified to hear his answer.

Chapter Eight

Neuro-ICU was a large room with seven beds and a central desk where nurses kept close watch over patients who had head and brain injuries. It was a netherworld of shadows illuminated by green and amber blips, of machines linked with lines and tubes, and of hissing sounds and electronic beeps keeping perfect cadence. Erin met the night nurse, Laurie, who took her and Mrs. Bennett to a more private room, separated only by a glass partition from the larger area.

"We have three other patients up here now," Laurie said, but Erin only half heard her because she couldn't take her eyes off her sister. Amy's head was swathed in gauze, and a tube protruded from her mouth. Too overwhelmed to speak, Erin stood by the bed and blinked back tears. Her hand reached out, then drew back.

"Don't be afraid; you can touch her," Laurie said.

"She doesn't even look hurt. She just looks like she's asleep."

"The only damage is to her brain. By tommorow you'll be able to see swelling in her face. Her eye area will probably turn black-and-blue."

Erin gently stroked Amy's cheek, careful not to brush against the apparatus. She hoped to see her sister's eyelids flutter, knowing that Amy hated being tickled. "What are all these tubes and wires for?"

"The oral tube is her ventilator. That wire is taped to her chest and leads to her heart monitor, and that tube in the back of her hand is an IV. She has a catheter too."

"My poor little girl," Mrs. Bennett whispered from the other side of Amy's bed. Erin swallowed hard and tried not to look at her mother. If she did, she knew she'd lose it.

"You can stay with her for now," Laurie said softly. "The waiting room is right down the hall. You can come in and out of here to check on your daughter whenever you want."

"I'll wait here for my husband," Mrs. Bennett said.

Erin trembled, unable to hold in her feelings any longer. "I'll go down there now," she said, suddenly desperate to get out of the machine-driven world of Neuro-ICU. "So you and Daddy can be alone with Amy."

She followed Laurie to a very large room that looked more like a luxury hotel suite than a hospital waiting room. The carpet was dove gray, the furniture light oak wood with burgundy upholstery. "It's brand new," Laurie explained. "We've tried to make it comfortable because families like to be near each other through these crises." The lights were dim, but Erin could see people piled in oversized chairs with pillows and blankets. "Our only rule is that you can't sleep on the floor," Laurie whispered. "Local church groups bring in the food. There'll be fresh pastry and coffee here in the morning." Laurie pointed to a wall where three pay phones hung. "Give out the numbers to friends, and they can call and talk to you."

Erin realized she should call and tell Ms. Thornton something. She glanced up at a wall clock. It was three A.M. "I'll call everyone tomorrow."

Laurie gave her a skimpy pillow and a thin blue blanket and left. Erin dropped into a chair, careful not to make too much noise. She felt exhausted and numb, as if she were trapped in a bad dream and couldn't wake up. She told herself that once this terrible night was over, they'd all go back in to see Amy, and she'd be awake.

Erin consoled herself with the image of Amy sitting up in bed and eating breakfast. "Amy . . ." she pleaded in a whisper. "Please wake up, Amy. If you do, I'll be your best friend." Erin buried her face in the blanket and wept.

Throughout the remainder of the night, Erin cat-napped, unable to relax in the foreign surroundings. Her parents settled near her, and she heard her mother leave often to check on Amy. Early the next morning Erin called Ms. Thornton, who promised to start the phone chain and pass along information about Amy's condition, which hadn't changed during the night. Erin also asked her to tell friends to stay away for the time being. She knew she couldn't stand visiting with a lot of people, no matter how good their intentions.

Erin called Travis, but his mother said he was asleep and promised to have him call her later. Erin hung up, realizing that, like her, he'd been up half the night and probably had slept no better than she had.

Inez came for a visit and so did a few neighbors. Shara stopped by late Sunday afternoon but didn't stay long. "Dad delivers a lot of babies at this hospital," Shara told Erin with a wave of her hand, "so I know my way around the red tape. Let me know if you want anything." Erin told her thanks but was too bewildered and overwhelmed to know what to ask for.

By afternoon the strangers in the waiting room were beginning to look familiar. Erin wondered who they all were and what patients they were waiting for, but she resisted talking to anyone. She didn't want to meet new people. She only wanted to get out of there and take Amy home.

In the light of day, Neuro-ICU didn't seem quite so formidable. The machines appeared less intimidating, and the sounds less hostile. Overhead TVs played softly despite the fact that the patients couldn't react to the programs. At the nurses' station Erin toyed with a plastic model of a human brain, tracing her fingers along the convoluted surface of the cerebrum and down to the dark mass of the cerebellum at the base of the model. She found it hard to comprehend that Amy's brain was so hurt that it had shut down.

"Fascinating isn't it?" a tall man standing beside the main desk said to her. He was dressed in a dark blue suit and had black hair and a mustache. "The average human brain weighs only three pounds, and yet it has the capacity to elevate mankind to the stars."

"Are you a doctor?" Erin asked.

"No. But I work with the staff here." His eyes were brown and kind. "Is that your sister back there?" He motioned with his head toward the glass wall.

"Yes, she was in an accident." Erin held up the plastic model. "Her brain's hurt and she's in a coma. She can't even breathe by herself."

"This unit is the best," the man said. "And the staff is tops."

Erin didn't find any comfort in his words. If everything was so medically advanced, then why didn't Amy wake up? If the human brain was so superior, then why hadn't it found a way to bring sixteen-year-old girls out of comas? She set the model down on the desk. "I'm going in to be with my sister," she told the man and walked away.

A nurse named Ellie was monitoring Amy's vital signs and making notations on a chart. Erin watched as Ellie performed several procedures. "What are you doing?" Erin asked, afraid that the nurse might try to hide something from her.

"Charting the results of her latest Glasgow test."

"What's a Glasgow test?"

Ellie showed Erin the paper with numbers neatly written in small boxes. "It's a standard for measuring a comatose patient's progress."

"Progress? But she never moves."

Ellie smiled. "Let me explain. We take temperature, pulse, and blood pressure. We check respiration—in Amy's case she's on a ventilator—and we do a few neurological tests and grade her on a scale."

"Like what?"

"For instance, we chart whether or not her eyes open. 'Spontaneously' equals a four, while 'none' equals a one." Ellie pointed to the bottom of the chart where the criteria was printed. "On 'Verbal Response'—you know, whether she reacts when you talk to her—there's a scale of one to five, with five being 'oriented' and meaning fully conscious, and one meaning 'no response.' For 'Motor Response' a five means she 'obeys commands,' and a one means 'no response.'"

She paused, and Erin examined the neat rows of charted numbers. "So where's Amy?"

"Right now she's a one-one-three."

"That's not good, is it?"

"The higher the score, the better."

"But she's a three on 'Motor Response,'" Erin said hopefully.

"Yes, she reflexes to pain."

"You hurt her?"

"Not really. It's an automatic reaction of the muscles to stimuli. Like when a doctor hits your knee and it jerks. It's the way we can judge the depth of her coma and her brain-stem functions."

Erin pointed to the paper on the metal clipboard. "And what's 'Pupil Reaction' mean?"

"How well her pupils react when we shine a light

into them. Another way of gauging brain-stem functions."

Erin's head was swimming with information and starting to ache. "The numbers will go up, won't they?"

"That's what we're hoping."

Erin wanted to ask, "And what if they don't?" but lost her courage. Of course they would go up. Amy was a fighter, and their whole family was going to stand by her and help her fight.

Later she went to the cafeteria with her parents to discuss a schedule for the upcoming week. "I don't want Amy alone," Mrs. Bennett said. "When she wakes up, I want to be sure that one of us is there with her."

"I can come after classes and stay till midnight or so," Mr. Bennett said. "We'll trade off the night shift, Marian, so that every other night we each get to go home and sleep in our own bed."

"And Inez can handle the shop in the mornings, so I can stay from midnight till about ten A.M. That way I can go into the boutique at noon and stay until closing."

"Spring break starts this Thursday, so I can be up here during the days," Erin offered. "In fact, I'm positive I can get excused absences through Thursday."

"All right," Mr. Bennett said. "Erin, you and I'll go home tonight. In the morning we'll go to school, and you can get your books and assignments. I'll work my regular class schedule so that the headmaster doesn't have to find a substitute at the last minute."

"We'll need another car," Mrs. Bennett said, and Erin felt guilt sear through her like a hot iron.

"I'll rent one for us," Mr. Bennett told her. "Erin can use our station wagon."

Mrs. Bennett said nothing more about the car situation, but Erin felt her resentment. After all, if she'd driven instead of Amy, there might never have been an accident. Then another thought came to her. What if *she* had been the one in ICU instead of Amy? That idea so terrified her that she felt sick to her stomach.

What would it be like to be trapped in a coma? To be—where? Where was Amy anyway? Her body was in the room, but where were her thoughts? Did she dream? Did she think? Was it like being asleep? Or was it worse? Erin had no answers. All she had was fear. It lodged inside her heart like a monster with tentacles and began to squeeze.

Chapter Nine

❦

The next morning Erin rode to school with her father. Outside the world seemed perfectly normal. A bright March sun made the day feel balmy, and azaleas bloomed in profusions of fuchsia, white, and pink in neighborhood yards. She wondered how everything could look so normal, so ordinary, and yet be so irreversibly changed at the same time.

"This is going to be rough on all of us," Mr. Bennett said with a deep sigh.

"We'll make it, Dad," Erin said, not at all convinced.

"According to Dr. DuPree a coma can be unpredictable. Sometimes a patient can be in one for years."

"Well, not Amy," Erin said with determination. "By the end of the week, she'll be awake and complaining."

"A physical therapist will come in soon and start exercising Amy's arms and legs to keep her muscles toned. Otherwise they can atrophy and waste away."

Erin stared out the car window and struggled for composure. It was hard to think of Amy being so silent and still. "Maybe I can learn how to exercise her and help out," she said.

"There's—uh—also the possibility of brain damage." Mr. Bennett said the phrase carefully, and Erin felt her father's eyes cut to her. "Even after she wakes up, it may take a long time for her to be all right again."

Or she may never be all right again. He hadn't said it, but Erin knew that's what he was trying to tell her. "She'll be fine, Daddy. No matter how long it takes, Amy's gonna be fine. If we all work together, she'll be just the way she was before." *Amy is only sixteen years old,* Erin thought. *She has to be all right.*

At school Erin was mobbed by concerned classmates and teachers as she collected her books and assignments. She forced herself to answer the same questions over and over, anxious to leave and go back to the hospital. She was almost out the front door when Miss Hutton hailed her.

The teacher with the high, funny voice Amy loved to imitate rushed up and said, "I'm so sorry. How could such a thing have happened to our little Amy?"

Erin gritted her teeth. Her sister wasn't Miss Hutton's "little Amy." "It was an accident," she said.

"Oh you poor dear! What a horrible, horrible ordeal for you all. And to think that this Saturday she'd planned to come with me to the Children's Home and play a clown for their big Easter party."

Erin recalled how Amy looked bobbing around her bedroom wearing the bulbous nose and floozy red wig. "She was looking forward to doing it."

"Well, when she wakes up in the hospital, you tell her not to worry about it. And you tell her that all the children will miss her terribly, but that she can come to next year's Christmas party and play the clown."

"I'll tell her."

"I'll find someone to fill in for her, but I've never had a nicer clown than Amy. And the kids are just crazy about her." Miss Hutton rested her briefcase on a nearby water fountain adding, "Before I forget . . . here's some of Amy's papers—assignments, tests, reports and such. They're graded, and I thought you might show them to her when she's recovering. The grades are good, so they might cheer her up." The older woman smiled broadly and handed over a sheaf of papers.

Erin mumbled "Thanks," and shoved them into her duffel bag, then left the school pondering Miss Hutton's words. She'd often thought of Amy as "scatterbrained" and "silly," as a show-off who could never say no. But she realized how warm and giving Amy was too. Erin told herself that she had much to share with her sister when she came out of her coma—and a lot to make up for.

At the hospital Erin relieved her mother, who looked about ready to drop. "You call me at home if there's *any* change," Mrs. Bennett told her before leaving. Erin promised, then settled in for the long afternoon vigil.

In the sun-filled waiting room Erin recognized a

few faces from the night before, but she kept to herself, too tired to socialize or make friends. She snuggled into a chair. A television soap opera droned in the background. The chair felt soft and cozy. Erin's eyelids drooped, and her head nodded downward.

She dreamed that she and Amy were unwrapping gifts, but Amy had a long hose attached to her mouth, and she couldn't laugh. Erin tried to reach over and pull the tube out, but her hand kept knocking against an invisible glass wall, and no matter how hard she tried, she couldn't get through it.

The warmth of the dream gave way to anxiety, and Erin's heart began to pound. She reached out toward her sister, who kept busy and was oblivious to her. She heard someone calling her name. From far away the voice beckoned, "Wake up, Erin. Wake up."

She jumped, suddenly awake, and found her arms wrapped around Travis's neck.

Confused, and then extremely embarrassed, Erin let go of Travis and pressed hard into the back of the chair. She mumbled his name, still trying to separate the dream from reality. What was he doing here in the middle of a school day?

"Are you all right?" he asked.

"I think so." Her face burned. "I–I guess I fell asleep."

He rose from his crouched position and dropped into the chair next to her. "You look tired."

"What time is it?"

He looked up at the wall clock. "One o'clock. I—uh—didn't go to school today. I called the hospital, but they only said Amy was in fair condition, so I decided to drive over and check things out. What's happening?"

"There's no change. She's still in a coma. My folks and I are taking turns staying round the clock until Amy wakes up."

"How long will it take?"

"The doctors don't know."

Travis's expression fell. "That stinks."

Erin shifted and straightened out her leg, which had cramped. She got a sudden idea. "Would you like to go in and see her?"

"I—uh—I thought only family could go inside."

"They'll let you in if I ask them."

He looked hesitant and wary. "Gee, Erin, I don't know. . . ."

She wanted him to come with her. Somehow she felt she owed it to Amy because Amy cared about him so much. "Please, Travis. When she's better, she'll ask if you came. You know how Amy can be if she thinks someone isn't thinking about her one hundred percent of the time."

"I'll never hear the end of it," he said, his smile softening the look of panic on his face. "After I took you to the concert and after I told her the details, all she asked was, 'Did you miss me?' As if I thought about anything else all night."

His confession stung Erin, making her realize how one-sided her feelings for him really were. She stood up. "Come on, Travis, come see Amy with me. Talk to her. The nurses said that it's important to talk to people in comas. They told me that patients often wake up and tell them that even though they couldn't respond, they remember hearing someone talking to them and encouraging them."

He hesitated but followed her down the hall. At the closed door of ICU, Erin explained the situation through a speaker in the wall to Becky, the daytime nurse. They were admitted, and Erin continued to lead him through the unit toward the partitioned area where Amy lay.

Amy's body was motionless, but Becky approached and announced cheerfully, "You've got visitors, Amy. It's your sister and a friend named Travis." Becky patted Amy's arm. The ventilator hissed, and Amy's chest rose up and down under the white sheet. Dark bruising had appeared around her eye sockets, and her coloring seemed ashen, not pink and glowing.

Erin stroked Amy's cheek. "Travis is with me, Ames. And when I stopped by school to get my books, everyone there asked about you. Even Miss Hutton." Erin felt as if she were talking to a doll. She glanced toward Travis, who had backed up all the way to the wall, his expression wooden. "Do you want to tell Amy anything?" she asked.

"No." He looked cornered, trapped. "I want to go now."

"But you've hardly seen her," Erin protested.

"I've seen her enough."

Becky stepped forward and told Erin, "Perhaps you could come back later."

Travis brushed around them and hurried to the door. "I'll see you outside, Erin."

He was gone, and Erin faced the nurse over Amy's bed. "I—I guess it was getting to him," she apologized.

"It's not unusual."

"I'd better go check on him."

Becky nodded, and Erin took one last lingering look at her sister and said, "I'll be back later, Ames, all right?" She felt a little foolish asking permission, because Amy couldn't answer. Erin turned quickly and left ICU to look for Travis.

She found him back in the waiting room taking long gulps from a can of cola. "Are you okay?" she asked.

"Sure." He shrugged and looked sheepish. "It was tougher than I thought, seeing her that way."

"She's going to be fine," Erin said. "It's gonna take some time, that's all."

Travis shifted nervously. "Listen, I bought her a stuffed animal, but I left it down in my car. Can I bring it over to your house later? Maybe you could bring it up to her, and she could have it in her room. Do you think that'll be all right with the nurses?"

Erin considered his plea. He'd bought Amy a gift, which was more than she had done. And maybe it would be a good idea to bring some of Amy's familiar things from home so that when she woke up, she'd see them and not be scared. "How about tonight? I'll be home after supper."

"I'll see you later," Travis said, and after he'd gone, she stared at the floor where he'd stood until her legs ached.

Erin ate a quick supper in the hospital cafeteria and returned to the waiting room only to see her mother sitting alone in a corner and smoking a cigarette.

"Are you relieving me, Mom?" she asked, feeling awkward.

Mrs. Bennett casually snuffed out the cigarette and said, "Don't look so disapproving, Erin. It settles my nerves, and it's better than taking tranquilizers."

"You don't have to explain it to me." The room was nearly deserted, and Erin assumed that the "regulars" were at supper and would be returning soon. "Travis came up today," she said. "But he didn't handle it too well."

"I'm not surprised. Dr. DuPree said he'll have another CAT scan run tomorrow. There's still a lot of intracranial pressure." Mrs. Bennett took out another cigarette and lit it.

"What's that mean?"

"It means that if her brain continues to swell, he'll have to operate to relieve the pressure."

The word "operate" made Erin's stomach lurch. "That sounds scary."

Mrs. Bennett tapped the ash off the end of her cigarette. "There's something else you need to be aware of, Erin. It happened this afternoon and gave me a lot of false hope."

"What?"

"Amy moved."

Erin gasped audibly. "You mean she might be coming out of the coma?"

Mrs. Bennett shook her head impatiently. "No, that's not it at all. I thought it was, but when I ran for the nurse, she explained to me that what I saw was simple spinal reflex. Nothing more. You know, like a knee jerking when it's hit in the right spot. So if you see her hand move, or her eyelids flutter, that's all it probably is."

Erin realized how much her mother's hopes had been dashed by the medical explanation of Amy's movement and wished she could take away her disappointment. "Thanks for warning me," she said.

Her mother blinked hard and crossed her arms. "I don't want Amy to be a vegetable, Erin. I don't want her hooked to machines for the rest of her life, unable to talk or smile ever again."

"That's not going to happen to Amy," Erin said fiercely. "The quality of Amy's life is important," Mrs. Bennett continued. "She's too young to live the rest of her life in a nursing home."

"That's not going—"

"Stop it, Erin!" her mother interrupted. "Of course it can happen to Amy. That's the bottom line when she comes out of her coma. *If* she comes out of it."

Erin wanted to clamp her hands over her ears. How could her mother be saying those things? How could she even suggest the hideous alternative to being kept alive by machines? She felt a growing pressure at the base of her skull and knew that a headache was coming on. "M—mom, please don't give up on Amy."

Mrs. Bennett reached out and tucked Erin's hair over her shoulder. "Is that what you think I'm doing? I'm not giving up. I'm just tired, and I feel so helpless whenever I go in there and see her lying so still."

"But she's *alive*," Erin said. "And that's what counts."

Her mother ground out her cigarette and stood. "Go on home, Erin. Wake your father at ten so that he can come down here and stay with Amy and me. I'll be home later."

Erin watched her mother head down to ICU, feeling as if her insides were being torn out. Why was this happening to their family? Why had she let Amy talk her into driving the car? If only she could turn back the hands of the clock.

"Are you all right?" The voice caused Erin to jump, and she turned to face a girl her own age with dark hair and wide gray eyes. "Sorry, I didn't mean to scare you," the girl said. "I'm Beth Clark, and I saw you come in the other night."

Erin mumbled a self-conscious greeting and wished Beth would go away.

"Why are you here?" Beth asked.

Erin told her, then realized that it was only fair to ask, "And why are you here?"

Beth stared off in the distance. "It's my mother." Her gaze found Erin's again. "She's dying, and her only hope is if somebody else dies before she does."

Chapter Ten

❧

"I don't understand," Erin said to Beth, taken aback by her extraordinary statement.

"My mom's had kidney disease for years. This past year she's gotten worse, so they put her on dialysis three days a week. She was an outpatient, so I dropped her off for treatments on my way to school and picked her up on my way home from school."

"I've heard about dialysis," Erin said slowly.

"It's being hooked up to a machine that does the work of the kidneys." Beth explained. "The machine cleans the blood, and each exchange takes about six hours."

Another machine doing the work of a human organ, Erin thought. "Let's hear it for technology," she said without sarcasm.

Beth sank into an upholstered chair, and Erin took the chair next to her. "Anyway, dialysis helps, but it's no way to spend the rest of your life. I've got a brother and two sisters, and we'd like to have Mom well."

"So what now?"

"She needs a kidney transplant. We've been waiting for a donor for months."

71

"Is that why she's here?"

"Not really. She got sick, so they checked her into the hospital, but she's getting better."

Erin found herself keenly interested. She'd read about kidney and heart transplants, and now here was a real-live person who needed one. "How will they find a donor?"

Beth toyed with a silver necklace. "Oh, she's been programmed into a computer bank. That way if someone dies and donates his organs, doctors can check for compatibility. You know, a good match of tissues so her body won't reject the new kidney. At home we're always on call. Everytime the phone rings, it could be the hospital saying they've found a donor. If that happens, we drop everything and go for the transplant."

"And if they don't find one?"

"They'll send her home again without one. This time they're putting a portable dialysis machine in our house, and she'll be almost one hundred percent bed-ridden. Our lives would be so much easier if they could find a kidney for her."

Erin saw sadness in Beth's eyes, and she felt sorry for her. But she saw the unfairness of the situation too. Finding Beth's mother a kidney meant that someone, someplace, had to die. The idea made her shudder. She didn't quite know what to say, so she changed the subject and asked about Beth's school.

It turned out that she was a junior at a huge public high school. She had a boyfriend—"the tall guy with red hair who sits in the corner with me during the evenings." Erin remembered seeing him.

Beth asked, "Was that boy who was here earlier your boyfriend? I saw you hugging him."

Erin reddened. "No, Travis is my sister's boyfriend. I was having a bad dream, and he woke me up, and I just grabbed him."

"He's cute."

"Yeah, well, he and Amy have been hot and heavy since before Christmas."

"Is that your sister's name? Amy?"

Erin nodded but found herself reluctant to discuss her sister's situation. She quickly looked up at the clock and said, "Gee, Beth, I've got to be going. Travis is stopping by my house sometime tonight, and I don't want him to wake my dad. We're all taking shifts, and it's Dad's turn to spend the night."

"No problem. I wanted to say hi to you sooner, but you kind of looked like you wanted to be left alone."

"I didn't mean to be antisocial, but it's been a tough few days. Some of the other people in here have tried to get a conversation going, but I just didn't feel up to it."

"Hey, that's okay, I understand. It's crazy. You spend night and day with these strangers, and the only thing you have in common is that somebody is really sick, maybe dying, and you sort of band together for support. When they leave, you never see

73

them again, but while you're here, together in this room, they're the best friends you have."

"You sound like the voice of experience."

Beth gave a wry smile. "Five times in the past fourteen months I've camped in this place. I sure hope they find a kidney for my mom soon. I feel like a hospital groupie."

Erin laughed and gathered her things. She promised Beth she'd see her the next day and headed for the elevator. Erin was halfway down before she realized that it was the first time she'd laughed in the past three days, it had felt good.

Erin let herself into her house and shivered. The silence was eerie. No lamps were lit, and the rooms were dark and chilly. She found a note from her dad saying he couldn't sleep and had gone to the library, and that he'd be home by ten to get ready to go to the hospital.

Erin deposited her things in her room, took a hot shower, washed her hair, and began to blow-dry it. She'd never felt so drained and sapped in her life, not even after a grueling dance performance. She stared at the mirror thoughtfully. She hadn't thought about dancing in days. There'd been a time when that was all she thought about. Funny how the focus of your life can shift so drastically.

Her fine blond hair danced about her head as the dryer worked. Terpsicord, Ms. Thornton, and Wolftrap seemed light-years away. She'd never even told Amy about Wolftrap. She'd been upset with her and had perversely held back the news. Yet Erin knew that if she *had* said something, Amy's response would have been totally excited and encouraging.

A lump rose in Erin's throat. There were so many things she wanted to say to her sister, so many times she'd growled at her or teased her that she wanted to take back. If only Amy would wake up, Erin swore she'd never be mean to her again.

Listlessly Erin finished dressing and wandered to the living room. She put on a cassette of Amy's favorite rock group and pulled out the stack of family photo albums. Her mother had kept them up-to-date, and Erin started with the one that featured Amy's birth. She'd just gotten past the photos of an infant Amy in the hospital nursery when the doorbell rang. Travis stood on the doorstep. She brought him into the living room and plopped onto the floor.

"I was just going through some old pictures," she explained.

He tossed the stuffed bear he was carrying onto the sofa and sat down beside her. "Amy?" he asked, pointing to a dark-haired toddler, holding two fistfuls of birthday cake.

"She was a terror," Erin said with a wistful smile.

"Is this you?" He indicated one of a six-year-old Erin dressed in a tutu with her arms poised over her head.

She made a face at her roly-poly image. "That was taken before my very first recital. Look at all that baby fat."

"There's no baby fat on you now," Travis said, and

his observation made her stomach feel fluttery. He was sitting so close that she caught his fresh, clean scent.

They flipped through the albums and watched the years parade past in a collection of color photos. Amy in her playpen. Erin on her first tricycle. Amy with her front teeth missing and clutching her school lunch box. Erin wearing a crown as May Day queen in the fifth grade.

"When was this one taken?" Travis asked.

Erin gazed at a blowup of one of her father's favorite photographs. Erin and Amy were running barefoot through a grassy field full of dandelions, their long hair streaming behind them, their mouths wide with laughter.

"I still remember that day," Erin said. "I was five and Amy had just turned four. I thought that field was the most beautiful thing I'd ever seen, that it was a place where a fairy princess lived. And all Amy wanted to do was run around and make the seeds fly off the weeds. I started to cry and asked Dad to make Amy stop, but of course she didn't, and I eventually got into the game too. We chased those seeds for over an hour. I can still see them floating away in the sky."

They stared at the photo in silence until a wave of melancholia engulfed her and she was afraid she might start crying. She looked at Travis, and his expression was blank. She wondered what he was thinking, and then she saw the cuddly stuffed bear on the sofa. "Is that for Amy?"

Travis followed her line of vision. "Yeah. She saw

it at the mall and made a big fuss about how cute it was. So I bought it for her."

"I asked the nurses if it was all right to bring some of her things from home for her room, and they said I could. Why don't you just bring the bear up to her tomorrow?"

Travis studied the bear for a long moment before speaking. "I'm not going back up there, Erin."

"What?"

"Not until Amy's sitting up in her bed and talking."

"But it may help her subconsciously knowing that you're in the room with her."

He looked at Erin as if she were crazy. "Erin, she doesn't know when *anyone's* in the room with her."

Erin snapped, "How do you know? What makes you an authority?"

"Take it easy," Travis said with a placating tone. "I'll keep calling for reports, and you can call me too. But I can't go back inside that room when she's so— you know—so out of it."

"She's unconscious. She'll wake up."

"She's in a coma. It's different."

By now they were both on their feet amid the jumble of photo albums. "It's just a deep sleep, that's all. It's a way for her brain to recover from being so banged around."

"Erin, face reality. She can't even *breathe* by herself."

Erin wanted to scream at him, but just then her father came home. "Is something wrong?" he asked.

Erin stood facing Travis, her heart pounding, her fists balled. "Travis was just leaving," she said tersely.

Travis mumbled apologetic words to Erin and her dad and retreated out the door. She longed to slam it hard against his back.

"What was *that* all about?" Mr. Bennett asked when she bent and started piling the albums.

"Nothing. He's just so negative about Amy's condition, and I got mad. He says he's not even going up to see her again until she comes out of the coma."

Mr. Bennett knelt down next to her and held her by the shoulders. "Don't be so upset about it, honey."

Erin felt tears well up in her eyes. "But she likes him so much, and he acts like he doesn't even care!"

"You can't expect everyone to handle this thing in the same way, Erin. Grief doesn't affect us all alike."

"Grief?" She said the word incredulously. "Grief is when you cry. Travis isn't crying. I guess he's too macho for tears."

"In other words, real men don't cry?"

She held her spine stiff and put a chill in her voice. "Real men stick by the people they say they care about. They don't have to bawl and blubber, but they *do* have to keep their promises. And Travis Sinclair told me he really liked Amy. Now he's not even going to go see her in the hospital."

She thought of all the fantasies she'd had about him, of how much she'd longed to have him as a boyfriend, and felt even more betrayed. "He's acting like a creep, Daddy. A genuine creep!"

Chapter Eleven

"Don't judge him too harshly," Mr. Bennett said. "There's more to grieving than crying. And there's more to caring than hovering over someone's bedside."

The lamplight glowed on the side of his face, and for the first time Erin noticed the bags under his eyes and lines around his mouth. He had a whole night ahead of him to spend in the hospital, and here she was taking out her anger at Travis on her father. "I'm sorry, I didn't mean to get so upset."

Mr. Bennett smiled pensively. "That's okay, honey, we're all on edge these days." He picked up an album and leafed through the plastic-covered pages. "I remember when she was just learning to talk, and your mom and I would ask, 'What does your sister want, Erin?' And you'd tell us, and sure enough, that's what it was. You two always seemed to understand each other. I think underneath you're very much alike, even though on the outside you have different styles."

He rose, crossed to the buffet, and rummaged through the junk drawer. "I got the birthday pictures back a week ago and tossed them in here for your mother to put in the album." He withdrew the packet and brought it over to Erin. "They turned out good, huh?"

Erin sorted through them—Amy grinning from behind her birthday cake, Amy holding up the car keys and special key chain Erin had given her. A lump wedged in Erin's throat. Could it have been only a few weeks ago that they were all so happy and carefree? "Yeah, Dad, they're super." She placed them carefully inside the back cover of an album.

"Maybe when this is all over, you mom will put them in order," he said. "Maybe this will be the birthday we remember most of all."

"Amy will wake up, won't she, Dad?" Erin hadn't wanted to ask the question but couldn't help herself. Her conversation with her mother earlier still weighed on her mind.

"The doctors aren't making any promises."

"If she doesn't, will we have to put her in a nursing home?" The idea made Erin shiver.

"What do you suppose Amy would want?"

"She'd want to come home."

"How would we care for her?"

"We could." Erin jutted her chin stubbornly. "Between the three of us, we could take care of her."

Mr. Bennett eased onto the sofa. He picked up the bear and stroked its fur. "The doctor asked us about putting a 'Do not resuscitate' order on Amy's chart this morning."

"Meaning what?"

"Meaning that should her heart stop suddenly, they wouldn't do anything to start it beating again."

Erin stared at him blankly as his words sunk in. The house was so silent that she heard the ticking of the hall clock. "You mean, let her die?"

Mr. Bennett kept studying the teddy bear. "She's going to have massive brain damage, Erin. She'll never be normal."

"But they can't just let her *die*. Please, Daddy, don't let them do that. They have to start her heart."

He turned anguished eyes on her. "Honey, Erin. Take it easy . . . it's all right. Her heart's very strong right now, so don't worry."

Erin had gone cold all over. She dug her nails into her palms, hoping the instant pain would keep her from screaming. "How could her doctors suggest such a thing? Aren't they supposed to do everything to keep a person alive?"

Mr. Bennett let out a deep, weary sigh and rubbed his hand over his forehead. "They are, Erin. But lately I've wondered, What's the distinction between prolonging life and postponing death? Can't you see the difference between the two?"

"What about, 'Thou shall not kill'?" Erin grabbed at the commandment as if it were a lifeline. "If they let her die, it's the same as killing her."

"But if they didn't have the machines in the first place, wouldn't Amy have died already? There's a saying that everything under the sun has a season, that there's 'a time to live and a time to die.' What about

Amy's time to die, Erin? What right does medicine have to tamper this way with her season?"

Erin was afraid she was going to be sick. Her father's questions were frightening her. She had never thought about such things before, and she couldn't think about them now. Especially about Amy. "But you said her heart's fine, didn't you?"

"Yes, honey, she's young and strong. They were only asking what we'd want done should she suddenly die, that's all. We live in a world where technology gives us options. They can restart her heart"—he paused and cleared his throat—"or they can let her go."

Erin pressed her lips together. "Well, I want them to start her heart again if it should stop. So that's my choice. What do you and Mom want to do?"

"The same thing."

Erin sagged and let out her breath. "I guess it's real complicated, isn't it?"

"It's very complicated. If Amy never comes out of her coma, we're probably dooming her to a life in an institution."

"But she may wake up," Erin countered, her voice quavering. "The machines are helping her live long enough for her brain to get better. That's the way I see it."

Mr. Bennett stroked the teddy bear's tummy. Erin wanted to throw herself in her father's arms, but she was too old for that. Too old to cry like a baby. "Thanks for talking to me, Dad. I—I'm glad you told me what the doctors asked."

"We're a family, Erin. Your wishes count too." He stood, smoothed his rumpled shirt, and plunked the stuffed bear on the couch. He said, "I'd better get ready and get down to the hospital so your mother can come home and get some sleep."

"Sure." Erin began to gather the photo albums, spread out in a jumble around her. "I'm going to clean up here and go to bed." He left the room, and Erin shut each book, being very careful not to look at any more pictures.

When she was finished, she picked up the teddy bear and hugged it to her breasts. It smelled new but also carried the sweet, pungent aroma of her father's pipe tobacco. She cuddled it tenderly and rocked back and forth on her knees until she heard her father leave for the hospital.

By Wednesday Erin had settled into a routine of relieving her mother midmorning and staying until one of her parents relieved her in the early evening. The monotony of the day was broken by Beth, who came straight from school every afternoon.

"I'm glad Easter break starts tomorrow," Beth told Erin as she nibbled on a handful of potato chips.

"Me too," Erin said, thinking of the plans she'd made a month before with Shara to go to the beach and stare at the college guys down from the northern campuses. There'd be no sun-filled vacation for her now.

She and Beth started a game of Monopoly. "How's your sister today?"

"The CAT they just did didn't show any more swelling, so at least they won't have to operate."

"That's good."

"But it didn't show the doctors anything else promising," Erin countered. "They'll do another one in a few days."

"Did you put the things in her room like you told me you were going to do?"

"Only some stuffed animals, but I want to put up her life-size poster of Tom Cruise on one of the walls tonight. The nurses didn't seem to mind when I asked if it was okay."

"Who would mind?" Beth joked. "At least when she comes out of her coma, there'll be something worth waking up for."

"Right," Erin agreed. "Whenever she comes out of her coma."

That evening at home Erin went into Amy's bedroom to take down the poster. She entered hesitantly, momentarily surprised. The room was spotless, neat, and orderly. Clothes had been hung up, papers stacked, pillows arranged on the tidily made up coverlet. It didn't look like Amy's room at all. "Inez . . ." she muttered. Hadn't her mother told her that one of Inez's friends was coming over to clean their house? Obviously, she'd come.

Erin walked around the room. It was too quiet and seemed foreign to her. Without Amy, Erin could scarcely stand to be in it. She stopped at Amy's dresser and fingered a pile of papers. She wondered if Amy would have to learn to read all over again. She'd seen a television report once about people who'd had brain damage and they'd had to relearn certain things as if they were babies. "I'll help you, Amy," she vowed, rearranging the pile.

She scanned the photographs stuck into the wooden frame around the mirror. Travis and Amy smiled out at her. She stared hard at his handsome face. He'd kept his promise and called once a day for an update, but Erin was cool to him. How could he refuse to come see her sister? She wondered what he'd be doing over spring break.

Erin turned toward the poster of Tom Cruise and spied Amy's makeup kit in the corner. She lifted it onto the bed and opened the lid. Tubes of greasepaint were scattered inside. The fuzzy red wig and the bright red nose were also there. False eyelashes and a pair of oversize rubber ears were wrapped in wads of tissue.

Erin went to the closet and dug around until she found the satin clown suit and floppy shoe coverings that extended outward a foot long. On the same hanger with the costume was a stiff white net bib with sequins. She ran her hand over the smooth satin. On Saturday Amy was to have appeared at the Children's Home. Erin wondered what the kids would be told. She wondered if they'd ask Miss Hutton, "But where's Amy?"

Unexpected tears welled up in Erin's eyes as she thought about the children. Why should she feel so sad about it? Why should she care? Amy couldn't be there, and that's the way it was. *But you can*, she thought, startled.

"I don't know anything about being a clown," she argued aloud.

You can go in Amy's place, the voice inside said.

"But I'll feel so stupid dressed this way."

It's for Amy. And the kids.

"This is the dumbest idea you've ever had, Erin Bennett," she announced. Yet even as she said it, Erin knew she was going to go find her father's Briarwood faculty phone directory and call Miss Hutton and volunteer.

Quickly she gathered up the costume and the makeup kit and hurried from the bedroom. Her pulse was racing, excitement carrying her down the hallway. She had something to do. Something to give to the kids at the Children's Home, and no matter how silly and foolish she felt about being a clown, she'd do it. For Amy.

Chapter Twelve

∽

Erin hid in the rest room at the Children's Home until the last possible moment. A glance in the mirror told her all she wanted to know about how she looked dressed as a clown. She looked ridiculous. Yet she was experiencing some sense of satisfaction in the achievement. When she'd called Miss Hutton, the teacher had been so delighted that she'd personally driven Erin to the Home, chattering and complimenting her all the way.

"This is so wonderful of you, Erin," Miss Hutton had said in her distinctive, high-pitched voice. "I did manage to find someone to fill in for Amy—a young man from Berkshire Prep named David. You'll meet him at the Home. But the more clowns the merrier, I always say." Erin only nodded and mumbled.

Miss Hutton barreled ahead. "The party will start in the activity room, then move out to the lawn where the staff has hidden about one hundred Easter eggs. I know you don't have much experience in this sort of thing, but the children are so fascinated by clowns that they won't notice. Most are five to ten years old, and they're so adorable."

Once at the facility Erin had retreated to the

bathroom to begin her transformation. She'd watched Amy several times and felt she could reconstruct her sister's clown from memory. First she applied a base coat of white greasepaint. Next she filled in a wide mouth of bright red well beyond the perimeters of her own lips and drew large red circles on her cheeks. She pasted on the false eyelashes and drew eyebrows that arched high on her forehead. The red wig and bulbous nose topped off her appearance. In many ways she looked like Amy, but the resemblance so disconcerted her that she drew a row of bright blue tears from the corner of one eye to the edge of her jaw.

She donned the satin costume, tied the bib behind her neck, and slipped the floppy rubber shoes over her sneakers. "Good grief, it's like trying to walk in swim flippers," she said, taking a few cautious steps.

Yet she *had* become a clown to rival any that performed in the circus, and she was sure that Amy would be proud of her. She announced, "Well, here goes nothing," took a deep breath, and edged out the door. One of the outsize rubber shoes got stuck in the doorway. "Drat!" she muttered, and struggled to pull it free.

"Need some help?" someone asked.

Erin jerked upright, only to have the shoe slip free and the door swing shut. She toppled backward and landed in the arms of another clown.

"Do you always throw yourself at guys this way?" he asked with a laugh, hauling her to her feet.

She felt totally embarrassed, then realized that he

couldn't see her blush because of all her makeup. "That wasn't funny," she said, squaring her shoulders. Even though he was wearing full makeup, she saw mischief sparkling in his blue eyes, and she thought of how silly she must look trying to act dignified in a clown face and outfit. Erin started to giggle.

The boy's face, already painted with a lopsided grin, smiled more broadly. "Hi, I'm David, fellow clown and court jester. You must be Amy."

Erin sobered quickly. "No, I'm Amy's sister. I'm filling in for her. She's"—Erin searched for an explanation—"sick."

"Too bad. I've heard she was terrific, and I was looking forward to working with her."

"You do this often?"

"Every chance I get. I have a magic act too, but my specialty is balloons."

"Balloons?"

"Yeah, I make animals and things for the kids out of balloons. Let me show you." He reached into the pocket of the billowing overcoat he wore, pulled out a balloon, and proceeded to blow it up.

Erin watched, fascinated, as he puffed and twisted and shaped the pliant elongated balloon. A minute later he held out a giraffe. "That's super," she said, taking it. "How do you do that?"

"Trade secret," he whispered. "What's your specialty?"

Suddenly Erin realized that she couldn't *do* anything. How had Amy managed these appearances?

What had she done to entertain her audience? "I–I don't-know. Like I said, this is my sister's gig."

David pondered her, tapping his fat clown shoe on the polished tile floor. The makeup around his mouth turned into a sad-sack frown. "You need a gimmick," he said. "Here, take my water flower, and every chance you get, squirt me in the face."

"Oh, but I couldn't. . . ." She backed away, but he whipped off the large plastic daisy from his lapel. A long thin hose led from the back of the flower to a bulb.

"You feed the hose down your sleeve and keep the bulb in your palm." He explained how the gizmo worked as he pinned it on her costume and pushed the tubing inside her sleeve along her arm.

Erin was amazed by his brashness but soon realized that he didn't think of her as anything but a fellow clown out for the biggest laugh. Just the way Amy would have acted. "Uh—thanks," she mumbled when he had finished.

"Try it." She squeezed the bulb, and a spout of water doused him in the face. "Outstanding," he said. "So, this is your first gig?"

"Yes. My last too," she added yanking at the constricting bib around her throat. "If I don't choke to death before the end of the day."

"Want to work up a little routine?"

"Like what?"

"The kids like it when you do pratfalls."

Erin looked skeptical, thinking of her dance aspirations. She didn't want to hurt herself. "Gee, I don't know. . . ."

"I'll do all the falling," David assured her. "You just trip me up."

"Are you sure?"

"Positive. I do this stuff all the time. I won't feel a thing."

Erin agreed, and they did a few practice moves. Each time David sprawled convincingly on the floor. Finally satisfied, he rose, dusted himself off, and offered his arm in courtly fashion. "Shall we adjourn to the activity room?"

Erin hooked her arm through his and curtsied. "Lead on, fool." They started down the hall, each lifting oversize rubber feet in cautious, exaggerated steps, being careful not to trip one another.

The activity room was packed with small kids and personnel, and in no time David had won their hearts with his antics and balloon creatures.

Erin followed his cues and tripped him often. She sneaked behind him and tapped him on the shoulder. The kids shouted warnings, but he turned and took a faceful of water. No matter how predictable her action was, the children squealed in delight. Behind the anonymity of the makeup, she was able to act with outrageous abandon.

When the staff director announced the start of the egg hunt, Erin was almost sorry. David helped form a line and led the children out into the sunshine. Erin didn't follow but hung behind. Without the shouts of the audience, the room seemed hollow, and she watched from the window for a few moments, then let out a sigh. For her the party was over.

"There you are, Erin," Miss Hutton said, coming in from the bright outdoors. "You were wonderful, dear. The children are asking for you. Won't you come help find the eggs with them?"

"I really need to get back to the hospital," she explained.

Miss Hutton's expression turned to instant understanding. "Well, of course you do. Let me get my purse and drive you home."

Erin watched David prancing on the lawn with a dark-haired girl who kept dodging him and laughing. An overwhelming sadness descended on her. "Thanks. I'll need to clean up before I go."

Miss Hutton touched her arm. "The children will long remember this day, Erin. Thank you for coming."

"I did it for Amy."

"You charmed everyone. So did that young man, David."

"Miss Hutton, if he asks about me, don't tell him who I am or where I've gone. I'd like him and the children to remember me as just a clown."

"If that's what you want."

It was what Erin wanted—to be associated with laughter. She took off the floppy shoes so that she could walk more quickly and started for the door. Her foot brushed against an inflated balloon, and it danced upward in the air. She caught it and held it up. It was tied off in the middle to form a heart, and she decided to keep it as a souvenir.

David was very talented, and he had the gift of laughter. Too bad she'd never see him again. She wondered what he really looked like, then decided she didn't really want to know. This day had merely been an interlude in time, a brief time-out from all the pain and turmoil in her real life. She tucked the heart-shaped balloon under her arm and hurried down the hall to gather her things and make a quick escape.

On Easter Sunday, Erin went to a small chapel service in the hospital. It felt strange not to dress in new spring clothes and go to church with her family, where the choir would sing Handel's *Messiah* and baskets of white lilies would line the altar and aisles. This year the Bennetts would be sitting in Neuro-ICU instead of in the sanctuary.

They ate Easter dinner in the cafeteria, but there was no sense of joy in the meal. "They'll do another CAT scan tomorrow," Mrs. Bennett said, pushing aside her half-eaten food.

"You should eat more, Marian," Mr. Bennett told her.

"How can I eat? How can I even think about eating when my baby's upstairs attached to wires and machines?"

Erin's eyes darted quickly between her parents. *Don't let there be a scene*, she pleaded silently.

"Well, how's starving yourself going to help Amy?" he argued. "I'll bet you've lost ten pounds."

"So what? I'd lose a hundred if I thought it would help her." She reached in her purse for a cigarette.

"Well it won't."

Erin scraped back her chair and flung her napkin over her plate. "Stop it! Just stop it! It's Easter Sunday. And . . . and . . ." Her voice broke. She wanted to scream at them, wanted them to understand how bad she felt and how much she wished she could turn time backward. "I'm going up to the waiting room," Erin cried, and fled to the stairwell. She bolted up the stairs, two at a time, and by the fifth-floor landing she could scarcely breathe. Somehow she made it to the seventh-floor landing, where she stood gasping for air, sweat trickling down her face and back.

Her legs felt rubbery, but she pushed through the stairwell door and let it slam shut. She had almost regained her composure by the time she reached the waiting room, and the moment she entered, she sensed an air of expectancy.

Beth rushed over to her, her eyes shining with exuberance. "I'm so glad you came! I was afraid I'd miss you."

"What's happened? Is it your mom? Is she going home?"

"Better," Beth said, her voice breathy. "They found her a donor kidney, and we're on our way to Gainesville for the transplant operation."

Chapter Thirteen

"You're leaving?"

"As soon as possible. The donor's on a ventilator. He was in a motorcycle accident and was declared brain dead real early this morning. His family decided to donate his organs, and my mom was matched by the computer."

"But why do you have to go to Gainesville for the surgery?"

"There's a transplant team waiting and ready to go at the University of Florida's School of Medicine. The man's other organs will be flown to other hospitals for transplantation, but Mom's well enough to travel, so we're flying there."

An absurd picture from a Frankenstein movie flashed into Erin's mind—the mad scientist robbing graves to give his creature life. Beth's news seemed so farfetched, but the look of joy on her face told Erin that it was happening for real. "I'm glad for you—for your whole family. What did they tell you about the donor?"

"Oh, they never tell you much. All we know is that he was twenty-three and healthy. And that his kidney is compatible." Erin nodded. It was true that he'd have no use for his organs now. Perhaps it was best that they could go to help someone else live. And without a new kidney, Beth's mom was pretty much doomed. Erin reached out and squeezed Beth's hands. "We didn't know each other very long, but I feel very close to you."

Beth gave an understanding smile. "It's the waiting-room syndrome I told you about. Life and death get people together real quick."

"It turns complete strangers into buddies, right?"

"Erin, I don't even know that boy's family in Gainesville, but I love them. I love them because they're saving my mom's life."

A film of tears formed in Erin's eyes. "How long before you come home?"

"About a month if everything goes perfect." Beth had once told Erin that there were no guarantees that the kidney would function properly once it was transplanted, but that the risk was worth taking. She wondered if she'd still be sitting in the hospital waiting room in a month. "You have my home number, don't you?"

"I'll keep in touch," Beth promised. Someone called to her. "I gotta go." She ran a few steps, then stopped and turned. "I hope Amy gets well, Erin. I hope she wakes up and goes home real soon."

Erin watched her leave and felt a hole opening up inside her. She would miss Beth. She glanced around the waiting area and for the first time realized that she was an "old-timer" in the room. The others had come and gone as their relatives had recovered. She sniffed and wondered how much longer she and her parents could live in this limbo. Then Erin remembered that it was Easter Sunday, and that made it especially fitting for Beth's mom to receive a second chance at life. After all, wasn't resurrection supposed to follow death?

Monday's CAT scan on Amy showed no improvement, and her Glasgow tests had lowered to a one-one-two status. Her eyes weren't opened, she didn't respond to verbal commands, and her motor response to pain had diminished.

On Wednesday Erin's parents decided that they should all try to resume a more normal schedule. "The hospital will contact us if there's any change," Mrs. Bennett said when Erin argued that she wanted to stay during the day instead of returning to school.

"It makes no sense for us to just hang around here day after day this way," Mrs. Bennett insisted. "It's killing me."

Mr. Bennett agreed. "Work is good for us, Erin. It'll keep our minds occupied. And if they call us, we'll be at Briarwood together so we can come here together."

Erin returned to school on Thursday, sullen and angry with her parents. Her classmates and teachers greeted and hugged her, and by noon even she had to admit that she was better off at school than sitting around the waiting room.

"We missed you over break," Shara told her at lunch. "I went to the beach with Kori and Donna, and we met some guys from Northwestern." She bobbed her eyebrows lecherously. "We were naughty but nice. I dated two of them at the same time."

Erin listened to Shara's tales with a twinge of envy. She felt as if she were caught in a time warp and wondered if her life would ever be back to normal. "I don't think that's what the term 'double dating' means, Shara."

Her friend laughed and said, "Spring Fling's Saturday night. I invited Kenny after all. I guess you won't be going, huh?"

Erin had forgotten all about the dance until that moment. She recalled how much Amy had wanted to go with Travis, and how she'd felt sorry for herself because she'd had no one special in her life to even think about asking. "I don't think I'd have much fun."

"Lots of girls will be there without dates," Shara ventured. "You could meet the gang and have a good time."

Erin gave a wry smile. "Not this year," she said. "I'd like to see your dress though."

"I'll wear it up to the hospital and show it to you. It's different," she added mysteriously.

After lunch Erin went to the gym for dance class. It had been so long since she'd stretched and danced that she knew she'd be sore by the next day. Yet she was looking forward to the familiar muscle aches too. She put on her leotards and tights and was stretching when Ms. Thornton came in.

"Erin!" her instructor cried and embraced her. "I'm so glad you're back in school."

Erin quickly brought her up-to-date on Amy. Ms. Thornton shook her head. "I'm sorry she's not better. I went to Washington over the break to see my family, but I thought of you every day. I saw Allen, the director at Wolftrap, and mentioned your name. I told him how good I thought you were."

For a moment Erin's heart leapt; then it plummeted to her feet. "I haven't danced since the recital, Ms. Thornton. And I can't dance now. Not the way I'd need to in order to be in shape for an audition with Wolftrap."

Ms. Thornton touched Erin's arm. "Erin, you're a born dancer. You deserve the best training so that you can share your gift with the world."

Erin thought of Amy hooked to machines. She deserved to share her gift with the world too. "It's too much to think about now, Ms. Thornton. How can I even ask my parents about me going to Washington all summer?"

Ms. Thornton nodded. "I understand, but please don't give up the idea entirely. There's always next summer," she added.

"Sure," Erin agreed. "There's always next summer."

Ms. Thornton started to leave. "Oh, by the way, I have a cassette for you in my office of Amy's readings from the recital. I thought you'd like to have a copy."

For a moment Erin was overcome by her teacher's kindness. She cleared her throat, struggling to hold onto her emotions. "I'd like that very much. Thank you. I'll pick it up when I'm done here."

Later, when she did get the tape, Erin slipped into a bathroom stall because it was the only place she could be alone. She wept silently, holding the tape in her palm, remembering the terrible night when her world turned upside down.

Erin didn't know how long she stood there, shut in the stall, but she started when she heard voices. Two girls had entered the rest room.

"Don't be a drag, Cindy. Let's double-date. Spring Fling's more fun when you go with a group," one girl said.

"Fat chance," the other female voice countered. "It's taken me six months to get a date with Travis Sinclair, and I'm not about to share the evening with all of you."

At the mention of Travis's name, Erin pressed herself against the metal wall. What was the girl talking about? Maybe she'd misunderstood.

"How'd you ever talk him into going anyway? What with Amy still in the hospital and all."

"I just took a chance and asked him. I never really thought he'd come, but it was worth a try. I almost fell over when he said yes."

By now Erin could scarcely breathe. She felt hot and cold all over. Travis was going out with Cindy Pitzer. It was as obvious as if she'd seen Cindy on the other side of the door.

"Don't you feel bad about Amy?"

"Of course. But I don't know her that well, and I was dating Travis before she came on the scene anyway." There was a pause in the conversation; then Erin heard Cindy snap, "Don't look at me that way. It's just one crummy dance."

"But if it works out . . ." the second voice admonished.

"If it works out," Cindy interrupted, "then we'll double-date the next time. Now hurry up, or we'll be late for last period."

Erin stood in the bathroom stall long after Cindy and her friend had gone. She couldn't believe what she'd overheard. Travis was going out with another girl while Amy lay in a coma! She was so angry, her whole body shook. *Well you're not going to get away with it, Travis!* she vowed under her breath.

She let herself out, gathered her things, and left school, cutting her final class. All the way home she plotted revenge. She didn't know what she was going to do, but she would do something to get even with him. Travis would pay for treating her sister this way.

Erin skipped school on Friday and spent the day walking around the mall, moody and brooding. Travis's betrayal goaded her, and it wasn't just Amy he'd betrayed. She felt as if he'd betrayed her too. Hadn't he told her how much Amy meant to him? Hadn't he ignored Erin because he "cared" so much for Amy?

That evening at the hospital, she shared her day with Amy in a one-sided conversation. She never forgot what the nurse had said about comatose patients being able to hear, and she babbled on about the latest fashions and the newest makeup colors, feeling guilty about withholding the information about Travis and Cindy.

When the nurse came in to take Amy's vital signs, she told Erin, "Your parents are in the private consultation room, and they want you to meet them there."

Erin knew the room Laurie meant. It was a cubbyhole next to the waiting room, where doctors took the families of patients whenever they wanted to discuss something private, such as the results of surgery. Erin went to the room and let herself in. Her parents were talking in hushed tones to Dr. DuPree. Her mother looked as if she'd been crying. "What's wrong?" Erin asked, instantly alert.

"We've been waiting for you, Erin," her father said. His expression was grim, guarded. "Dr. DuPree was just going over the latest Glasgow test results."

"So what's the score?" Erin licked her lips. Her mouth had gone dry.

Dr. DuPree cleared his throat. "We've lowered Amy to a one-one-one."

Erin's stomach twisted into a knot. Suddenly she felt trapped and cornered. "Why are we in this room?"

"Your mother and I want you to talk to a man we met with earlier this evening," Mr. Bennett said. As if on cue the door opened and a man entered. He was tall and had black hair and a mustache. Erin's brows knitted together. She recognized him, but from where?

"Hi, Erin." The man thrust out his hand. "I'm Roger Fogerty."

Memory clicked into place. Neuro-ICU. A model

of a plastic brain. Words from a stranger with kind brown eyes. She'd asked, *"Are you a doctor?"* He'd answered, *"No. But I work with the staff here."* Erin took his hand, hesitant, wary. "Why are you here?"

His grip was firm and warm. His eyes caught and held hers hypnotically. "I'm with the Florida Organ and Tissue Donor Program."

Chapter Fourteen

〜

Erin blinked, bewildered. Why would someone from the organ-donor program be here? Was one of Amy's major organs failing? Did they want to try some experimental transplantation technique on her? "I–I don't understand. . . ."

"This is always a difficult conversation for me to have with families, Erin. Would you like to sit down?"

"No."

Mr. Fogerty laid a briefcase on the table. Dr. DuPree stood beside him, and her parents sat rigidly in chairs on the other side of the table. Their shoulders were touching, but Erin thought they somehow looked miles apart. Mr. Fogerty snapped open the case and pulled out some papers. "I spoke with your parents earlier, Erin. Now I'd like to tell you about the donor program. About how the donation of organs can extend the lives of others. And about how some sort of meaning can be derived from your sister's tragedy."

"Donors are dead people."

"That's true, and—"

"Amy's not dead," Erin interrupted. "I've just come from her room."

Mr. Fogerty glanced quickly at the Bennetts. Dr.

DuPree came forward and leaned across the table. His voice was gentle as he told her, "Her pupils are fixed and dilated. The results of her EEG show that she's had no brain activity for about six hours."

Erin's gaze flew to her mother, who lifted a trembling chin. Erin took a step backward. Dr. DuPree continued. "We've run many tests, Erin. Blood-flow studies to the cerebral area, CAT scans—the newest, the best tests—and they all indicate that Amy is brain dead."

"Dr. DuPree has determined that there's absolutely no hope of recovery," Mr. Fogerty said very gently. "Now it's time to consider your alternatives. And donating Amy's organs is one of them."

Stupefied, Erin sputtered, "So that's what this is all about? You want to use her organs, and you need our permission?"

"The entire family has to be in agreement," Mr. Fogerty said.

Mrs. Bennett said, "You seemed pleased for your friend Beth's mother when she got news about her kidney transplant." Her face looked haggard and haunted, and Erin recalled how pretty her mother liked to keep herself.

"Th—that was different. The guy was already dead."

"Erin," her father spoke so quietly that she had to strain toward him. "So is Amy."

The room was silent. Erin heard the sound of her own blood rushing to her ears. "I don't believe you." But the look on her parents' faces took away her assurance. "I was just in her room, and I know she's alive."

"If we unhooked her from the ventilator, she'd stop breathing in minutes, and all her organs would begin to fail," the doctor said.

So that was the way it was, Erin thought. Amy was supposed to be dead, but without the machines her organs would be no good to them. She jutted her chin. "Well, I don't agree about donating her organs."

"Why?" her mother asked. "Shouldn't *something* positive come out of this hell? To help balance what's happened to Amy? Someone can't run out to buy sodas and just die! It makes no sense."

Erin felt as if she'd been slapped. *She* had let Amy go buy the sodas. Erin laced her fingers and cupped her hands demurely in front of her. "As long as the machines are doing their job, then maybe she can get better. But if you turn off the machines, then she'll die for sure."

"Haven't you heard a thing we've said, Erin?" Mrs. Bennett's voice sounded as tight as a wire. "Amy *is* dead."

Mr. Bennett silenced his wife and went to stand in front of Erin. "Baby, listen to me. Don't you think this is the hardest decision I've ever had to make? Kids are supposed to outlive their parents, not the other way around."

His face was contorted with pain, and Erin felt panic inside herself. She wanted to smooth it away for him. She wanted him to smooth it away for her. "It's not fair," she whispered through trembling lips.

"I agree," he said. "None of it's fair. And because I've seen so many unfair things in life, I've come to realize that while we can't expect fairness, we can expect mercy. And right now the merciful thing to do is to accept the results of the tests and turn off the machines."

The doctor took a step toward Erin. "Erin, please believe us. Technology is what's keeping your sister breathing." The lamp's light sent silver reflections off his hair. "You know, it used to be that doctors declared a man dead when he stopped breathing. And then we decided, 'No. He's not dead until his heart stops.' But we learned how to start hearts again, and we learned to build a machine to breathe for him. So we had to change the way we determine dead. Brain activity is our standard today."

"And donating organs is about the only good thing that can come out of something like Amy's death," Mr. Fogerty added.

Erin turned pleading eyes to her parents. "You can't let them do that. You just can't let them turn Amy off and then give her away in pieces."

"Stop it!" Mr. Bennett cried. "Is that what you think we're doing? I'd cut off my arm if I thought I could change what's happened to Amy. I'd donate any organ I had, if I thought it would save her. I'm her father, for God's sake. I gave her life. She's half of me." Tears glistened in his eyes.

Erin felt cold and numb, and a lump in her throat felt the size of an iceberg. She recalled a movie she'd seen in which a giant computer had become "human" and tried to take over, and after much combat had been turned off. Its lights went out one by one as it begged for another chance. What if Amy was like that? Dependent on the machines, crying to get out of the arena where she was trapped between life and death? "Labs make mistakes on tests," she said.

Dr. DuPree shook his head. "Not this time. I'm declaring her brain dead, Erin. And once death is declared, and the family agrees to donate a victim's organs, we can't turn off the machines." His voice was tender and compassionate. "We must maintain her bodily functions if we're going to take her up to surgery and retrieve her organs for donor transplantation."

"Retrieve?" Erin said the word bitterly. "Is that what you call killing somebody so you can take their organs?"

"Erin!" her father said sharply. "That's uncalled for and not the point of this discussion at all."

By now Erin felt sick to her stomach and so icy cold that her teeth were chattering. "Why should I believe you? First you ask if you can put a 'Do not resuscitate' order on her chart, and now you want to 'retrieve' her organs. Why can't you just keep her alive until the great world of technology finds some way of making her better?"

"It doesn't work that way," Dr. DuPree told her. "Once brain death occurs, the body begins to deteriorate in spite of the machines. We have only a few days at the outside if her organs are going to be viable for transplantation."

"That's why I'm here, Erin," Mr. Fogerty explained. "I want to answer any questions you might have about organ donation."

She glared at him, suddenly furious at this stranger. "Well, I don't have any questions. You aren't going to cut up Amy."

"There's no disfigurement, Erin," Mr. Fogerty said. "She'll look the same as she does now."

"Is that why you were in ICU the night they brought Amy up? What do you do, Mr. Fogerty, hang around the halls waiting for someone to be declared brain dead so you can move in and take their organs?"

"Erin! Stop it!" Mrs. Bennett cried, rising to her feet. "They're just trying to help."

"I won't stop it," Erin yelled. "I won't, because I'm the only one who can keep them from taking Amy into surgery for dismantling." Her anger kept boiling, and all she wanted to do was hurt all of them.

Dr. DuPree and Mr. Fogerty didn't flinch. She hated them most of all. "I don't agree to 'organ retrieval,'" she said hotly, spitting the words like venom. "You'll have to find somebody else to give away."

Mr. Bennett sat back down heavily, reminding Erin of a balloon that had lost all of its air. "You're just upset. You don't know what you're saying." He looked to Dr. DuPree. "Give us some time together."

The men left, and Erin faced her parents. "Don't try to talk me out of it," she warned. "I'm not going to change my mind."

Her mother was crying openly. "Do you think we *want* to do this? For the love of heaven, Erin, just *think*! Amy's dead, and nothing's going to change that.

But we have the chance to make something good come from it." She fumbled in her purse for either a tissue or a cigarette.

"Leave her alone, Marian," her father interrupted on Erin's behalf. "It's too much for her right now. Just let her think about it."

Erin bit her lip until it bled. There was nothing to think about. She wouldn't change her mind. Her mother sagged down into the chair and buried her face in her hands, and her father put his arm around her shoulders. Erin felt left out and utterly alone. "I'm going home," she said. "And I'm going to bed. I'll come back up in the morning and check on my sister. Maybe something will have changed by then."

Erin left them. All the way home she silently warred with herself, her parents, the doctors. She couldn't believe that they were giving up. That they were turning Amy over to some faceless program that would take her apart and send her away to be placed inside somebody else. In spite of knowing Beth and how much it meant to her family to receive a new kidney, this was different. This involved her sister, and Erin didn't want to donate her organs like money to a charity. And deep down she clung to the hope that as long as she said no, some miracle might happen, and Amy would begin to rally—that all the tests would be wrong, and that Amy really was alive.

Inside her house she flipped on all the lights because the place seemed so empty, but even the blaze of lamps couldn't disperse the gloom.

Her mind felt numb. She thought about calling Shara but realized she couldn't talk about it. There was no one for her to turn to about this. Erin headed for her bedroom, got as far as Amy's door, and stopped. She reached out and grasped the knob, turned it, and stepped inside.

It didn't look like Amy's room. It was too neat and orderly, everything stacked and in its place. Slowly Erin walked around, visualizing it as it would be if Amy were home. "The bed would be unmade," she said aloud.

Erin pulled back the covers and tossed the pillows. "And there would be clothes all over." She went to the closet, tugged things off hangers, and heaped them onto the tumbled bedcovers. "And there'd be stuff sticking out of drawers," she said, pulling sweaters and lingerie so that they spilled out of the drawers.

"And Amy wouldn't approve of all these dumb papers in all these dumb stacks." She grabbed up a handful and flung them in the air and stood while they rained down on her like giant pieces of confetti.

"Her makeup would be all over the vanity table." Erin opened bottles of foundation and perfume and compacts of eye shadow and powder and blusher. She scattered some crumpled tissues and smeared one with Amy's favorite shade of lipstick.

Erin caught sight of the photos edging the mirror frame, Travis grinning out at her. She pulled the photo from its place and studied it. Memories from weeks before came back to her.

Amy asking her to work for her at the boutique. *"Pretty please. I'll be your best friend."*

Amy talking about the concert. *"I came up with an alternate plan. I told Travis you'd go with him."*

Amy at her birthday party saying, *"Life isn't fair,"* and *"I'll never be late again. Promise."*

"I hate you too, Travis," Erin told the photograph. She picked up Amy's eyeliner and drew a pointed beard on Travis's chin and horns coming out of his head. She wanted to tell him about Amy and what the doctors wanted to do with her. She wanted to see the expression on his face when she told him, "They say she's dead, and they'd like to cut out her heart and give it away. You know, for the good of humanity."

Suddenly she decided that that's exactly what she would do. Saturday night when he came home from taking Cindy to the dance, she'd be waiting for him. She'd tell him, and then she'd throw the teddy bear at him and suggest that maybe Cindy would like it for her collection. After all, how many people could say they owned a stuffed animal that once belonged to a brain-dead girl?

Chapter Fifteen

The next morning at the breakfast table, Erin and her parents sat in a strained and total silence. Erin assumed they hadn't seen Amy's room and was a little disappointed. She wanted a fight—they were all acting too polite and reserved to each other, and she guessed their strategy at once. *Leave Erin alone. Give her plenty of space. Sooner or later she'll come around.*

Erin sipped orange juice without tasting it and swore she wouldn't change her mind—ever.

"I'm going into the boutique for a while," Mrs. Bennett announced. "I've got to focus on something else."

"And I'm going by Briarwood," Mr. Bennett said. "I've got a hundred papers to grade, and since it's Saturday, there won't be any interruptions."

"I'm going up to the hospital." Erin's words were crisp and delivered like a dare.

"We'll go by tonight," her father said, clearing his throat and avoiding Erin's eyes. Erin left without even saying good-bye.

In Neuro-ICU the day shift greeted Erin as usual, but she sensed something different in their attitudes. They were nurses, and their profession was for the living, and Amy was, well, somewhere in between. Inside the cubicle where Amy lay, Becky was checking her vitals. Erin asked, "If she isn't alive, why do you bother?"

Becky removed the blood pressure cuff and hung it on the wall. "We want to maintain proper body temperature and keep her oxygenated."

"Why?" Erin asked sharply. She felt as if they were maintaining Amy for some scientific experiment.

Becky stared straight at her, and for a moment Erin thought she saw the nurse's eyes glistening. "She's a *person* to me, Erin. A human being who I know was loved because your family has shown their love every minute Amy's been in this room. I didn't know her, but I care about her."

Erin almost unraveled on the spot. Ever since the organ-donor possiblity was mentioned, she'd regarded the medical staff as enemies. She didn't trust them anymore. "I'll be back," she muttered, and fled out of the unit. In the hallway she collided with Shara.

"Whoa! Hey, Erin. I've been looking for you." Shara eyed her narrowly. "Are you okay?"

"Fine." Erin sniffed, clinging to Shara's arm. The appearance of her friend, wearing her familiar trench coat, seemed magical, and Erin realized just how badly she needed an ally. "It's been a rough night, that's all."

"Want to sit in the waiting room and tell me about it?"

They settled in the sunlit room, which was now

almost empty. Only emergency surgeries were performed on Saturday, so unless you were waiting for an extremely critical patient, there was no reason to hang around. Erin plucked at an armrest. "Th—they say Amy's . . ." Erin couldn't get the words out.

Shara touched her arm. "I know."

"How?"

"Rank has its privileges. My dad's on staff here, remember? He checks on Amy every day for me."

Erin dropped her head wearily against the back of the chair. Knowing that Shara had been checking on Amy's case all along comforted her. "So you know they want us to donate Amy's organs."

"Asking is SOP—standard operating procedure. There are plenty of people who need transplants, and not enough people donating their organs to go around."

"I think it's ghoulish. How can they ask such a thing? Especially when the tests might be wrong and Amy might suddenly start to improve. If they just give her enough time, I know she'll wake up from her coma."

Shara jammed her hands into the pockets of her trench coat and tugged it tighter. "You up for a little tour?" Shara asked.

"Tour of what?"

"Come with me. You'll see."

Curious, Erin tagged after Shara to the elevators, which they rode down to the fifth floor. When the doors opened, they stepped out into a corridor painted pink and blue with nursery pictures stenciled on the walls. "This way," Shara said.

They rounded a corner and faced long horizontal windows that looked into a room filled with row after row of Lucite bassinets of newborn babies. Nurses in gowns, gloves, and masks changed diapers, wrapped and rewrapped blankets, and juggled crying infants.

"Babies?" Erin asked, dumbfounded.

"Cute, huh? I used to come here a lot when I was growing up. Daddy seemed to always have to deliver a baby in the middle of the night, so Mom and I would come and have breakfast with him. He was always so busy that if we didn't meet him here, whole weeks would go by without us having a single meal together." Shara pressed her nose to the glass and pointed to one baby whose tiny face was puckered with a cry. In the next cart another slept, oblivious to the noise. "Anyway, while we waited for him, I'd stand here and watch the babies. They were like living dolls, and I always wished I could hold them."

Erin watched the infants with their eyes scrunched shut and their mouths shaped like rosebuds and their hands balled into doll-sized fists, until she felt a softening sensation inside her. "Bet it's loud in there."

"You need earplugs."

"Okay, you're right, Shara, they're cute. So what?"

"Let's go around the corner." Shara took her to another window, but the babies in this room were different from the others. They were wired to machines and monitors, some so small that they could fit inside a grown man's hand. Ventilator tubes snaking out of their mouths were held fast by crisscrosses of white tape. The walls of their chests rose and fell rapidly, little stocking hats covered hairless heads, and their skin was so thin that Erin could see their veins and count their ribs. "Neonatal-ICU," Shara explained.

"I—I've never seen anything so tiny," Erin whispered, mesmerized by the scraps of human life attached to tubes and wires.

"They're able to save more and more of the ones born prematurely," Shara said matter-of-factly. "It's a good thing," she added, "but I wonder, is it the right thing?"

"What d'you mean?"

"Dad and I talk about it a lot. He's delivered some babies who are so premature that there's no way they can make it. And if by some miracle they do, they're so physically or mentally damaged that their whole life is spent in an institution."

"But they're alive."

"That's true. Daddy says that a doctor takes an oath to heal and restore and to relieve suffering." Shara looked Erin in the eye. "At the very least he's to do no harm. But still, I wonder—just because medicine *can* do something, *should* it be done?"

Vaguely Erin caught on to what Shara was implying. "Medicine's created a monster, right? We have the means to heal, but not the wisdom. Is that what you're saying?"

"Something like that. What wisdom is there in

117

keeping a person alive above all other considerations? Why should doctors keep restarting someone's heart if he's never going to get well?"

Erin's own heart thudded. "Or why not turn off the machines on a person who—according to all the tests—is brain dead?" She spoke caustically, raising her shield of anger to protect herself from her best friend's words. "If this is a lesson in how I ought to okay the hospital's game plan for Amy—"

Shara grabbed Erin's arm. "No way. But I've seen my dad work and worry over babies like these when there's no hope for them. But because he's delivered them, he feels responsible for keeping them alive." She stared hard at one baby in a corner of the room whose legs and arms were no bigger around than the width of two adult fingers.

"Dad says that God made us to live with dignity. Instead, medicine and science get all caught up in the technicalities . . . in the heroic measures. We put all our efforts into keeping a person alive at any cost. It's as if winning the battle is more important than the person."

Erin mulled over Shara's words. She'd known Shara for years. They'd talked on the phone about a million silly things, but she'd never realized what her friend thought about things as serious as they were discussing now. She pressed her fingers into her eyelids and softly said, "Shara, I hear what you're saying. But I can't give up on my sister. I just can't!"

Shara sighed. "No one's saying you should give up as long as there's hope."

"But I can't give up my hope just because of some stupid tests. You said yourself that they make advancements and breakthroughs in medicine every day. Maybe there'll be one tomorrow that'll help Amy. If they take her now and remove her organs, then what hope will she have?"

Very gently Shara told her, "Erin, it's not going to work that way for Amy. There's no cavalry coming in medical breakthroughs to save her."

"Unexplained things happen every day. Something still could happen to bring her back."

"They can't keep her on machines much beyond tomorrow," Shara said. "I've asked my dad to explain what happens. Once brain activity ceases . . ." She left her sentence unfinished.

Unable to respond, Erin studied the infants connected to the equipment. She understood the medical consequences of Amy's condition: without brain activity, the body simply wasted away. She cleared her throat and pressed the palms of her hands against the glass. "Crazy, isn't it? *Their* brains are working fine. It's their bodies that are struggling."

Erin stepped away from the window and turned toward Shara. "Thanks, Shara. Thanks for bringing me here and thanks for being my friend. I—I'll think about everything you've said."

They stood together in an intimate silence. Finally Shara broke it. "Look, I've got to be going. The dance is tonight."

The dance. Travis dating Cindy. Erin forced a smile. "You have a good time." They started toward the elevators. "I thought you were going to show me your dress."

Shara glanced up and down the hall. "I'm wearing it under my coat."

"Let me see."

Shara opened the coat. She wore a cream-colored tuxedo, complete with ruffled white shirt, rhinestone buttons, and red satin cummerbund. "I told you it was different. Kenny's wearing a black one just like it. What d'ya think?"

Erin nodded her approval. "It's terrific."

"We're both wearing high-top sneakers, and I've got a silk top hat too."

Erin couldn't help feeling envious. How she wished her life had not grown so complicated and so sad. "You have a ball, and call and tell me all about it," she told Shara.

"I will." Shara hugged her. "I'll be home tomorrow if you need me to come up here."

Minutes later Erin drove aimlessly through the streets crowded with Saturday afternoon shopping traffic. She passed a baseball field where a Little League game was being played, and a mall where a radio station was doing a remote broadcast. How was it that the world could be going on in such an ordinary way?

Erin kept fighting back tears and wishing there was somebody she could go to. An image of her father floated into her memory. She saw herself as a small girl sitting with Amy on her dad's lap while he read them a book of fairy tales. How safe she'd felt then, intoxicated by the scent of his pipe tobacco and after-shave.

She glanced out the car window and got her bearings. She wasn't too far from Briarwood, and more than anything she wanted to be with her daddy. She wanted him to tell her that everything was going to be all right. That like Sleeping Beauty, Amy would wake up if the right prince came along.

Chapter Sixteen

Erin walked the halls of Briarwood slowly, touching the rows of lockers as she passed. The smell of chalk dust and white paste and old books saturated the air, and her heels made a forlorn echoing sound as she went.

She passed the trophy cases and paused to read the plaques and ribbons and trophy inscriptions. *All City Champs—Soccer, 1978, 1980, 1983. Best in State—Debate Team, 1973, 1981, 1985, 1986.*

So what? Erin thought. Where were those girls now who'd brought back the trophies? Did the winners ever think about the awards sitting preserved and polished behind a glass wall? Why did wood and brass endure while life evaporated into the wind? It didn't seem right.

She sighed and shook her head. The thoughts were too heavy and the questions too complex. An ache had begun between her temples. She hoped her dad had some aspirin in his desk.

Erin moved quickly until she spotted her dad's classroom, the eerie quiet unnerving her. She might have barreled headlong inside, but something made her stop short in the doorway. Maybe it was that sound—a sound she knew but couldn't quite place until she looked inside the room.

Her father was sitting at his desk, which was covered with papers, his arms resting on the wooden desktop and his face buried in the fabric of his jacket. He was weeping. Great, racking sobs were making his shoulders heave, and the sound he made was like that of a person whose soul was being torn away.

For a stunned moment Erin stood and watched. *"Real men don't cry. Is that it?"* he'd asked her the day they'd looked through the photo albums together. And she'd answered, *"Real men stick by the people they care about."* Her heart pounded. *Oh Daddy. Poor Daddy*, she thought.

For a brief, panic-stricken moment, she didn't know what to do. She wanted to go to him and hold him, but she knew his tears were too private, too sacred for her to intrude upon. Erin flattened her back against the wall outside the door and shut her eyes, but the image of her father was burned into her mind forever.

Slowly she slid down the wall, biting her lip and resting her forehead on her knees. The tears came in quiet streams, and somehow she felt connected to her father by a cord of grief, as a spider's web connects two tree branches by its shimmering threads.

Erin parked her car on a side street near Travis's house and waited for him to return from the dance. She checked her watch. It was well past midnight.

"Cinderella's coach should have turned into a pumpkin by now," she said to herself.

While she waited, she carefully plotted her strategy. Travis lived in a fine old house on Bayshore Drive. When he pulled into his driveway, she'd call to him and make him cross to the bay side of the street, where she'd confront him. They'd be alone, and she'd say everything that was on her mind. He was a louse and a creep, and she'd make him pay for abandoning Amy.

When his headlights turned into the driveway, her mouth went dry, but the hard, cold knot of anger gave her the courage to call to him. Travis hesitated, so she called again, then watched as he jogged hesitantly across the deserted avenue.

"Erin?" he asked, coming closer. "What are you doing here?"

"I want to talk to you."

"Now? It's one o'clock in the morning. How long you been waiting?"

"Never mind. Did you have a good time at the dance?" Her question was laced with acid.

"Yeah." He drew the word out slowly. "Is that why you're here?"

"Of course. I just *had* to know if you and Cindy had fun at the dance. If you had a few laughs about old times and old girlfriends."

Erin knew that her barb had hit home. Travis glared at her. "Butt out, Erin. My life's none of your business. Don't you know? Life's short. We have to grab all the gusto—go for the gold. Know what I mean?" He turned, but she grabbed his arm. "Let go."

Years of dance training, coupled with anger, made her strong, and she tightened her grip. "I'm making it my business for my sister's sake."

"Has something happened to Amy?" His tone was wary.

"You mean you still remember her name? How interesting. I would have thought you'd forgotten it by now. You haven't been to see her in ages, have you?"

"I saw all I wanted to see that day in the hospital."

"And what did you see, Travis?"

"I saw Amy lying there like a vegetable." He broke her hold and started up the sidewalk that encircled the bay. Erin went after him. His strides were longer, but she kept pace. "I owe you nothing, Erin. Get out of my face."

"Well you owe Amy—you owe my sister plenty!"

He spun toward her, seizing her shoulders. His expression had become fierce. "I told you once that I'd never met anybody like Amy. She was wild and a little bit crazy, and we had a million laughs together. But when I walked into that hospital room, when I saw her lying on that bed with tubes and wires and hoses—" His voice quavered, and it surprised Erin. He dug his thumbs into her arms until it hurt. "*That* wasn't Amy. That was some shell."

"It *is* Amy," Erin insisted through clenched teeth.

"It's Amy's body, but it's not Amy's—" He searched for a word. "Where *is* Amy, Erin? Where's that special *thing* that made her Amy? That made her *real*. Tell me."

If her arms hadn't been pinned, Erin would have slugged him. She hated him. Hated him for asking a question she couldn't answer. She searched desperately for a way to hurt him. "Well, I think Amy's really up in that hospital trying to wake up. *If* they don't take her into surgery and remove her organs for medical science first."

Travis's grip loosened, and she saw his confusion. "What are you talking about?"

"You don't know, do you? If you'd been up to see her, you'd know that yesterday they declared her brain dead."

For an instant he looked as if he might be sick, and Erin stepped back, rubbing her arms and feeling confused. It was the reaction she'd wanted, wasn't it? Hadn't she come to hurt him? He said, "I—I didn't know."

"Well, with your big date with Cindy and all, I can see how it might have slipped by you." She reached inside her jacket and extracted the teddy bear. "Here's a little something I thought you'd like to have back," she said, holding the bear toward him. "Maybe Cindy would want it."

Travis knocked the bear from her hand, then turned and braced his hands on the cement railing. "You've got a mean mouth, Erin."

She wanted to leave him alone to think about how he'd wronged her sister, but her feet suddenly felt like lead weights. "I told them that they weren't going to cut up my sister and give her away. I said that I didn't care what their stupid tests showed, *I* wasn't giving up on my sister." She paused. "Like some people have."

"You think just 'cause I don't hang around Amy's bedside that I don't care? That I don't hurt?"

"You have a strange way of showing it, Travis."

"What am I? A robot?" His voice dropped, and Erin had to lean closer to catch all his words. "See, your problem is that everybody has to act exactly the same way for it to be legitimate with you."

"That's not true."

When he glanced up, she could have sworn that there were tears in his eyes. But he blinked, and then there was so much shadow that she couldn't be sure. "So you do penance by hovering over your sister and making sure everyone feels guilty for not caring the way you want them to."

"You're crazy."

"Am I? If they tell you she's dead, Erin, why can't you believe them? Let her go. For everybody's sake, let Amy go."

She shook her head vehemently. "Doctors have been wrong before."

"But what if they're not wrong?"

"You're not getting off that easily, Travis. I know what you're trying to do. You're trying to confuse me so you don't have to admit you're so disloyal to Amy that you're dating before she's—" She stopped the flood of words because she'd been cornered by them.

"Before what, Erin? Finish the sentence."

She started to tremble. Below her, waves continued to hit the seawall, and her head began to pound. "Drop dead," she told him.

"This is the way I deal with it, Erin. Cindy doesn't mean anything to me but I'm going on with the rest of my life because it helps me get through, because life is too short to waste."

Erin felt defeated. "I should have known telling you anything about Amy was a stupid thing to do."

"I can't change what's happened to Amy. And neither can you."

They stared at one another in the moonlight. The scent of jasmine mingled with the salty smell of the bay. Travis glanced up and down the sidewalk that wound along the water. "You know, I've suddenly got the urge to go for a run," he said. "At this hour you don't have to get out of the way for other joggers. Yeah, the world's pretty empty right now. And I'd never have figured that out if you hadn't come by tonight, Erin. So—uh—thanks for the tip."

Erin, silent, watched him run away. She had nothing left to say to Travis. He was a total stranger, and Erin wondered why she'd ever liked him, why she'd ever been jealous of Amy over him.

Erin picked up the stuffed bear and started to heave it out into the bay, but she stopped. The bear's glass eyes glittered in the streetlight. "You're such a mess, teddy bear," she said. "I'm sorry. You didn't do anything wrong."

Erin cuddled the bear and started to cry. As she stared at Travis's figure, now just a speck in the moonlight, his plea kept coming back to her. "*Let her go, Erin. For everybody's sake, let Amy go.*"

Chapter Seventeen

"Erin, what are you doing here this late? Your parents left hours ago," Laurie, the night nurse, said when Erin stepped through the doors of Neuro-ICU.

"Yes, I know," Erin said. "I stopped by the house to get some things and told them that I was spending the rest of the night up here. I just want to stay with Amy." The clock on the wall read three A.M., and as Erin walked through the unit, she remembered how bizarre the machinery had seemed at first. Now her senses had become anesthetized to the blinking green lights and the rhythmic sounds she knew were sustaining life.

She stepped inside the glass-walled cubicle and set down her duffel bag at the foot of Amy's bed. "Hello, Amy," she said, squeezing her sister's hand and willing Amy to squeeze hers back.

"I'll bet you're wondering why I'm here," Erin said. "Okay, so you're not wondering, but I'll tell you anyway." The steady hiss of the ventilator was Amy's only response.

"I miss you. You probably never thought I'd say something like that. But the house is sort of empty without you." Erin felt her head begin to pound, and she pressed against her temples. "Oh by the way, I trashed your room. I know you would approve. I mean, if you could have seen how they cleaned it up— even the dust bunnies were gone."

Erin smoothed the sheet over Amy's chest. "And I need to tell you one other thing, Amy. I—uh—went to see Travis tonight. He had a date. It was with Cindy, but I don't think he had a very good time. We sort of argued about him dating and all. It made me so mad, Amy—I don't know how he could do that to you. But that's not really what I want to tell you about Travis." She took a deep breath. "You see, Amy, all these months—even before Christmas—I've sort of liked him. I mean, I *really* liked him. I thought I loved him." Erin's palms were sweating. Why was it so hard to get the words out? "Remember the night I went to the concert with him? I wanted to go *so* bad, and then when you sort of arranged it to happen . . . I couldn't believe it! But you know what? He never stopped talking about you the whole night. I guess I knew way back then that he never could have been *my* boyfriend."

Erin watched the ragged line of her sister's heart monitor. "I've thought a lot about it, Ames, and I realize that I didn't really love *Travis*. I just wanted to love *someone* and have somebody love me the way it is in books and movies. Maybe someday it will be that way for me, but it won't be with Travis. I hope you understand about me liking him behind your back." Amy's chest rose up and down in cadence with the ventilator.

"So, how will I tell you when my Mr. Right comes

along? How will I let you know if you're never gonna wake up?" Erin placed her palm along her sister's cheek. The skin felt dry and cool. Abruptly she stood and paced to the foot of the bed. "Look, Amy, I didn't mean to get all mushy on you. Forget all that junk about Mr. Right. I brought some stuff for you." She reached into the duffel bag and pulled out a book. "Remember this? Daddy used to read it to us when we were little."

"Nursery Rhymes." She read the title aloud. "Remember how we'd both sit on Daddy's lap and he would read to us? It used to get me mad because you always had a zillion dumb questions like 'Why did the man put his wife inside a pumpkin?' or 'How come she cut off the tails of the poor blind mice?'" Erin shut her eyes and tried to block out the images from her childhood. "Geez, Amy, we never had any of the answers. I'm sorry."

She switched on the light over the hospital bed. "Speaking of Daddy, he's taking all of this kind of hard. And I don't think Mom's doing so good either. They look older, Amy. I guess we all do."

Erin pulled a chair next to the bed and opened the book. She read a few of the nonsensical rhymes, until her eyelids got heavy and the words began to blur and run together. She realized she hadn't slept for two days.

"Let me borrow your pink sweater, Erin. Please? I'll be your best friend." Erin jerked awake. For a moment she was disoriented, then she spotted the book lying on the floor near her feet. She reached up and

flipped off the fluorescent light and listened to the steady rhythm of the ventilator. *In, out. In, out.* Across the room a child crouched bedside the machine wearing a flannel nightgown and holding a teddy bear. Her dark hair looked ruffled as if she had just woken up.

Erin shot out of the chair. Her heart raced as she stared hard into the shadows, but now she saw only the wall and a towel on the floor. She was hallucinating. Agitated, Erin fumbled with the light switch. "You ruined my pink sweater, you know. Oh you were sorry and all that, but it didn't take away the pizza stain on the front."

"Oh let me go! Please. I've had my license for a whole week, and I still haven't had a chance to use the car."

"How about if we go together?"

"I want to drive by myself this time. Pretty please? I'll be your best friend."

Erin felt herself growing angry as she spoke about the sweater. "You're so careless, Amy. Why can't you be more careful? Why can't you be more responsible?" Suddenly she felt foolish. Hadn't the doctors told her Amy was beyond hearing? Erin quelled her anger with a long sigh and took up her vigil in the bedside chair.

"I have something for us to listen to." Erin unzipped her duffel bag and fumbled for the cassette player. "Ms. Thornton gave me a tape of the dance recital, and I thought you'd like to hear your reading. You were pretty good. Even if you were always late for rehearsals and—" Erin stopped, because her fingers had encountered a sheaf of papers. She withdrew the packet, saw Amy's name, and remembered the day Miss Hutton had given them to her. At the time she'd shoved them into the bag and forgotten about them.

Erin put on the tape and leafed through Amy's old tests and quizzes and book reviews. The music from the recital sounded. Shara's voice sang and Amy's voice read:

> *"O Lord, thou has searched me and known me. . . . I will praise thee; for I am fearfully and wonderfully made. . . . Whither shall I go from thy spirit? or whither shall I flee from thy presence? Thine eyes have seen my unformed substance; and in thy book they were all written, the days that were ordained for me. . . ."*

Erin stopped listening to the tape and began reading one of the papers that Miss Hutton had given an A +.

Subject: English
Assignment: Essay
Date: February 9
Name: Amy Bennett

Sisters

> *My very first memory is one of my sister's face. Erin was wearing a cardboard*

crown she'd gotten at a hamburger place, and she told me she was a princess and I was her maid. I had no reason to question her—princesses don't lie—so I served her tea and sneaked cookies from Mom's pantry, and when I was caught I took my licks. (Maids are always supposed to be loyal to their employer, especially when that person's a princess.)

Whenever she dressed up in her tutu and toe shoes, I thought my sister was the most beautiful girl in the world. And when she was six and went off to school without me, I sat by the window and cried all day long. She must have felt sorry for me because when she got home she told me, "School's not much fun. They make you line up just to go to the bathroom." Then the next year when I had to go to school, I didn't want to!

Erin and I shared a room until I was eight and my grandmother died. Then Erin got her own room, and I cried about that because I missed her. I also got all her hand-me-downs, her old toys and books, her case of the chicken pox, and all the valentines from the boys she didn't like in the third grade.

But she taught me stuff too. She taught me how to spit water through the space between my front teeth. She taught me how to get even with mean boys ("Don't hit them—shove them!"), and she taught me how to use makeup and how to put together neat outfits. She also taught me that you should never keep people waiting. (This is something I'm still working on, but at least I know I should be on time, and someday I'm going to surprise her and never be late again.)

Sometimes I hate being the "baby" of the family. It's awful being told "You're too young," and "Why can't you behave like your sister?" But Erin took up for me lots of times and once got punished for flushing Dad's pipe tobacco down the toilet (I wanted to see it swirl in the bowl and turn the water brown).

In two years Erin's going off to college, and it'll be a time of new freedom for me. No more sharing the bathroom. No more waiting for the vanilla ice cream to be eaten before we buy chocolate because vanilla's Erin's favorite. No more being fussed at because Erin's room's neat and mine's a mess. No more borrowing her car, her hair spray, or her pantyhose. No more sister's shadow to live in. I'll miss her like crazy. (Of course, I can't tell her because I'd never live it down.)

In summary, I believe that sisters are more than blood relatives. Over time they either become friends, or they wind up kill-

*ing each other! Sisters are made by living
every day with each other and wearing each
other down until the rough spots are smooth.
They're made by sharing secrets you'd never
tell Mom, and out of doing things for each
other just because you feel like it, not because you have to. I guess you could say sisters are "grown," not manufactured, in a
very special place called a family.*

Erin finished reading and let out a long, shuddering breath because it felt as if something heavy was
pressing against her chest. She had never known—
never even guessed—that Amy had felt that way
about her. So many times Erin had simply brushed
Amy aside, ignored her, or worse—teased and kidded
her. Especially when they'd been younger. Now she
saw that Amy had always cared about her . . . had
loved her.

She brushed away moisture from her cheeks.
Grown, not manufactured, Amy had written. *Fearfully and wonderfully made*, Amy's voice had said on
the tape. Erin gazed at her sister's body. The eyelids
were slightly parted, and she could just make out
Amy's once-blue eyes, now glassy like doll's eyes.
"Fixed and dilated," Dr. Dupree had said.

"Where are you, Amy?" Erin whispered.
Through the years she'd asked, "Where's Amy?" a
hundred times, but now the question took on a different meaning. Amy's body breathed, but it wasn't
alive. Her heart beat, but it was a mechanical thing—

a pump. The essence of Amy—her soul, her will, her personality—was gone. All that was left was an illusion, a trick done with machines. The days that had been ordained for her had run out—for Amy time was over.

Erin felt a sense of resignation, of finality. She touched the tube protruding from Amy's mouth, fingering the tape that held it in place. Gently she rested her head on her sister's breast and listened to the heart beating strong and steady.

Erin shut her eyes, lost herself in the echo of false life and whispered, "Good-bye, Amy. I love you."

Chapter Eighteen

❧

"Erin, are you absolutely sure you want to do this?" Mrs. Bennett asked over the conference table in the consultation room.

"I'm sure." Erin rubbed her eyes wearily, ignoring Dr. DuPree and Mr. Fogerty, and concentrated on her parents. In truth she was totally drained and exhausted. She was tired of fighting the inevitable.

"Once you sign the papers," Dr. DuPree said, "we'll gather the organ-retrieval team and take Amy upstairs for surgery."

"There are people who will benefit this very day from your generosity," Mr. Fogerty added.

Erin held up her hand. "Please, spare me the details."

"You don't really want to do this, do you, Erin?" her father asked.

"It doesn't matter anymore. Amy's dead. I believe that now, so what difference does it make if we donate her organs?"

"We have to be in agreement."

"I'm in agreement," she said dully. She watched her mother hunch over the table and scratch her signature on the bottom of the consent form. Mrs. Bennett slid the paper to her husband, who signed it too. Erin noticed that his hand was trembling.

Dr. DuPree took the paper. "Would you like to see your daughter one last time?"

"Yes," Mrs. Bennett said, and as Erin followed her parents to Neuro-ICU, she couldn't help thinking that this is how a condemned person must feel as he walks to his execution.

At the door of the cubicle, Mr. Bennett turned and said to the assembled staff, "My family and I want to thank you for all the care and support you gave us."

"We'll pack up her things and send them down to the Patient Consultant Office," Becky said. "That way you don't have to come back up here."

Erin saw that Becky had tears in her eyes. She wanted to reach out to her and say, "It's all right. You did everything you could. I'm not mad at you anymore." But she said nothing.

The three of them went into the cubicle where Amy lay. Erin walked to the opposite side of the bed from her parents, feeling strangely detached, as if she were standing outside herself and watching a movie.

"Good-bye, baby girl," Mrs. Bennett whispered. She didn't touch her daughter.

"Good-bye, Princess," Mr. Bennett said.

Erin said nothing, because she had already told Amy all she'd wanted to say. But she did want to touch her sister one last time while her skin was warm, while her heart still beat and her chest still moved with the flow of air into her lungs.

Erin stroked Amy's arm. She looked alive. She

felt alive. *An illusion*, she reminded herself. The fingers on Amy's hand twitched and flexed. "She moved! Amy moved," Erin said, incredulously.

Dr. DuPree rushed into the room. "It's spinal reflex," he said, patting her shoulder. "I assure you that's all it is, Erin."

"No! I saw her move."

"Erin, honey—" Mrs. Bennett said, her voice anguished. "I saw her move once too. Remember, I told you. But it wasn't real. Amy's dead, Erin. She's really dead. Please believe us."

The expression on everyone else's faces told Erin that her mother wasn't lying. She kept staring at Amy's hand, but there was no more movement, no more sign of life. "How can you be sure? How do you know?" she fired at the doctor.

"Because nothing else has changed. Her pupils are still fixed and dilated—"

"Stop it!" She was crying and couldn't stop. "Nothing's real around here! Everything's fake!"

"Perhaps a sedative—"

"No! I don't need one. I need to get out of this place. It's rotten. It stinks! Just go ahead and take Amy upstairs and get it over with. Do you hear me? Get the whole thing over with!"

Her father reached for her, but Erin backed away, found the door, and bolted. She ran down the hall, desperate to get away from the hospital. In the car her hands were shaking so badly, she could hardly get the key into the ignition, and once she did, she was crying so hard, she could barely see to drive.

Erin never remembered how she got home. She simply found herself parked in the driveway, and the next thing she knew she was in her bathroom. The odor of the hospital seemed to cling to her skin and clothes, making her gag. She wanted to be sick, but her stomach was too empty.

Erin felt dirty. Still crying, she stepped inside the shower and turned on the water full blast. Like fine needles the hot water stung her face and arms. She picked up the soap and ran it up her arms, across her blouse, and up her neck. If only she could get clean again.

She turned her face upward and let the water pour over her, trying to wash away the cloying smell of death that was strangling her.

Chapter Nineteen

The Bennetts kept Amy's funeral simple, choosing to have only a grave-side service for their family and a handful of friends. Erin would have liked for Beth Clark to be there, but she was still in Gainesville, where her mother was recovering from her transplant operation. Erin asked Ms. Thornton to come, and of course Shara, whom she asked to sing.

"What song would you like?" Shara had wanted to know.

"You choose," Erin told her. "Something special for Amy. Something for all of us."

Shara hugged her. "Oh, Erin, I'm sorry. So sorry."

"It's almost over," Erin told her. "Just one more day, and it will all be over."

The April morning of the burial smelled fresh with the promise of summer, and the vivid colors of the sky and grass made the day seem more like a garden party than a funeral. Wildflowers bloomed, butterflies danced, honeybees gathered pollen. Erin wondered how the world could look so beautiful, how creation could be so active on such a day of sadness.

Her parents had dressed in black. They both wore sunglasses, and her mother had bought a hat with a wide brim that flopped low over her forehead. Erin had decided to wear white. "It's the color the Japanese wear for mourning," she'd told her mother when she'd started to express disapproval. "Besides, I don't think Amy would have wanted everyone dressed in black. Too drab."

They sat together in a row, facing Amy's coffin, which was surrounded by baskets of flowers. During the service Shara leaned over to ask, "Are you all right?"

"Yes, I am," Erin told her. Her eyes were dry, and she meant it. "I guess I got everything out at the hospital. This part almost seems like an afterthought."

Erin tried to concentrate on the minister's words but kept getting distracted by the world that surrounded them. Somehow it seemed to her that all creation was dancing, and she began to sway slightly to the silent, secret music of clouds and sunlight, flowers and insects.

At the foot of her chair she spotted a dandelion. She plucked it, and inspecting it, realized how perfectly it was made. Its head was a symmetry of seeds that resembled stars, each connected to the central core. *Earth and sky*, Erin mused. She was holding a tiny universe in the palm of her hand! Trying to be inconspicuous, she raised the dandelion to her lips and blew gently; then she watched as the seeds scattered and sailed away.

The minister finished his eulogy, and Shara stood. Erin listened to her friend's voice but kept watching the dandelion fluff floating in the air.

"Amazing grace, how sweet the sound,
That saved a wretch like me.
I once was lost, but now I'm found,
Was blind, but now I see."

Was blind, but now I see. The words bounced around in Erin's mind like echoes off empty walls. She caught her breath in wonderment. Suddenly she *saw*, truly *saw*, something she hadn't seen before. Because of the gift of Amy's eyes, someone was able to see the beautiful world again. And because of the gift of Amy's heart, someone else was able to breathe the fresh, clean air for another day.

The flowers, the butterflies, the greening of the grass, told her that life was cyclic, season after season. It came, it went. It came again. And that just as the dandelion had shed its seeds to take root and grow again, Amy had given herself to all the tomorrows of someone else's life.

Erin gazed at Amy's coffin, draped with a mantle of pink roses, and knew with certainty that Amy wasn't in it. Maybe her body would be buried, but the person of Amy, her spirit, would not. For Amy was with Erin still and would live in her heart for all the days of her life.

Around her, chairs rattled, and with a start Erin realized that the funeral service was over. Her father reached out and took her hand. "We made it, honey."

"Yes, we made it."

Her mother leaned against her husband and he

cradled her to him. He slipped his other arm around Erin. "I'll bet Amy would have liked the service," Mrs. Bennett said.

"She would have liked it," Erin agreed.

Her parents started for the long black limo parked on a narrow roadway, but Erin lingered behind. Shara stood next to her, sniffing back tears. "Your song was perfect," Erin told her.

"Thanks. I was afraid my voice would break up." Shara eyed her. "I know this is an awful day for you Erin, but you look . . . well, settled. Sort of peaceful."

Erin lifted her face toward the sun. White clouds billowed overhead. "I feel peaceful."

Shara said, "I always envied you, Erin, because I always wanted a sister."

Shara's confession surprised Erin. Seeing fresh tears pool in her friend's eyes made Erin want to comfort her. "Sisters are special, and they have something very special between them." Erin smiled mysteriously. "But you know, Amy and I were much more than sisters—we were best friends."

Time to Let Go

I'd like to express my appreciation to Roses Colmore-Taylor, M.Ed., of REACH, Chattanooga, Tennessee.

. . .

Blessed are they that mourn: for they shall be comforted.   —MATTHEW 5:4 (KJV)

Chapter One

~

"By your silence I sense that you'd rather be anywhere but here talking with me. And I'm also assuming it wasn't your idea to come."

Erin Bennett glared at Dr. Roberta Richardson and released an exaggerated sigh. "There's nothing to talk about. I don't need a psychiatrist to pick my brain apart."

"I'm not a psychiatrist; I don't dispense medications in my practice. I'm a professional counselor, a family therapist, and your parents are concerned about you and thought I could help—"

"Help how? I'm perfectly fine. It's my parents who need counseling."

"Why do you say that?"

"Because they're the ones who're making me come here. There's nothing wrong with me. It's *them*."

Dr. Richardson pressed her fingertips together and leveled soft brown eyes at Erin sitting on the other side of the polished oak desk. Quietly she said, "'Perfectly fine' seventeen-year-old girls don't have incapacitating, unexplained headaches."

Erin winced, remembering the fierce pain that

1

came on with little warning. The doctors had referred to them as "migraines," even though they weren't altogether typical of most migraines. Erin didn't care what they called them. She only knew that they were interfering with her senior year at Briarwood. "I'm sure there's a good explanation," she said stubbornly.

Dr. Richardson opened the manila folder on her desk. "According to all the testing you've undergone in the past two months, there's no physiological reason for them. 'No reasonable medical explanation,'" Dr. Richardson read from the open file folder. "Looks as if they covered everything from brain tumors to epilepsy."

Erin shuddered, remembering how they'd injected dye into her veins and taken endless X-rays of her head while she lay perfectly still on a hard metal table. *Like a corpse*, she thought. *Or a person in a coma*. "They just haven't found the cause yet. Doctors don't *know* everything. Just because they can't figure it out is no reason to tell my parents that I'm some kind of a nut case."

"I know you're not a nut case, but aren't you concerned about your headaches?"

Erin felt her anger and resentment turning into tears, but she held them back. "Yes," she whispered, miserably, wanting to add, *"More than anything*." In the past month Erin had gotten sick twice at school and had to go home. Sometimes she had bad dreams in which her head was hurting, and when she awoke, she really did have a severe headache. "But I'm taking medicine for them," Erin told

Dr. Richardson. In the previous few months, Erin had been popping aspirin every day, and when her parents dragged her to a specialist, he gave her stronger pills that relieved the headaches but also wiped her out.

"Sometimes medications only relieve symptoms and never deal with the cause," Dr. Richardson continued. "Good health is more than treating bodily ailments. Human beings are made up of *soma*—body—and *psyche*—soul. I believe that you shouldn't treat one without treating the other."

"Are you saying that my headaches are all in my imagination?"

"Absolutely not. They're real enough. But it's important to look at the whole person, not just the malady, before seeking a cure." Dr. Richardson shoved the folder aside and said, "I'm glad you're here, Erin, and I'd like to get to know you better."

Erin felt like saying, "I don't want to know you better," but thought better of it. She didn't want her parents coming down on her the way they were always coming down on each other. Her mother was forever working at her boutique, and when she *was* at home, she was yelling about something or other at her husband.

Erin didn't think her father was doing so great either. He stayed away from the house, using his teacher's job at Briarwood as an excuse, but when he was home, he acted so withdrawn that he might as well be gone. Maybe if Amy were still around, things would be different.

It had been a hard summer after Amy's death, but with the new school year half-over, life was back to normal. If only her parents would stop their fighting. And if only she didn't have these blasted headaches—

"How's school going?" Dr. Richardson was asking.

"All right," Erin said, forcing herself to concentrate. The topic seemed safe enough, so she continued. "Ms. Thornton—she's the dance teacher at Briarwood—announced today that we're doing a joint play production with Berkshire Prep."

"The boys' school? When?"

"After Easter."

Dr. Richardson glanced at her desk calendar. "Only two months from now. Sounds like a big task. What's the play?"

"West Side Story."

The willowy, brown-haired therapist smiled. "That was always one of my favorites. I saw the movie five times when it first came out in the sixties. Are you going for a part?"

Erin fidgeted with the buttons on her blouse. "I love to dance. I'd like the lead—Maria."

"You sound as if you may not try out. Why?"

The headaches, she thought, refusing to meet Dr. Richardson's eyes. "No reason. I guess I'll go for it. Auditions are next Monday, and the Berkshire drama department is supposed to come to our school for them."

"I guess it makes sense to do a joint production. It wouldn't be much fun playing a love scene with a girl dressed up like a guy, would it?" Dr. Richardson leaned across the desk and added, "I hope whoever gets the role of Tony is *gorgeous*."

Erin hadn't thought about the male lead until then. "It doesn't matter to me. Just so long as he's good."

"Do you have a boyfriend? Maybe he won't want you to play opposite some other guy. Would that be a problem?"

Erin felt herself tense up. The last boy she'd cared about had been Travis Sinclair. Dark-haired, brown-eyed, Berkshire Prep senior, Travis. Amy's Travis. The betrayer. "No. I'm too busy with dance and school. I don't have time for a boyfriend."

"Really? You're so pretty—"

Erin stood. "Look, I don't want to talk anymore today. I've got stuff to do, and I'll bet you have other people to see. People who really need a shrink."

Dr. Richardson rose and stepped forward. "Your hour's not up, Erin. You don't have to leave."

"This is a stupid idea, coming here to talk about my headaches. I feel fine, and I haven't had one in a week."

"Until we figure out what's causing them, they won't stay away. Won't you let me help you, Erin?"

The bright, airy office seemed suddenly small and confining. Erin wanted out. But she kept seeing the stern set of her mother's mouth as she'd told her, "You're going to see this counselor, and that's final. We've spent a fortune on medical tests, and everything's come back negative."

Erin had shouted, "Would you rather they'd found some horrible disease?"

"How could you suggest such a thing?" Her mother's eyes had filled with tears, and Erin wished she could have taken back the words. "We have to get to the bottom of this. I've already lost one daughter. . . ."

". . . week, same time?"

With a start Erin realized that Dr. Richardson was talking to her. "What?"

"Can you come back next week, same time?"

"I—uh—guess so. Sure."

Dr. Richardson smiled brightly. "Good. We can get rid of these headaches, Erin, if you trust me and let me help."

Erin didn't believe the therapist for a minute, but she'd go just so her parents would stop nagging her and shouting at each other. "Nobody has to know that I'm seeing a counselor, do they?" She dropped her gaze to the sea green carpet.

"Our discussions are in strict confidence, Erin. Only the people you choose to tell need ever know."

Fat chance! Erin told herself. She'd never let anyone find out. It was humiliating. "I still think the other doctors gave up too soon."

"Then prove it by working with me." Dr. Richardson's voice held a challenge.

Erin stared straight ahead as her mother's worried face floated in her mind's eye, along with the distant memory of her father crying over the decision to turn off Amy's life-support machines. "I guess I don't have any choice, do I?"

"See you next week."

Erin left without answering.

Chapter Two

"How did your meeting with Dr. Richardson go? What did you think of her?"

Erin shoved the food around on her dinner plate, figuring the best answer to her mother's question. "She was okay."

"Just okay? I liked her a lot when I met with her. I honestly think she can help you, Erin—"

Erin let go of her fork, and it clattered against her plate. "Look, this whole thing is your idea, you know. I never wanted to go see a counselor in the first place."

"It's for your own good. We only want to see you happy and well again."

"I'm *happy* going to school, dancing, planning for graduation and college, and doing things with my friends."

"Now don't go making too many plans. I'm not convinced that you need to go away to college. After all, the University of South Florida is a perfectly fine place, and it's right here in Tampa, so you could live at home—"

Here we go again, Erin thought. She interrupted her mother. "But USF doesn't have the dance department that Florida State does. I've told you that before."

"And if you're not well by September, you can't possibly consider moving away," her mother said stubbornly.

"I'll be okay, Mom."

"It's not a stigma to need help, Erin. There are lots of people—"

"Stop it," her father said curtly. "Erin, calm down. And Marian, get off Erin's back."

Mrs. Bennett glared at Mr. Bennett. "It was *your* idea too. We both agreed that she needed counseling."

"That's the point. It's *her* counseling. We agreed not to discuss her sessions, that she could talk about them only if she chooses."

"She's my daughter, my *only* daughter. I just want her to get well and lead a normal life again."

"It's her life, isn't it?"

They continued arguing, but Erin had stopped listening. She'd heard it all before over the past months, and no matter how it started, they always ended up in a yelling match, with Erin feeling like the catalyst. They argued about her, around her, because of her. Sometimes she heard them well into the night, and she had to cover her head with her pillow to shut them out.

It hadn't always been this way. They'd been happier together once, even as much as a year ago. Before Amy's accident.

"That's right," Mrs. Bennett was shouting. "Just walk right out in the middle of supper. That's the way to solve the problems—run away from them."

Mr. Bennett threw his napkin on the table and stood. "I've lost my appetite. I'm going to the library. I have papers to grade."

Mrs. Bennett followed him out of the dining room. "We certainly wouldn't want your family to get in the way of your job now, would we?"

"Me? What about you? You're always working late at that store of yours."

"I own my own business, and I have to manage it. I'm the boss, and the place would fall apart if I wasn't around."

"Well, since you're so indispensable, you won't miss me tonight."

"You've never turned down the money the store brings in, have you? And besides, it's going to take ten years to pay off our medical bills."

Erin squeezed her eyes shut, as if to block out the voices. What was happening to them? Why had her parents turned into strangers, and why was her family falling apart?

When Amy had been alive, their dinner table had been fun. She could still see Amy making them all laugh with her silly faces and involved stories about school. Sometimes, the way Amy hogged the limelight had irritated Erin, but now, looking back, she saw that Amy had definitely brought their family together. She'd acted as a kind of unifying force, compelling them to interact whether they wanted to or not! Erin suddenly realized that she'd give anything to have meals together again where they laughed and kidded instead of fought and argued.

She blinked away tears and began to clear the table, trying to ignore Amy's chair. It stood empty, yet ready and waiting, as if its former occupant might one day return.

Breathless, Erin slipped into the Briarwood theater back door and hurried to join the people sitting in a semicircle of metal chairs on the brightly lit stage. Her friend, Shara Perez, caught her eye and waved her over to the seat she'd been saving next to her. Ms. Thornton was talking to the group, and Mr. Ault, from the Berkshire drama department, stood beside her.

"Sorry I'm late," Erin whispered to Shara. "Did I miss anything?"

"Just the usual pep talk," Shara whispered back. "They'll start the auditions in a few minutes."

Erin heard Ms. Thornton saying, ". . . going to be a terrific production. Mr. Ault and I will be assigning major roles by Wednesday and passing out a rehearsal schedule on Friday. I expect every one of you to make every rehearsal. If you can't come to one, you must contact either me or Mr. Ault. Is that clear?"

Erin darted her eyes nervously, feeling as if Ms. Thornton was talking directly to her. Erin knew she had an excellent chance at the lead, but if she missed rehearsals because of the headaches, then Ms. Thornton might not choose her. Only the day before, during church, another one had come on her, and she'd spent the rest of Sunday in bed because of it.

Mr. Ault stepped forward. "Since this is a cold reading, we'll pass out the scripts now. Take a few minutes to look them over; then we'll have everybody break into smaller groups for the principal parts and let you read individually."

When she'd received her script, Erin asked Shara, "Are you going to read?"

"Don't have to," Shara told her. "Ms. Thornton already told me I'll be the singing voice of Maria. That way the lead only has to be responsible for her lines and the dancing. In fact, most of the parts will have stand-in singers. That way more people can participate."

"And those of us who can't carry a tune won't have to ruin the roles by attempting to sing," Erin observed. "That's pretty clever of Ms. Thornton."

Shara smiled. "I thought so, because those of us who can't dance won't have to worry about falling on our faces."

Pinky, a senior and a pixie-sized girl with black hair and a fiery Spanish personality, read for the part of Anita, the leader of the Puerto Rican girls. Erin's palms began to sweat because the reading for Maria was next, and by now she had her heart set on the part.

Erin read a scene, and when she was finished, Mr. Ault said, "I want you to try another one. But this time I want you to interact with the male lead."

He studied the group of boys who'd come forward for Tony.

Erin did too. One guy was particularly attractive, tall and lean with straight chestnut-colored hair and sexy smoke-colored eyes. She glanced at Shara, who gave a discreet thumbs-up gesture. All at once Erin realized that doing the play might be more fun than she'd originally thought.

Mr. Ault said, "David, come give this a try."

The dark-haired boy moved aside, and another one stepped forward, one not nearly so handsome. Erin judged him only about an inch or two taller than herself. His blond hair was tousled, a bit too long, hanging over his eyebrows in front and brushing his collar in the back. His eyes were bright blue, and they sparkled with mischief. He was wearing baggy checkered Bermuda shorts and a flamboyant floral-print shirt, socks that sagged and torn tennis shoes. Erin stared. Surely Mr. Ault was joking!

"Hi. I'm David Devlin," he said as he stood in front of her, offering a grin that lit up his face. "Did anyone ever tell you that you're the most beautiful girl this side of paradise city?"

Erin felt her mouth drop open and color creep up her neck.

"Uh—Erin? Do you want to get on with the reading, please?" Ms. Thornton's voice penetrated her trance. Totally flustered, Erin fumbled with the pages and dropped the script. The onlookers shuffled. David stooped, retrieved her booklet, and handed it back with another disarming smile. Erin took an instant dislike to David Devlin.

She snatched the booklet, found her place, and read the lines stiffly. David's expression grew serious as he fell into the character of Tony with amazing skill. At the end of the scene, Mr. Ault called, "Good job. You want to try it, Andy?"

Another boy came forward, and after he read, Mr. Ault sent in another one. Seth—Mr. Smoky Gray Eyes—read last with her. Other girls did the scene with each of the boys, and finally it was over.

"Okay, take a break," Ms. Thornton directed.

Shara hurried over to Erin. "You're a cinch," she said. "I saw Ms. Thornton and Mr. Ault taking notes the whole time."

Erin did several leg stretches and bend-overs to relieve the tension that had collected in her muscles. "Well, I certainly hope that they don't pick that David idiot to be the male lead," she said.

"Why not?" Shara said. "I think he's sort of cute. Not knock-you-out-cute, but adorable cute."

"So are three-year-olds, but I don't want to be in a play with one."

"As an objective bystander, allow me to tell you that he gave the best reading."

Erin rolled her eyes. "Just my luck." She took a chair to one side while activity buzzed around her and voices echoed in the cavernous theater. Beyond the lights the stage and seats were swallowed up by darkness. The wooden stage floor looked dusty, and the scrim curtain swayed slightly with a draft.

An unexplainable sense of loneliness descended on her. She stared at the others, feeling distant and removed. She loved the theater because she loved to dance, but she'd never wanted to be an actress. It had been her sister Amy who'd had greasepaint in her blood. Amy should be reading for a part. If only . . .

"I meant it when I said you're beautiful."

David Devlin's voice intruded into Erin's thoughts, and she looked up to see him standing beside her. "Just drop it," she told him sourly.

Instead he dragged a chair over and plopped down beside her. "So you're a dancer. I'm an actor. At least that's what I intend to be. Broadway and everything."

"Does that mean you can't dance?" she asked. "You can't take the male lead if you can't dance, you know."

"I can shuffle along," he said. " 'Course I'm not a pro, but I've taken classes before. Still, I'm a better actor than dancer, and I can sing. How about you?"

She ignored his question, saying, "You talk like you've already landed the part. You're not the only one trying out." To make her point Erin inclined her head toward Seth. She also hoped to convey to David that she found Seth a lot more appealing than she did him.

"He's decent," David said. "But I'm going to be playing Tony."

His attitude irritated her. "You'll excuse me if I cheer for the other guy."

David laughed. "You're pretty sure you're

going to get Maria, aren't you? What's the difference?"

"I—I am not sure at all," Erin stammered.

"Then why didn't you read for any other part?"

Disarmed by his logic, Erin was seething. "Well if you're a 'sure thing' for Tony, then I guess I should have read for another part." She stood, dropping her script.

David scooped it up. "You gotta learn to hang onto this thing, Erin."

Intent on brushing him off, Erin spun, only to have the back of her heel catch on the rung of the metal chair. It clanked and clattered and would have fallen if David hadn't reached out to steady it. "For a dancer you're a little clumsy," he teased. "Still gorgeous, however."

She couldn't think of a snappy put-down, and she considered throwing her script at him. Instead, she stalked off while he called, "See you on Friday, 'Maria.'"

Chapter Three

"If he gets the part, I'll quit." Erin shoved dance gear into her duffel bag in the girl's locker room while Shara watched.

"Boy, I haven't seen you this worked up since Travis Sinclair took Cindy Pitzer to last year's Spring Fling dance."

"That was different," Erin snapped. "Amy was comatose, and that creep was dating someone else while he was supposed to be Amy's boyfriend. I hated him then, and I still do." She glared at Shara for making her remember. "I dislike David Devlin for entirely different reasons," she said.

Shara opened her locker and took out an apple. "Then you'd better consider quitting. According to the other guys at tryouts, he's the best. He wins every forensic competition and placed second in state in drama as a junior last year."

"What are you, a reporter?"

"I just asked a few questions, that's all. Besides, what better way to get to know Seth? Remember, the one with the sexy eyes?"

So Shara was interested in Seth. Erin hid her disappointment, saying, "No. They all seemed alike to me."

Shara buffed the apple on her shirt. "What's with you anyway, Erin? You're always snarling at people, and you're negative about everything. I was hoping that this play would be something fun we could do together."

"Nothing's wrong with me. I just happen to think David Devlin is a jerk, that's all."

"I don't think so," Shara countered. "Afterwards, after you stormed off, we were all getting acquainted and talking, and David had us in stitches imitating teachers at Berkshire. I laughed until I was crying, and I don't even *know* the teachers at Berkshire." Shara chuckled. "I can still picture him."

Exasperated, Erin slammed her locker door shut. "That sounds so juvenile. I wouldn't want to be a part of *ragging* on teachers. My father's a teacher here, remember?"

"Well, if we're all going to be in this play together, then you'd better join in. It's going to take all of us working like crazy to bring it off."

Erin realized Shara was right. She'd been in enough dance productions over the years to know how much hard work went into them. "We've got a couple of months, so there's plenty of time to get to know everybody." She zipped up her bag. A knot of tension had gathered at the base of her neck.

"The sooner, the better," Shara said. "I like the music, don't you?"

Erin was relieved that Shara had changed the subject and was forgetting their earlier disagreement. She didn't mean to argue with her friend. "Yeah, it's good music."

Shara broke into the words from the song "Tonight" and whirled around the locker room, her soprano voice echoing off the empty walls.

Erin listened to Shara's beautiful voice. It reminded her of springtime, and suddenly she imagined dandelion seeds floating above Amy's casket. A dull ache began to inch its way up her neck and lodge in the back of her head. "Be careful, or you'll fall down," she said to Shara.

Shara stopped twirling, then reached out and steadied herself on the bank of lockers. "Whoa! You're right. How do dancers twirl around and not get dizzy?"

The ache had spread to her forehead, and her eyes began to hurt. She rubbed them. "You have to focus on an object and every time you turn, you have to make sure you come back to that object."

"I guess that's why I sing," Shara said with a shrug. "Less danger of falling over."

Erin dropped to a bench. She began to see pinwheels of color, and the throbbing increased in her temples.

"Hey, you okay?" Shara asked. "You look white as a sheet."

"Did you drive your car today?"

"No, Dad dropped me off on his way to make hospital rounds. What's wrong, Erin? Another headache?"

Erin never tried to keep the headaches a secret

from her friend. Her parents had asked Dr. Perez for the names of specialists to treat her when the headaches had first started. "It came on real sudden."

"You want me to drive you home in your car?"

"Could you, please?"

Shara quickly gathered up their things. "Do you have your pills with you? Maybe you should take some."

"Yes, you're right." Pain stymied her. Why hadn't she thought of that? She found the pills, took two without water, and leaned against the lockers. Her breath was shallow. "I wish it didn't hurt so bad."

"Your doctors still haven't found what's causing them?"

"Not yet." By now Erin was feeling sick to her stomach. She gripped Shara's hand and allowed her friend to lead her out of the gym. Outside, the late-afternoon light stabbed at her eyeballs like hot needles.

"This isn't right, Erin," Shara muttered. "You can't go on this way. How are you ever going to do the play—"

Erin dug her nails into the blond girl's palm. "*Please*, don't say a word to Ms. Thornton, Shara, okay? Not one word."

"You know I won't. But I can't stand to see you hurting like this."

"I want that part, Shara. And I'm not going to let these stupid headaches stop me." She was dizzy now and very nauseous. She braced herself on the car while Shara fumbled with the key.

"Even if you have to play opposite David Devlin?" Shara asked shakily.

Erin tried to nod, but every movement sent fresh waves of agony shooting through her head. "Even that," she whispered, falling across the seat as the door opened.

"You need to think of your headaches as a *friend*, Erin," Dr. Richardson said Thursday afternoon in her office.

"There's nothing friendly about them," Erin retorted.

"The headaches are your body's way of letting tension out. We'll be detectives and try to give this friend some tangible features."

Erin thought it was a dumb idea, but rehearsals started the next afternoon, so she was desperate to do something about the headaches. "Okay. How do we start?"

"We look for a pattern. For instance, when do they occur most often?"

"No particular time." She shrugged. "They're just *there*."

"When did you have your last one?"

"Monday, after play tryouts."

"Did the tryouts go well for you?"

"I got the lead."

"Congratulations," the counselor said heartily. "But did the competing make you tense?"

"Not really," Erin answered honestly. "I've been auditioning for dance roles all my life. It's part of the fun."

"Was it easy being with the other kids? Didn't you tell me Berkshire was doing the production with you?"

"When you go to an all-girls school, being around guys is different at first. But some of them are really good-looking. Except one. His name is David, and I don't like him very much. But I'm going to have to adapt, because he got the part of Tony."

"What don't you like about him?"

"He came on too strong, I guess. He acted too friendly, sort of Mr. Personality, Life-of-the-Party, you know the type? He wasn't the one I wanted to get the part either."

"What did the others think of him?"

"Shara, my best friend, likes him. She says he's a real comedian."

"Is that when your headache started?"

"No. It was later, in the locker room. But I don't see how David could have set it off. He's more like a pain in the rear end."

Dr. Richardson laughed. "What about the headache before that? When did it come on?"

They spent some time listing what Erin could recall when each headache started. Most of the events were hazy because of the pain. Still, the pattern seemed undiscernible, and she told Dr. Richardson as much. "Don't be discouraged," the therapist said. "Something's here, we just haven't singled it out yet." Dr. Richardson studied her notes briefly. "The headaches started about a year ago, is that correct?"

"More or less. They got worse over last summer. They slacked off when school started, but they seem to be coming more often now. Since it's spring, couldn't it be allergies?" she asked hopefully.

"But you've never had allergy problems before."

"So? Allergies could explain everything. I think my parents should take me to an allergist. Don't you?"

Dr. Richardson tapped her pencil on her notepad. "We won't rule it out, but let me ask some more questions first. What happened in your life about a year ago?"

Erin knew what the therapist wanted her to say, so she chose the most direct, hard-hitting words she could. "I'm sure my parents already told you that my sister, Amy, was in a car wreck and in a coma for three weeks before she died. I'm not 'retreating from reality,' if that's what you're thinking."

"Where did you hear that phrase?"

"From one of the doctors Mom took me to in the beginning. I know that my sister's dead and nothing's going to bring her back."

Dr. Richardson frowned. "It was unfair of that doctor to make a diagnosis without a thorough evaluation. We need to look at the total person, not just body parts."

"That's the way they treated Amy," Erin said

ruefully. "There was a doctor for her brain, one for her heart, one for her other organs. They just sort of parceled her out in pieces." Erin shook her head to chase away the images of machines and monitors and antiseptic smells.

"You're telling me that you hated to see her in that condition, aren't you?"

A lump filled Erin's throat; she swallowed it down. "I know they were trying to save her life, but still it was like she was just some sort of lab experiment. I've accepted Amy's death," Erin added. "I know I won't see her again until I get to heaven. So it still doesn't make any sense for me to have the headaches."

Dr. Richardson leaned over the desk and touched Erin's shoulder. "Your heart hurts, Erin. It hurts so bad, it's making the rest of your body hurt too. The headaches may involve Amy's death, but I believe there's more to it than that."

"But what?"

"That's what we're going to find out together."

"Don't you just *love* Friday night at the mall?" Shara asked Erin as they passed in front of a plate-glass window filled with bright spring fashions. "Everybody's here."

"It's too crowded," Erin said. "If I fell down, I'd get squashed."

"Don't be negative. Maybe if you fell down, you'd get rescued."

"By whom? Have you seen some of the scuzballs hanging around this place?"

Shara let out an "Eek!" of exasperation. "Then let's count tonight as a celebration of the first rehearsal."

"It was chaos, and you know it."

"True, but it gave me plenty of time to flirt with Seth," Shara said with a dimpled smile.

"And me too much time to avoid my leading man."

"But why do you want to? David's so sweet, and he seems crazy about you."

"He's crazy, all right," Erin muttered.

"He's got a smile that lights up the stage, too," Shara insisted.

"If you think he's so terrific, then let's trade. I'll take Seth."

Shara made a face. "David doesn't know any other girl is alive. Sorry, Erin, he's absolutely zeroed in on you." Shara patted her shoulder. "Tough life, having some guy drooling at your feet."

Erin started to retort but heard someone call her name. She turned to see a girl with short reddish hair weaving her way toward her. Erin's eyes narrowed. She knew the girl but couldn't quite place her.

"It's me, Beth Clark. Remember? From the hospital last year. My mother needed a kidney transplant, and your sister was in a coma. How did it ever turn out for her?"

Chapter Four

Seeing Beth again was like seeing a ghost. For Erin she was a painful reminder of the hospital and endless days of waiting. Erin stared at her, unable to speak. Shara must have realized her friend needed rescuing, because she said, "I'm Shara Perez, Erin's friend. I used to sit with her in the waiting room."

Beth nodded. "I remember you. How's Amy?"

"She—uh—she . . ." Shara stuttered.

"She died," Erin interrupted.

Beth's face looked stricken. "Oh, I'm so sorry."

"We donated her organs."

Glancing around, Beth asked, "Would you like to go to the food court and talk?"

"Sure," Erin said, marching off swiftly in the direction of the mall's fast-food area while the others tried to keep up. Once they'd bought drinks and settled at a table, Beth said, "I'm really sorry about Amy."

"You were still in Gainesville when we had her funeral. Then later—" she shrugged and let the sentence trail. "So how's your mom doing?"

"All right. But not perfect."

26

"I thought that getting a new kidney would make her well."

"She still has to take medication to suppress her immune system so she won't reject the transplant. The doctors are having a hard time finding the right combination. She's depressed a lot."

Beth let her gaze wander, and Erin sensed there was a lot she was leaving out. "So, how are you doing?" Erin asked.

"As well as can be expected."

"How's that boyfriend of yours?"

"We called it quits. Between schoolwork and all the stuff I have to do at home, I didn't have much time for him."

"What stuff?" Shara asked.

Beth took a sip of her soft drink. "Taking care of my sisters and kid brother. Mom's not able to do much housework, or even cook, so I have to make sure it all gets done."

Shara grimaced. "What a drag."

"So what's going on in your life?" Beth asked, and Erin told her about the play. "Sounds exciting. I was in a play at my school last year, but I didn't have the time to go out for one this year. Who's in it from Berkshire? Maybe I know some of them."

Erin ran through several names. Shara added, "You forgot David Devlin. He's got the lead."

"David?" Beth said, breaking out into a grin. "I know him. He's *so* good! And funny too. You're going to have a ball playing opposite him." Erin held her tongue in spite of the "told-you-so" smirk

Shara gave her. Was she the only person in the universe who didn't think David was Mr. Wonderful?

Beth glanced at her watch. "I promised Mom I'd be back in an hour. It was great to see you again, Erin."

"Same here."

"Uh—maybe you could call me and remind me about the play. I'd like to see it."

Erin suddenly felt very sorry for Beth, thinking how hard it must be for her at home. Even though her family had its problems, at least *her* basic routine had remained about the same. "I'll let you know," Erin told her.

After Beth had gone, Shara asked, "Do you want to hit a few more stores?" Erin shook her head. "Are you getting a headache?"

"No," Erin said, both relieved and disappointed. On the one hand, she didn't want to face the pain, but on the other she could now be reasonably certain that her headaches had nothing to do with seeing someone who she associated with those horrible few weeks before Amy died. She made a mental note to tell Dr. Richardson. They were no closer to discovering the reason for her headaches than before.

"Quick! Duck! Devlin's got a can of slime, and he's hitting everybody!"

Seth's shout made Erin flatten herself against the wall the second she emerged from the theater's dressing room. *What now?* she wondered irritably. The rehearsal had gone well, but now that everyone was supposed to be getting ready to leave, David was pulling a stupid prank.

She heard kids giggling and saw Shara slip behind a partially painted flat with Seth. Erin calculated the fastest route to the outside stage door and away from the dumb game. She inched along the wall, spied the door, and prepared to make a dash for it. Suddenly all the lights went out.

Erin froze, hearing muffled screeches and kids banging into chairs and props. Someone yelled, "You're dead meat, Devlin!"

Erin crouched, trying hard to remember the path to the door. An arm shot around her waist and pulled her close against a warm body. A melodramatic voice rasped in her ear, "Now you're mine, my pretty!"

"David!"

"Shh," he warned. "Don't give away our position."

"Don't you dare slime me," Erin hissed.

"What? I'd sooner deface the Sistine Chapel. No, you're my hostage."

"Let go of me!"

"Can't," David whispered. "Seth and Andy have cans of slime too. It's them against us now."

"I don't want to play."

David seized her hand and pulled her behind him. "Too late. If they see you with me, you'll get slimed for sure."

From the far side of the stage, Andy yelled, "Pinky, turn the lights on."

Great, Erin thought. Everybody was involved

in the foolishness. She tried to tug away from David, but his grip was tight. "In here," he said, pulling her down into a large wooden box.

"Where are we?" she asked.

"Prop box," David said. "I cased it out when I got here tonight. They'll never find us in here."

"You mean you *planned* this?"

"Of course. The cast needs to lighten up and have some fun. And so do you."

"Ms. Thornton and Mr. Ault will have an attack."

"What are they gonna do, fire us?"

Erin knew he was grinning, even though she couldn't see his face. "I don't want to be here with you," she said, hoping to sound icy.

"So where would you rather be with me? Just name it."

Outside, Pinky shouted, "I found the lights!" The lid of the prop box was closed, so Erin saw only a small stream of light through a crack. Andy called, "Come on out, Devlin. I promise to make this as painful as possible."

David scrunched lower and, not knowing why, Erin ducked in tighter next to him. She could tell by the sound of Andy's voice that he was standing right outside the box. Her heart pounded and she held her breath.

Next to her, David coiled. He dropped her hand. She sensed what he was going to do and pulled to one side. With a rebel yell, David flipped up the top of the box, stood, and sprayed a startled Andy directly in the face.

"He slimed me!" Andy wailed.

Erin peeked over the edge of the box in time to see five kids emerge from the shadows and surround David, who skidded to a halt.

"We've got him now," Seth said. "Tighten the ranks," he ordered. Shara, Pinky, and three boys locked arms and slowly closed inward.

David shook his can of slime and shrugged. "Gee fellas, I'm all out," he said.

"Prepare to *die*, alien," Seth said.

Erin climbed out of the box, wide-eyed, torn between wanting to see David get his just rewards and wanting to see him outwit his friends one final time. Seth hit the nozzle as David did an elaborate pratfall. The movement was so quick, so well timed, and so effortless, that no one saw it coming. The slime spewed across the small circle and doused Shara and Pinky, while David rolled like an acrobat, sprang to his feet, and darted away.

Erin felt struck by déjà vu as an image of a similar pratfall flashed through her mind. She struggled to bring the memory into focus, but it eluded her like mist, and the screaming and laughing around her pushed the memory even further out of reach.

Soon everyone scattered, still laughing and talking, to clean off the messy slime. Erin, haunted by David's pratfall, heard him organizing a trip to McDonald's. "Hey, Erin, can you come with us?"

A hard knot of tension was forming at the base of her neck. "I—I can't."

He walked over to her. "Are you mad?" he asked.

"No. I just can't come tonight."

"Maybe next time?" Erin started to feel desperate to get away. Shara walked past, and David caught her arm. "Can you persuade Erin to come with us?"

Shara questioned Erin with her eyes. The knot was growing, and Erin felt the tightness inching up her skull. She had to get out of there fast and drive home while she still could. She kneaded the back of her neck, hoping Shara would get the message. "I really can't," she said.

Shara understood. She tucked her arm through David's and said, "Oh no you don't, wise guy. You're not going to stand here flirting with Erin while the rest of us clean up this mess. Come on."

Erin quickly gathered her things and left. Somehow she made it home, where she took her headache medication and crawled into bed. Nausea made her gag, and she writhed on the cool sheets praying for the pain to go away. But every time she closed her eyes, the image of David's pratfall replayed in her mind.

She didn't know why. She couldn't explain it. Yet she was completely and absolutely convinced that somehow David Devlin was mixed up in the headache's arrival.

Chapter Five

"You want me to pull David from the cast, and you won't even tell me why? Erin, that makes no sense."

Erin tugged at the leg of her leotard and avoided eye contact with Ms. Thornton. "I don't mean to cause problems. It's just that I—uh—I don't get along with him too well."

"Artistic differences? Come on now—he's an excellent actor, and you're much too professional to be pitching a temper tantrum."

Erin couldn't stand for Ms. Thornton to think badly of her. In spite of her being a teacher, their relationship was more like a friendship; yet she couldn't run the risk of being around David and having another headache either. What if one came on during the actual performance?

Ms. Thornton's eyes narrowed. "He didn't try something with you, did he? I mean, it's obvious he's smitten, but is he harassing you?"

"Oh no. Please, that's not it at all."

Ms. Thornton reached out and took Erin's arm. "What is it then? Tell me. I want to help."

Erin caught the reflections of the dancers'

bodies dressed in contrasting leotards and tights in the wall of mirrors, and she wished the floor would open up and swallow her. How could she tell Ms. Thornton the truth? Maybe she'd decide to replace *her* instead of David. "It—it's nothing. He sort of gets on my nerves, that's all."

"Hardly a reason to drop him from the play," Ms. Thornton said. "You know, Erin, you're the best student I've ever had, and you have a wonderful sense of professionalism. You have a future in this business, and you'll often have to work with people you aren't nuts about. You may as well learn how to do it now."

Erin felt silly and foolish. "Forget I said anything."

"It's forgotten," Ms. Thornton said, smiling. "In fact, Mr. Ault is working with David privately to bone up his dance numbers. He has a decent voice, so we'll let him record his song numbers on cassette for playback in the actual performances. In fact"— the teacher paused and measured Erin in the mirror—"I've been considering asking you to work extra with him too. In light of our discussion, will that be a problem?"

Erin's heart sank. "Of course not. I'm a professional, remember?"

Ms. Thornton grew serious. "Look, honey, I know it's been a tough year for you, but you seem to be doing well. Are you?"

"Um—all right. Some days are better than others." No use pretending to Ms. Thornton that her life was a bed of roses, but no sense in dumping the whole truth on her either.

"I want you to think again about taking that Wolftrap scholarship this summer. The offer's still open."

Erin was half-afraid it would be. She wanted it, but if the headaches didn't go away, if Dr. Richardson couldn't help her discover the cause . . . She faked a bright smile. "Let's see how I do with this play. I mean, if David and I don't kill each other before it's over."

Ms. Thornton smiled. "You'll figure out a way to get along with him. He *is* kind of cute," she added. "And he's certainly attracted to you."

Erin rolled her eyes. "That's the last thing I need."

"Or the first," Ms. Thornton said, then began doing leg lifts on the bar while Erin stared blankly in the mirror.

Erin found her mother in the garage sorting laundry. "Um—have you see any metal chain out here?" she asked.

"All I'm seeing is a week's worth of dirty clothes," her mother complained. "What do you need a chain for?"

"It's for the rumble scene in the play—the big gang fight."

"This place is such a mess, you'll be lucky to find anything."

Erin glanced around at the piles of junk, heavy

with dust and grime. "Looks like we need another family workday. We haven't had one of those in"—she wrinkled her brow—"way over a year."

"No one has time anymore to do anything around here."

"I could make the time," Erin said quickly, seeing it as an opportunity for them to do something together as a family. So what if it was grungy, dirty work? At least it would bring them together for a day.

"I'm swamped at the boutique, and I know your father won't take his nose out of his books long enough to do anything as mundane as garage cleanup."

Erin hadn't counted on her mother's animosity toward her father. She was suddenly sick and tired of all their hassling. "What's the matter with you two? Do you always have to be at war with each other?"

Mrs. Bennett shoved a load of laundry into the machine. "You couldn't possibly understand—"

"Is it me? Is it something I've done to make you both angry?"

"Oh, of course not, darling. You're all we have." The tears brimming in her mother's eyes shocked Erin. She hadn't meant to make her cry. "Why if it weren't for you—" Her mother's sentence trailed, and Erin felt panicked. If it weren't for her what? Would her parents break up? Mrs. Bennett grabbed her, hugging her fiercely. "Don't you see? You're all that's left. I—I can't stand the thought of losing you."

"You won't, Mom," Erin mumbled, confused and a little scared by her mother's wide emotional swing from anger at her husband to clingy tearfulness over her daughter. And what did she mean about "losing" her? She was moving away to college next year. They'd discussed it many times. If only Amy were still with them, then perhaps it would be easier to leave. Amy was *supposed* to have been at home another year.

Awkwardly Erin broke free and skirted her father's overloaded workbench. "I—uh—I have to find that chain."

She searched hurriedly, eager to get away. Suddenly she saw it on a stack of boxes next to an old trunk against the cement block wall. The black lettering had faded, but each container was marked "Amy" in her father's neat writing.

"What's wrong?" her mother asked from across the garage. "Did you find it?"

"Yes," she said, unable to take her eyes off the boxes and trunk. She remembered the day her parents had cleaned out Amy's room and packed away the total accumulation of her sixteen years on planet Earth.

"You should go through this stuff," her mother had said through her tears. "There'll be things you'll want to keep."

"Not now," Erin had told her. "Maybe someday."

Her father had taped each box shut, and her mother had wept, "My baby, my poor baby."

"That won't help, Marian," her father had admonished. "We have to get on with life, and crying about Amy won't bring her back."

Erin blinked, and the vivid pictures from the past faded to the dingy darkness of the garage. She grabbed the chain, dragged it toward the washer and dryer, and stuffed it into a paper sack. "Ugh, it's all rusty. You'd better wash up in the laundry sink," her mother said.

Erin stared at the rust that had stained her hands brown. She quickly washed them, watching in macabre fascination as soap and water cleaned away the red brown stain that reminded her of dried blood.

David was late for their special rehearsal with Mr. Ault, and Erin grew angrier by the second. She adjusted her leg warmers and did several arabesques in the center of the stage before asking, "Where is he? We've been waiting twenty minutes, and I told my mom I'd work at her store this afternoon."

Mr. Ault shrugged. "David's never been punctual. I'll have to remind him again that we must start on time."

They heard the outside stage door bang, and seconds later David bounded across the stage and skidded to a halt, saying, "Sorry," and flashing a boyish grin.

"Well, it's about time," Erin mumbled.

"It was my sister's birthday, and I had to do my bit."

"You have a sister?"

"Yeah. Jody. She turned eight today."

"Let's get started," Mr. Ault said, cuing up the cassette for the musical number during which Tony and Maria meet at the neighborhood dance amid the rivaling gangs. "This is slow. The rest of the cast is frozen in motion, the lights dim, the spot comes up and pulls Tony and Maria to the center of the stage. They look with wonder at each other and then . . ." He put Erin's hand in David's and made them face one another.

David's fingers felt warm. Since he wasn't tall, she only had to raise her chin slightly to look him in the eye. "I'll try not to damage your feet," he told her.

"I only dance on the bottoms," she said, hoping a little humor would relax her.

David turned on his famous megawatt smile. She noticed a white substance smeared along his jawline and squinted at it. "What's wrong?" he asked.

"There's some kind of white stuff on your neck."

He dropped her hand and wiped his face. "Greasepaint. I thought I got it all off."

She wondered why he'd been wearing white greasepaint but didn't want to ask. *No use getting too friendly*, she thought. They danced for a few minutes to Mr. Ault's instructions. David was amazingly light on his feet and a quick learner.

He pulled her closer, and she rested her cheek on his shoulder, all the while keeping pace to the music. He was muscular and solid and smelled like sunshine.

"That's good," Mr. Ault said. "Remember, you two are beginning to fall in love here. . . . No, Erin, don't stiffen. Relax. That's better. Now, 'Tony,' spin her slowly, push her outward . . . pull her back . . . yes, very good. Now stop dancing and act like you're about to kiss her."

David's face dipped lower. Erin's heart began to hammer. When his mouth was inches from hers, Mr. Ault said, "Hold it. Perfect. Now, at this point Tony and Maria will freeze, the spotlight will widen, the lights will come up, and the others will dance around them."

Erin scarcely heard him, because David's mouth was coming closer. By reflex her eyes closed and her chin tilted, and David's lips brushed over hers. The contact jolted Erin out of her trance. Her eyelids opened wide; she brought up her palms and shoved hard against David's chest. "Don't do that!" she cried.

"What's the problem?" Mr. Ault groaned. "It was going so well."

David staggered backwards, throwing up his hands in innocence. "My mouth slipped," he explained.

"You're not supposed to kiss her here, hot lips," Mr. Ault said. "Not until act three."

"He's such a pain!"

"Come on, Erin," the teacher admonished. "Let's try to be professional. David, back off."

Erin squeezed her eyes shut, afraid she was

going to cry. Why *was* she overreacting? She felt a throbbing and a tightening in her temples. How was she ever going to make it till the play opened in six weeks? "This is just supposed to be for blocking out the dance moves," she said. "He—he caught me off guard, that's all."

"Can we try it again?" Mr. Ault asked. "And this time, David, keep your lips from 'slipping.'"

David saluted and took Erin in his arms again. "Loosen up," he said. "It was just a kiss."

Erin glared at him. They made it through the number several more times, and when Mr. Ault was finally pleased and had dismissed them, Erin hurried to get her things, because the pressure in her skull was building. At the stage door David stopped her before she could get outside. His expression was serious and contemplative. "Why don't you like me?" he asked.

Erin tried to shrug him off. "You surprised me, that's all."

"I don't think so. You haven't liked me since day one."

"I—it isn't personal."

"How else can it be? You don't even know me. We've never even met before."

Something about him nagged at the back of her mind. "I'm sorry. Really." She seemed to be saying that phrase a lot lately.

David tipped his head to one side, and his eyes gleamed with mischief. "Would you like me more if I gave you a present?"

"I don't want anything. I have to go." She tried

to step around him, but he dodged in front of her, pulled a balloon from his pocket, and proceeded to blow it up.

"I'm really a nice guy," he said between puffs of air. "Kids and dogs are nuts about me. I'm gonna make you a dachshund out of this balloon to prove it." He twisted the balloon into shape. "Don't look so surprised. See, at heart, I'm really a clown."

In that instant Erin knew exactly where she'd seen David Devlin before.

Chapter Six

❦

"You didn't recognize him until he said the word 'clown'?" Dr. Richardson asked, tapping her pencil on the side of her notepad. "Why not?"

"The first time we met, we were both wearing full clown makeup. White greasepaint, fake noses, wigs, big sloppy costumes—there's no way I could have known who he was when he auditioned for the play. When we performed at the Children's Home together last Easter, I didn't even know his last name." Erin was relieved and elated that she'd solved the mystery of why David made her feel uncomfortable. "I guess that I disliked him because he reminds me of when Amy was in the hospital."

"A lot of things must remind you of Amy. But not everything that reminds you gives you a headache."

Erin fidgeted in the chair. She was so sure she'd hit on the solution to her headaches generated by David. "I was just making an observation," she said testily.

"Did you tell David about meeting him before?"

"Oh, no," Erin said. "I don't want him to know."

"Why?"

"I'd feel stupid talking about it. He didn't know Amy. And I'll never be a clown again. So why bring it up?"

Dr. Richardson pushed away from her desk and sat back in her chair. "Do you know what a support group is, Erin?"

"It's a group of people who have something in common. There's a support group at Briarwood for girls with divorced parents, and they meet once a week."

"I oversee a grief support group for young people who've lost a parent or a sibling or even a friend."

"So?"

"I'd like you to meet with us."

"I meet with *you*."

"You'd continue to meet with me, but you'd also meet with them. We gather in my conference room on Friday nights."

"I don't think so."

"Why?"

"I'm pretty busy already. Between school and dance classes and now the play, I don't have much free time. If I have any, I work in Mom's store."

"You could make time."

"I really don't want to come." Dr. Richardson looked at her expectantly, so Erin continued. "I don't want to sit around with a bunch of strangers and talk about Amy."

"Talking often helps—both you and the others. It helps you realize that you're not alone, that other

people have been through the same thing and feel
similar emotions."

"No one feels like I do. And talking won't bring
Amy back."

"But facing your feelings can help *you*."

Erin wanted to scream. Why did the counselor
keep firing dumb suggestions at her? "Look, I need
to cut today short. I've got lots of homework tonight." She stood. "I thought you'd be glad that I
figured out why I didn't like David."

"I'm not sure that's all of it."

"What do you mean?"

"I think there's a deeper reason why you feel
uncomfortable around this boy."

"Like what?"

"We're looking for the answers together, aren't
we?"

"In other words, you want me to figure it out
on my own," Erin said. If Dr. Richardson knew
what was wrong, why wouldn't she tell her?

"Please consider coming to the support
group."

"I said I was too busy." She stood and crossed
to the door. "I've got play practice too, so I gotta go
now."

The therapist picked up her appointment pad.
"I'll put you down for next week," she said.

Erin nodded, but deep down she doubted
she'd make the appointment. She was tired of talking about the past, and so far nothing much had
changed. She still got headaches. And now, with
the counselor pressuring her to come and spill her

guts in front of a bunch of strangers . . . Why would she talk to strangers about things she couldn't even discuss with her own parents?

Friday night after rehearsal some of the cast went out for pizza, and Shara all but dragged Erin along. At the pizza parlor six of them squeezed into a booth. Wedged between David and Andy, Erin grimaced at Shara on the other side of the dimly lit table. The aroma of tomato sauce and cheese made Erin's stomach growl. "And you said you weren't hungry," David joked.

"I said I didn't want to come," Erin corrected. A part of Erin really wanted to be there, but a part of her felt cut off and distanced from the others. It made no sense to her. "I've got to work at my mom's boutique tomorrow."

"So what?" Seth asked. "Do you turn into a pumpkin at midnight?"

The others laughed, and Erin felt her face flush.

"I've got a show to do, but I can't let a small detail like being up at seven A.M. deter me from pizza," David offered, drawing the attention away from Erin.

"Where?" Seth wanted to know. "Maybe we'll drop by and throw tomatoes."

David flipped water on him from his water glass. "I wouldn't notice even if you did. I don't actually wake up until noon. Just ask my science teacher," he joked.

"Lots of fun things come in the morning," Pinky told him.

"Name three."

"Santa Claus," said Shara quickly.

"The Tooth Fairy," Andy added.

"Unconfirmed," David told him. "Many suspect she comes late at night."

"Sunrise," Erin said quietly, remembering how Amy used to hate getting up in the mornings too. "Sunrise comes early in the morning." The others looked at her oddly. *How could I say such a stupid thing?* she thought.

"That can be confirmed," David interjected hastily, as if to cover for her.

Seth cleared his throat, and the awkward moment passed when the waitress brought a pizza, still sizzling from the oven. David divided up the pie and continued with a string of stories that kept the others laughing

Erin half listened, concentrating instead on picking the mushrooms off her slice of pizza. She flicked them absently, wondering where her hunger had gone. Her stomach was knotted for some reason, and she just couldn't eat.

"Something wrong with the food?" David asked.

"I'm just not a mushroom fanatic."

"Not a mushroom fanatic!" David feigned horror. "But mushrooms are our friends. In fact some of my best friends are mushrooms. Consider Seth here. . . ."

A tiny smile curled Erin's lip as David quickly started another conversation, this time about basketball. David did have the gift of charm and a ready wit, something she'd always envied in people. Amy had been that way, she thought. She set her piece of pizza down and tuned into what Andy was saying. ". . . no way, Devlin. You've got your hopes pinned on the wrong team. The Celtics are gonna take it all."

"In your dreams, buddy. How could you ever pick the Celtics to come out on top? Get with it, man! You'd have to be brain dead to pick them."

For Erin the world seemed to stop spinning, and the walls of the room closed in on her. *Brain dead*. She stood rapidly, pushing Andy out of the booth.

"Hey!" he yelped.

Erin didn't care. She only knew she had to get out of there before she screamed. She felt as if she were running through a thick fog. She heard Shara shout, "Erin! Wait!" She even felt a hand grab at her. But she wrenched away and ran to the door. People were staring, but it didn't matter. She had to get outside and into the cool night air.

She ran across the parking lot to her car and dug frantically through her purse. *Where are the stupid keys?* She climbed into the front seat and spilled the contents of her purse in her lap. She found them, finally, and jammed one into the ignition. She never got to turn it, though, because someone yanked open the passenger door, jumped in, and tugged the key from the switch.

Erin turned furiously toward the intruder, David Devlin. "Go away!" she shouted. "Go away and leave me alone!"

Chapter Seven

"I mean it," Erin said through clenched teeth. In the light from the overhead street lamp, she saw David's tortured expression.

"I'm sorry, Erin. I—I didn't know."

"Didn't know what? Give me my keys."

"I didn't know that you had a sister who died."

"Who told you?" Her chin lifted defiantly.

"Shara did, the minute you ran out. All I heard her say was that your sister had been brain dead after a car wreck; then I ran out after you."

"Shara's got a big mouth. The truth is I'm sick to my stomach."

David reached for her, and she shoved him away. "My keys." She held out her open palm.

"Talk to me," he pleaded. "Tell me what happened."

"If you don't give me my keys and get out of this car, I'm going to start screaming." Her hands were shaking, and tears were straining behind her eyes. Why didn't he go away and leave her alone?

"No," David said.

She lunged. He tossed the keys into the backseat and grabbed her wrists and pulled her toward him. She struggled to break free, fought to hold back the tears, but she couldn't do either. With a strangled cry the dam broke.

David held her, and she didn't resist because the fight had gone out of her. She didn't know how long she wept, but eventually the tears subsided, leaving her as limp as a rag doll. She fumbled in her lap for a tissue, while David stroked her hair. She eased back into her seat, but David held tightly to her right hand. "I haven't cried like that since . . ." Her voice sounded raspy. She remembered the day that her parents had signed the organ-donor papers for Amy and she'd stood in the shower wearing all her clothes and cried. ". . . well, for a long time." She was embarrassed, because no one had ever seen her lose it that way.

"Are you still mad at me?" David asked.

"No, you had no way of knowing."

David took a deep breath. "I wouldn't have hurt you for the world, Erin. My dad always tells me that I talk too much."

"It doesn't matter." Outside, people drove cars out of the lot, but Erin felt isolated and alone with David, as if they were the only two people in the world. She rolled down her window, and the night air cooled her hot, tearstained cheeks.

"Tell me about your sister," David said. "What was her name?"

"Amy," Erin told him. It seemed strange that he didn't know. For years everybody she'd known had known Amy too. "She was sixteen, a sophomore at Briarwood."

"You must miss her a lot."

Fresh tears came up, but Erin blinked them away. "Yes." David reached out and ran his thumb across her cheek. "I must look awful," she said, sorting through the mess in her lap for her hairbrush.

"Not to me." Without warning her heart began to thud. She glanced at him shyly. He took her hand. "I think you're beautiful."

She shrugged self-consciously. "You didn't get to eat your pizza."

"I don't like mushrooms either."

All at once David seemed different to her, kind and caring, not crazy and foolish. She was ashamed that she'd judged him before getting to know him. "I'd better get this stuff put away. I really do have to get home."

"I'll help." He held the purse while she scooped her belongings into it. "What time do you have to be at work tomorrow?" he asked.

"Not until three o'clock," she said, embarrassed that inside the pizza parlor she'd made it sound much earlier than that.

"Good." David reached over into the backseat and hunted for her keys. "I'll pick you up at ten."

"What? But—but—"

"No 'buts.'" He handed her the keys and opened the car door.

"But where are we going?"

"I have a show to do, and I want you with me. And I want to introduce you to the second-most-important woman in my life."

"Who . . . ?"

David got out. "Tomorrow," he said, shutting the door and jogging back to the restaurant.

"But . . ." Erin said to the empty car. Slowly, thoughtfully, she started the engine and pulled out into the light flow of traffic. "The *second*-most-important woman?" she asked aloud. Did that make her the first? Erin smiled despite her confusion over David.

That night she lay in her bed and remembered how gentle he'd been with her, how he'd let her cry herself out, holding her and hugging her. She noted something else too. For the first time in months, she felt peaceful, as if the tears had washed away the hard knots that lived inside her stomach and along her spine. And she also realized that she'd told him about Amy and didn't have a headache.

"Couldn't you have put your makeup on when you got there?" Erin asked, staring at David as he drove, dressed in his full clown gear.

"It's a kid's birthday party," he said. "Can't spoil the illusion by going off to the bathroom and changing when I get there, can I?" He looked over at her and grinned. Even under the white greasepaint and big orange mouth, she recognized his electric smile. He looked exactly as he had a year ago—oversize baggy suit, yellow curly wig, and bowler hat perched on his head. A flower she knew squirted water was stuck in his lapel.

"People are staring," Erin said as a car passed them and the driver did a double take.

David waved. "That's the trouble with the world. It's too conventional."

David might be indifferent to what others thought, but Erin wasn't. It was one of the things that made her and Amy so different. Amy never cared what others thought, while to Erin it had always mattered. Maybe that's why Amy, and now David, made friends so easily; and why it had been so out of character for Erin to dress in Amy's clown makeup the year before and fulfill Amy's commitment at the Children's Home. "People hardly expect to see a clown driving down the freeway," Erin told him.

"Careful, sweet-face, or I'll douse you with water. But then, I don't want to spoil my routine for you."

Erin almost told him that she knew his routine but decided that it would take too much explaining. "So who's this all-important woman I'm supposed to meet?"

"She's a regular doll," he said mysteriously. "You'll love her."

Erin wasn't too sure. David parked his car in front of a two-story brick house on a tree-lined side street off Bayshore Drive. She could smell the salt water in the breeze. He took Erin's hand and led her up the sloped driveway. The door of the side entrance flew open, and a little girl with blue eyes and dark blond hair barreled out and grabbed David around the waist.

"Whoa," he said, laughing and hugging her. She made several gestures with her hands, and

David responded with rapid gestures as well as words. "I know I'm late, but I told you I had to pick up a friend."

The girl turned toward Erin who watched, fascinated as the child's fingers flew in more gestures and signs. "This is Erin," David said, shaping her name with his fingers. "We're in the play at school together."

The girl measured Erin with wide, unblinking eyes. Caught off guard, Erin didn't know how to respond. "This is my sister, Jody," David said.

Erin was at a momentary loss. Why hadn't David told her that his sister was deaf? "I—um—hello, Jody."

"Watch," David told her. "This is the sign for 'Hello.'"

Erin repeated it awkwardly, and Jody giggled, then turned back to David and signed something. David laughed. "She thinks you're pretty," he told Erin. "And she wants to know how I got such a pretty girl to date *me*."

Just then a woman flung open the screen and ushered the three of them inside a big, sunlit kitchen. "David, the kids are waiting for you in the den."

"Well, I can't keep my public waiting, can I?"

Twenty children sat on the floor in a semicircle, and they giggled and pointed when David entered. Erin hung toward the back of the room, where she watched as David performed. He did magic tricks, made animal shapes out of balloons, and managed a few pratfalls in between. Watching him, Erin felt her throat grow thick. She kept remembering how well they'd worked together at the Children's Home, and she couldn't understand why she hadn't told him about it before now. She felt that she was deceiving him in some way.

"Isn't he wonderful?" the mother of the birthday child whispered in Erin's ear.

"Yes," Erin said.

"We've known his family for years. My daughter, Tracy, and David's sister, Jody, started at the same school for the hearing impaired when they were both two."

"That young?" For the first time Erin perceived that in spite of all the laughter, the room was strangely quiet to be filled with twenty children. "Are all these kids deaf?"

"That term's inaccurate," Tracy's mother said. "Some are more handicapped than others. Tracy and Jody both are considered 'profoundly deaf'— they can't hear anything. Others have some hearing with the use of special hearing aids. They all attend a special school where they're taught a combination of signing and lipreading. They're all taught to talk too, but since speaking depends so much on hearing, they don't sound like regular kids to the rest of us."

"In other words, you can't imitate what you can't hear?" Erin asked.

"That's right. Eventually we want to mainstream Tracy and Jody."

Erin knew that mainstreaming meant putting

kids with handicaps into regular classrooms. "Was Jody born deaf?" she asked.

"No. When she was a year old, she caught meningitis, and it left her without her hearing."

"She's a pretty girl."

"Yes, and she absolutely adores her big brother. He's a nice guy and very talented."

Erin watched as David brought Tracy from the audience and made quarters appear from behind her ears. Then he presented her with a bouquet of flowers that seemingly materialized from under his coat.

When it was time to serve the cake, Erin helped Tracy's mom pass it among the children, then she and David slipped out the back door. In the car David tugged off his hat and wig and red false nose and tossed them to the backseat.

"I'm impressed," Erin said. "You had them eating out of your hand."

He grinned, and his orange-painted mouth stretched cheek to check. "All women under the age of ten fall at my feet."

"It must be your humility that attracts them."

David snickered. "That's one of the reasons I keep you around, Erin. You never let me forget I'm a mere mortal."

"*Someone* has to remind you."

They rode in contented silence for awhile. "How about a Coke?" David asked.

"Sounds good. You look like you could use one too. Your face is running."

David laughed and swiped at the greasepaint with a tissue. It smeared, making his dark-penciled eyebrows smudge over his forehead. He turned into the driveway of a McDonald's and parked.

"You're not going to drive through?" Erin asked incredulously.

David got out of the car, came around, opened her door, and offered her his hand. "Why?"

"Well because—I mean—your makeup and all. People will stare."

"Stop caring what people think, Erin. Life's too short to live it by other people's rules. Come on, let's go in." Still she hesitated. He held out his hand and added, "If you do, I'll be your best friend."

Erin felt as if a giant hand had clutched her heart. "Why did you say that?" she asked, her voice trembling. "Why did you say that to me?"

Chapter Eight

"What did I say?" David asked.

For a moment Erin couldn't get it out. "'I'll be your best friend,'" she finally said.

They were standing in the middle of McDonald's, in everyone's way. "Let's sit down, all right?" David led her to a booth in the back.

Erin slid across the vinyl, another knot forming in her stomach.

"Now what's wrong with being best friends?" David asked.

"It—it was just something my sister used to say all the time."

David shook his head and sighed. "I have no way of knowing these things, Erin, and I hate having to be on my guard around you all the time. I probably picked it up from the kids—they say that all the time."

His attitude irked her. She at least wanted him to be sorry. "Can I have that Coke now?"

While David ordered, Erin stared pensively out of the window, wondering about her feelings toward him. Sometimes he got on her nerves, yet other times he seemed so sensitive and kind.

When he returned, she saw that he'd been to the men's room and removed the greasepaint. *Chalk one up to sensitivity*, she told herself. "So how did you ever get into clowning?" Erin asked, attempting to lift the cloud that had fallen between them.

David sat across from her. "My mom tells me I was born a comedian. Anyway, after Jody was diagnosed as deaf, I noticed that her eyes always followed me whenever we were in a room together. I used to make gestures and faces to make her smile."

"She does have a pretty smile." Pretty smiles seemed to run in his family, though Erin didn't want to tell him that.

"Thanks. When Jody started at the special school, our family learned how to sign so that we could communicate with her. When she was little, she'd throw terrible tantrums if we didn't understand her. We couldn't let her get away with it, but I understood how frustrating it was for her when no one could figure out what she was trying to say."

Erin knew what he meant. She'd been the only one to understand Amy's baby babble when they'd been small. "So you became her interpreter?" Erin asked.

"That's right. My parents would ask, 'David, what's she saying?' Anyway, I began to pantomime and entertain her. And one thing led to another until I had such a routine down, that I began performing at birthday parties and hospitals to make extra money."

"Is that why you've decided to become an actor?"

"Partly. You know, deep down clowns are really serious people. They see the good and bad in life and help people laugh about both."

"But sometimes there's nothing funny about life."

David shrugged. "Not to me. I think that hurting gives us a way to measure being happy. How can you know one without knowing the other? It's the difference between doing a hard dance move and an easy one. Which would you rather do?"

"The hard one's more challenging, so I feel better if I do it well."

"That's the way I feel about life. Why walk around desensitized? Why go for the easy moves when the hard ones make you feel better? I watch Jody deal with other peoples' ignorance every day. People who don't understand her handicap and who laugh at her whenever she tries to talk because she sounds weird to them. Sometimes it gets her down, but most of the time she keeps right on going." David balled the wrapper from his straw and bounced it on the tabletop. "I decided that making people laugh is sort of my mission in life. So I do my clown bit whenever I can. I'm doing the Special Olympics in June."

"Isn't that when all the handicapped kids compete in sports events out at USF?"

"Yes. Jody and some of her friends are competing. The organizers are always looking for people to help with the events." David snapped his fingers and added, "Say, maybe you'd like to help out! You know, if you have the time."

An image of Amy surrounded by machines and hoses, and with tubes sticking out of her mouth and arms, caused Erin to recoil. She couldn't face spending the day around kids who looked imperfect. Yet there was no way she could tell that to David. "I—I don't know. June's a long way off. We still have the play to get through."

"Speaking of the play, are you really going to make me meet you at the theater Monday morning at seven to practice our dance moves?"

"Absolutely."

David groaned and dropped his forehead dramatically against the table. "I can barely walk that time of the day, much less dance. Are you always such a slave driver?"

Erin recalled how Amy always groaned about getting up early. "I'm going to college to study dance theory, so I need to spend a lot of time practicing if I'm going to be good. Don't you practice so you can get better?"

"I practice," David said, his blue eyes holding hers. "But I never forget that it's supposed to be fun."

"And you think I do?"

"I think you need to loosen up and not take things so seriously."

"Life *is* serious," she countered. "And it can sometimes be too short."

"That's the point." David took her hand, lacing

his fingers through hers. "If it *is* short, shouldn't you have some good times along the way? Shouldn't you give everything you can to the people you meet?"

Erin pulled away, because a tightness was beginning to crawl up her back into the base of her skull. "I have to be at my mom's store soon. We'd better go."

David studied her so openly that Erin began to squirm. At last he said, "We clowns make people laugh and forget about their problems. The strange part is that whenever we do, we forget about our own problems. So, I'm going to see to it that you lighten up and let yourself go if it takes the rest of the school year."

"You do that," Erin said, standing because of the tightness that was inching slowly into her temples. David didn't understand, and she could never describe to him what it was like to have someone close to you die; to have a family of four suddenly become a family of three, and to feel like a sole survivor—a leftover that parents fight about.

"Are you going to Spring Fling?" Shara lay on Erin's bedroom floor tossing raisins into the air and trying to catch them in her mouth.

"When is it?" Erin asked.

"After spring break because Easter comes so late. You missed it last year, and since we're seniors, this'll be our last opportunity to go."

"I missed it because that was the day my folks

had decided to donate Amy's organs to medical science, and I couldn't hack the idea."

A hundred unspoken things passed between the two girls, but Erin couldn't bring herself to discuss any of them. Her fight with Travis after he'd taken Cindy Pitzer to the big formal dance stood out most vividly in Erin's mind.

Shara cleared her throat. "Well I think you should come this year."

"Who are you going with?"

"I've already asked Seth. Why don't you ask David so we can double?"

"David!"

Shara sat up. "Why not? You two are getting along better. I can tell by the way you act toward him at play practices."

"'Getting along better' doesn't mean I want to date the guy."

"For crying out loud, you're not gonna *marry* him. It's just a dance, and we could have a lot of fun double-dating. Don't be a party pooper."

Erin stretched, grabbed her toes, and bent to touch her forehead to her knees. It was true that ever since last Saturday she had been friendlier to David—in spite of the fact that he'd stuffed a toy snake into her duffel bag, and when she'd unzipped it, the snake had sprung out and almost given her heart failure. Yet he'd also stuck a rosebud under the windshield wiper on her car. There was no predicting what David was going to do.

"I don't know, Shara. I don't want to encourage

him. It's just another month until the play, and then I won't see him anymore."

"It doesn't have to be that way. You could date him until you go off to college."

If my parents let me go off to college, Erin thought. She and her mother had had another fight about it the other day when Erin couldn't work because of a headache. "I don't want to start anything with David."

"One dance," Shara pleaded. "We can go shopping for new dresses, then on the night of the dance make them take us to dinner—we can even stay out all night. Come on, it's our last big blowout before graduation."

Erin felt herself wavering. While David wasn't her ideal choice for a lasting memory of high school prom night, it might be the last time she got to do something like that with Shara. They *were* best friends, and they had gone to the Fling as sophomores and had had a blast. Yet so much had happened to her since that carefree sophomore year. Erin wondered if she'd ever feel that way again. "I'll think about it," she told Shara.

"Good." Her friend's face broke into a smile. "Then all we have to get through is the play and finals. After that"—Shara snapped her fingers—"we're off to college and the real world."

Erin agreed with a smile she didn't feel. Didn't Shara understand that Erin already had been thrust into the "real world" the day Amy died and the doctors harvested her organs for transplantation? "Do you want to her my newest tape?" Erin asked, changing the subject.

"I would, but I gotta go. I told Mom I'd clean my room today. She threatened to ground me if I don't."

Erin surveyed her bedroom. Everything was in order. She wondered why she was so fastidiously neat when most of her friends weren't. "I've been gone so much, I haven't been around to mess it up," she said, feeling as if she should defend her tidiness.

"You're the perfect daughter, Erin," Shara said. "My mother would *kill* to have me as organized as you. But I never will be. I'm messy, and I don't care."

After Shara had gone, Erin traced a path around her room, absently studying her belongings. The dance posters, the paraphernalia that she'd collected through the years, had once meant so much to her. Now she wasn't so sure. When had it changed? When had it stopped being important and started being just a bunch of old stuff?

The phone on her bureau rang, startling her. She grabbed the receiver.

"Erin?" The girl's voice on the other end sounded quiet and breathy.

"Who's this?"

"It's me, Beth Clark. Oh, Erin, could you meet me at the mall? If I don't get out of my house, I'm gonna go nuts."

Chapter Nine

Erin met Beth at the food court in the mall, where they bought Cokes and sat in cold metal chairs under pink-striped umbrellas. Beth looked thinner to Erin, and there were dark circles under her eyes. "Thanks for coming," Beth said.

"No problem. What's up? You sounded desperate."

"I *am* desperate. I don't think I can stand it for one more day in my house."

Shocked, Erin asked, "What's wrong?"

"It looks like my mom's kidney is failing."

"The transplant?"

"Yes," Beth said miserably.

"What happens if it does?"

"They have to find another donor."

"Gee, Beth, I'm really sorry."

Beth groped in her purse for a tissue. "It's horrible living in my house. We're all so scared, and I'm trying to keep it all together. I cut school three days last week just to get housework done and take care of Mom."

"What about your dad?"

A tear trickled from the corner of Beth's eye. "Dad left."

Erin stared, openmouthed. "Left?"

"He said he couldn't take the pressure any-more, and he packed up his things and took off about a month ago."

"Maybe he'll be back—"

"I don't think so. He hasn't even called to check on us. Not once in four weeks. My parents haven't gotten along for a while, you know. I guess this was just too much for Dad to handle."

Beth's situation made Erin feel as if lead weights had been hung on her heart. "Isn't there someone you could tell?"

"What am I supposed to tell? That I can't hack it? Do you know what Social Services does when it thinks kids are being neglected?"

"Social Services?"

"You know. The department for child welfare."

Erin nodded, pretending she understood. She only knew about welfare and such things through newspaper articles and TV news stories. Suddenly she wished she'd paid more attention to them. "What do they do?"

"They can come in and take us away from Mom and put us in foster homes, that's what. That would kill my mom. And it would be all my fault because I couldn't keep things together."

"But that's not fair. It's not your fault."

Beth slumped in her chair. "I'm thinking of dropping out of school."

"But you're only got a few months left till you graduate!"

"I'm barely scraping by now. My grades stink,

and they're not going to get any better until my mom's well. At least if I drop out and stay home, I'll be there for my brother and sisters."

"But there must be some other way. What does your mom say?"

"Oh, Erin, she's much too sick to even realize what's going on. She goes for dialysis every other day again—I can't dump this on her!"

"You gotta tell someone, Beth."

"I'm telling you."

"But I can't do anything to help."

"That's not true. Just telling you about it has made me feel better. I swear, I thought I was going to explode if I didn't get it out."

Erin wasn't sure she wanted Beth's burden. Beth might feel better now, but Erin was suddenly down in the pits. "I—I still think you should talk to somebody who can help you figure out what to do." For a moment Erin considered telling Beth about her own therapy, but she lacked the courage.

"I'll be okay," Beth said. She grasped Erin's arm. "You won't blab about this will you? You won't tell anyone and get me in trouble?"

"I don't have anybody to tell." She surprised herself with her confession. There was a time that she might have taken it to her parents, but now with so much tension in her own house, she couldn't talk to them anymore. She felt helpless. "How much time have you got before you have to be home?" she asked.

"An hour, tops."

Erin hauled Beth to her feet. "Then let's make the most of it. We'll do some shopping."

"Oh, I can't." Beth avoided Erin's eyes, making Erin realize that she probably didn't have any money for shopping.

"Um—I'm going to our spring dance—it's sort of like a prom—and I haven't had a chance to go shopping for a dress yet. Maybe you could help me pick something out."

Beth gave her a grateful look. "I really don't want to go home yet. Mom's resting, and I don't have to start supper for an hour. It would be fun to look at prom dresses—even though I won't be going to one."

In the department store Erin tried on several styles of dresses, and before long even she was caught up in the fun, despite her little white lie. She certainly hadn't decided to go to Spring Fling. Still, Beth seemed lost in the fantasy, and Erin was glad to help her forget her problems for even a little while.

Erin honestly hadn't meant to buy anything, but when she tried on a strapless dress in ice blue, Beth exclaimed, "That's gorgeous!"

The dress set off her eyes and ivory complexion like nothing else she'd owned. Before she knew it, Erin had bought it. "The guy you're going with will drool when he sees you in it," Beth said as they left the store.

The guy she was going with was the Invisible Man, Erin thought. "I really appreciate your helping me find something."

"It was fun for me too. I wish I . . ." her sentence trailed. "I'm glad I called you, Erin. Thanks for listening to me."

"I want you to keep calling me. Anytime. Please."

Beth agreed. "Just remember your promise to keep it a secret."

"I won't say a word. Don't forget, my play's next month. Please try to come."

Beth left, and Erin stood in the mall while people surged around her. Someone bumped her, and she spun, feeling like a leaf in a current of water with no control.

"What do you mean you bought a prom dress?" Shara stood in the center of the theater's dressing room with her hands on her hips. "I thought we were going shopping together."

Erin hadn't meant to upset Shara. She simply mentioned the dress in the course of conversation, hoping to brighten the mood after the rotten rehearsal they'd just had.

"And besides, when did you decide to go to the dance? When we talked the other day, you acted like it was the drudgery of the year."

"Shara, don't make such a big deal about it. Beth called me—you remember her—anyway, she was down in the dumps, so we met at the mall and started shopping just for fun."

"But you *know* how much I wanted to shop for dresses with you. Geez, Erin, that was a lousy thing to do."

"I bought a dress, Shara. It's not a federal offense, you know."

"Well excuse me for feeling like a reject!" Shara picked up her things and breezed out of the room.

"Terrific," Erin muttered, and chased after her. In the narrow hall she collided with David, who had already collided with Shara.

"What's the rush?" he asked.

"I have to go shopping for a dress," Shara said.

"Maybe I have one you could borrow," David said, grinning.

"I doubt it," Shara said. "We're not even the same size."

"I have a very nice wardrobe," David countered, tossing his arms around both their shoulders and tucking each under an arm. "You don't know what you're missing."

"I'll pass," Shara said.

"I already have a dress," Erin added, holding Shara's eyes with her own. "But I'm glad I ran into you because I do want to ask you something."

He bowed from the waist. "From your lips to heaven's ears."

"Briarwood's having a big dance, and Shara's asked Seth, and we thought it would be fun to double, so I'd like to know if you want to come with me." Her palms had gone clammy, and she could hardly believe what she was saying.

David blinked and then broke out into his dazzling smile. "Aw right!" Impulsively he caught her in a bear hug, lifting her off the ground.

"Save it for the dance numbers," Erin said, exasperated and flustered. Why did he have to act like such a kid?

Shara looked confused. "I'll call you later, Erin. I'm going to go tell Seth."

Alone with David, Erin felt timid. She hadn't meant to ask him; it had just happened. "I'll—um—get all the details to you tomorrow at rehearsal."

"Is this my day or what?"

"It's just a dance."

"But it's with you. A princess going with a frog."

Erin rolled her eyes. "Knock it off."

"You got a new dress?"

"Yes."

"What color?"

"Light blue."

David looked thoughtful. "I've got just the frock to match it," he said, and sauntered off.

A moment later his comment hit her. David Devlin was just crazy enough to show up in a dress, Erin thought. "David, wait! You're not going to embarrass me, are you?"

David turned innocent blue eyes on her. "You mean like wearing my clown makeup to the dance? Or is it something else you had in mind?"

"Let's just leave it for now," she told him. Wearing clown makeup to Spring Fling was something that Amy might have done. A terrible sense of melancholy stole over her as Beth's problems, the fight with Shara, and the memory of Amy bombarded her.

David caught his hand behind her neck and pulled her close. The teasing had gone out of his eyes. "I really want to go to the dance with you, Erin. Even clowns have their serious side."

That night her headache was the worst one she'd had in weeks. The medication didn't help, and it was nearly dawn before she fell into an exhausted sleep. Erin was in a stupor when her alarm sounded, so she told her mother to let her sleep in till noon, then she'd go to her afternoon classes.

The sunlight was streaming in her bedroom window when Mrs. Bennett barged in and shook Erin's shoulder. "Wake up, Erin. You have some explaining to do."

Erin opened her eyes and tried to focus. All she saw was her mother's grieved, tearful expression. "What's wrong?" Erin sat up slowly.

"Dr. Richardson just called. She said you've missed your last two appointments. What's going on? Why have you been lying to me?"

Chapter Ten

Swamped with guilt, Erin pulled the covers tighter as if to hide from her mother's wounded expression. "I didn't lie."

"You *said* you were going to therapy, then didn't go. What do you call it?"

"I got tied up with play practice and schoolwork and all. I just missed a couple of times."

"But you *must* understand the importance of this therapy in solving the mystery of your headaches," Mrs. Bennett admonished, twisting a wadded tissue as she spoke. "I want you to be well again, Erin. I couldn't stand it if something happened to you too."

By now Erin was starting to get angry—she hated the guilt trips her mother kept sending her on. She tossed off the covers and jumped to her feet, but the medication made her woozy, and she swayed.

Her mother reached out to steady her. "Just look at you—you're so groggy you can hardly stand up. Don't you realize that therapy is your only hope for getting rid of your headaches forever?"

"And don't you realize that sitting in that office

all by myself and having somebody dig around inside my head stinks?"

"Of course it's tough, honey. But you have so much ahead of you—college, career, family—everything. Why, someday you'll have kids of your own, and then you'll understand how I feel."

Kids of her own. She was the last of the Bennett line, because her father had no brothers or sisters. "Being married and having kids doesn't sound like such a hot idea to me."

"Why do you say that?"

Erin wanted to shout, "*Because yelling and fighting and leaving isn't fair.*" Instead she walked past her mother and started getting clothes together for school. "I need to get dressed."

Her mother took her arm. "Erin, please promise me you'll go back to Dr. Richardson this Thursday."

Her face looked pinched, and her tone sounded so pleading that Erin felt fresh waves of guilt. "Okay, I'll go."

"I'm counting on you to keep your promise." Mrs. Bennett sounded relieved.

"I'm your 'responsible' daughter. . . . Isn't that what you always used to tell me?"

"You still are."

Her mother stroked Erin's hair, and yet it was as if a great gulf separated them, and Erin didn't know how to get across. "Then I can't let you down, can I?"

"It's for your own sake," her mother called as Erin hurried toward the bathroom.

Erin shut the door and leaned against the wall,

fighting tears and feeling as if the weight of the world were on her shoulders. She turned on the faucets, and after the bathroom had filled with steam, she breathed deeply to relax and try to ward off a recurrence of her headache. The breathing exercises worked, and soon she felt better. Before climbing into the shower, she took her finger and wrote in the steam on the mirror: "Amy doesn't live here anymore." Then she smeared the words away and quickly showered and dressed.

Dr. Richardson treated her as if she'd never missed an appointment. Erin was relieved, because she couldn't have stood another lecture. The counselor's office seemed comfortable and homey, with framed passages of needlepoint on several of the walls. Curious, Erin thought, that she'd never noticed them before. She pointed at one. "Where'd you get these?"

"I do them. They relax me." It had never occurred to Erin that the therapist might have a life outside of her office. "What do you do to relax?" Dr. Richardson asked.

"I dance. The physical exercise makes me feel good."

"I tried aerobics once," Dr. Richardson said, "but there was nothing relaxing about grunting and sweating." She wrinkled her nose to make her point.

Erin giggled, glad that they weren't probing into her mind right away. She studied the intricate scrollwork of one particular needlepoint and read aloud, "'Is there no Balm in Gilead; is there no physician there?' What's that mean?"

"Gilead was a place in the Middle East where a legendary balm with miraculous healing powers was supposed to have come from. You simply smoothed it on, and all your diseases disappeared. Caravans used to bring it out of Gilead to sell to the rest of the known world."

"Too bad you can't find some of it and rub it into my head."

Dr. Richardson tapped her desk with a pencil. "For me the balm of Gilead is what I try to apply to people's hearts and souls, because healing begins from the inside out."

"Do you think I'll ever get well?"

"The fact that you're here, trying, encourages me."

"But just talking doesn't seem to be doing much."

"Aren't there longer and longer gaps between your headaches?"

"Yes, but I still can't figure out what's triggering them. I've been fine for a while, then the other day I was just talking to David, and bang—one hit me hard."

"How are you and David getting along?"

"Better." Erin felt her cheeks color. "I asked him to our school's formal dance."

"I'd say you were doing better. What changed your mind about him?"

Erin laced her fingers together in her lap. "We

talked. I went with him to see his clown routine, and I met his kid sister. She's deaf."

"But there's still something about him that sort of gets under your skin, huh?"

Dr. Richardson's perception amazed Erin. "It's like he *likes* being different, as if he goes out of his way to be outrageous."

"And that seems to bother you."

Erin stared at the carpet for a moment, trying to put her thoughts into words. "In the beginning he actually brought on some of my headaches, but now, in some weird way, he helps keep them away. I can't figure out why."

Dr. Richardson didn't say anything right away. When she did speak, her question seemed off the topic. "Erin, tell me what your sister Amy was like."

Startled, Erin looked up. "Cute. Everybody liked her, but she had some pretty annoying habits. She was *never* on time, and she could talk me into doing anything for her—which used to make me really mad. But I couldn't help myself. She'd always rope me into doing whatever she wanted. She was never serious about anything, except wanting to be a great actress. Like the world was waiting for Amy to make an appearance. She didn't take life very seriously. But then David says I take life *too* serious—" She stopped talking as insight swept over her.

"You look surprised. Tell me what you're thinking."

"It's Amy and David. They're a lot alike, you know? I—I never realized that until now."

"How does that make you feel?"

Erin wasn't sure. "Strange, that's all. Gee, I don't see how the world could handle *two* Amys."

"But David's David."

"Yes, that's true. They're different, but they're alike too. He does silly, goofy things like Amy would. We had a slime fight after rehearsal one day. When Amy was in the eighth grade, she led a Jell-O war in the school cafeteria."

"Does it make you feel sad to remember?"

"No," Erin said slowly. "But it makes me want to see her and talk to her again."

"If you could see and talk to her, what would you share?"

Erin shook her head. "I don't know. And I don't feel like talking about it right now."

"There are several kids your age in my support group who've lost a sister or brother."

Lost. The therapist made it sound as if the person could be found. As if death wasn't final and irrevocable. Erin thought of Beth, who might be "losing" her mother.

"Will you think about coming? We'd love to have you."

"Maybe. Look, I've got to get back to school for evening play practice. My dad's got a meeting at school tonight too, and his car's in the shop, so I have to give him a ride home." Erin knew she was making an excuse to bow out of the session early but didn't care. She wanted to leave.

Dr. Richardson walked her to the office door, where Erin turned and gestured toward the framed needlepoint about Gilead. "If any caravans pass through selling that stuff, buy some for me."

Dr. Richardson asked, "Do you know what 'debridement' is, Erin?" She shook her head. "When a person's been badly burned, the dead skin has to be removed, or debrided. The skin is literally scrubbed off the wounds."

Erin grimaced. "That must hurt."

"It's very painful, but unless it's done, the burn victim can't begin to heal."

"So what's that got to do with me?"

"There's something inside you—something about your sister's death—that's trying to get out. Your headaches are an expression of that 'something.' These sessions with me, and meeting with the support group, is a kind of debridement for your psyche. No matter how much it hurts, it has to be done so that you can be all right again."

"So there is no magic balm?" Erin asked wistfully.

"Only in the figurative sense. And you can't buy it either, you have to seek it on your own."

Erin sighed and left, unsure if she had the strength for the hunt.

The play rehearsal went so smoothly that Ms. Thornton and Mr. Ault let everybody go home early. Not wanting to linger afterward, Erin quickly gathered her things and hurried to her father's classroom. She approached the room cautiously, unable to forget the day she'd stopped by the school and discovered him weeping. She'd never told him, but the memory of his tears haunted her still.

Erin stopped at the closed door, listened, then knocked.

"Come in," Mr. Bennett said. Erin entered to see him putting papers into his briefcase. "Hi," he said, and smiled. "I thought I'd be the one waiting on you."

"We got out early. Are you finished?"

"I sent the Lowerys home with their promise to make Pam work harder in my class. She's bright enough, but she just doesn't apply herself. She's not nearly the student your teachers tell me you are, Erin."

She shrugged. "That's me . . . little Miss Einstein."

"Don't make light of it. I know it must be tough putting in time for that play and still keeping up with your schoolwork."

They walked to Erin's car and got in. The night had turned cool, and the smell of rain was in the air. She turned on the engine. In the glow of the mercury lamppost, the outside world looked colorless.

Her father asked, "Say, I've got an idea. How'd you like your old man to treat you to a hot fudge sundae?"

Surprised, Erin asked, "But we've got school tomorrow, and it's already after ten." Big drops of rain splattered against the windshield. She turned on the wipers.

"Oh, come on. It'll be like old times. Just you

and me and Amy and—" His voice stopped, and Erin's heart squeezed. Rain pummeled the car. The headlights cut a sweeping arc through the darkness, and Amy's ghost wedged between them in the seat.

Chapter Eleven

Erin was the first to recover. "I think a hot fudge sundae sounds yummy," she said with an enthusiasm she didn't feel.

"Me too," Mr. Bennett said quietly.

Erin drove cautiously, because the rain made the road slick. At the minimall she parked, and they ran for cover into the old-fashioned ice cream parlor, where waiters were dressed in white shirts and red-striped vests.

Once in a booth, Erin asked, "Are you gonna call Mom?"

"She said she'd be going to bed early, so I don't think she'll miss us." Mr. Bennett didn't meet Erin's eyes as he spoke.

They ordered, and once the waiter had gone, Mr. Bennett asked, "Do you want to talk about what happened in the car?"

"What happened?"

"When I said Amy's name. I didn't mean to, but for a moment I forgot she wasn't with us."

Erin felt panic, because she was certain she saw a mist cover his eyes. "That's all right," she said quickly. "Dr. Richardson says it's good to talk about her."

"How's it going with the counselor?"

"She says I'm making progress."

"She wanted us to come in as a family at first."

The news surprised Erin. "So why didn't we?"

"Your mother felt it wasn't necessary. You were the one with the headaches."

Erin wasn't surprised by this information, but it still annoyed her. Why did her parents act as if *she* was the only one with a problem? Couldn't they see how they were growing apart? "I'm really trying hard to get well, Dad. Honest."

"I know, and I'm not sure it's something you should be going through by yourself."

Their ice cream arrived, and Erin ate a spoonful of whipped cream, but it was too sweet, and the taste clung to her mouth. "Dr. Richardson thinks that I'm not over Amy's death."

"Who is?" he asked heavily.

"It's been over a year," Erin said.

"Is there a time limit on these things?"

"I guess not. I miss Amy too." For a moment Erin's voice sounded thick. She wanted to tell him, "*But Daddy, I'm still here.*" Instead, she asked, "I guess no one can ever take Amy's place, huh?"

Mr. Bennett shoved his sundae aside. "You and Amy were always so different from one another. Maybe it was because you were the firstborn, and your mother and I wanted so many things for you. Parents go a little overboard for the firstborn, you know."

"You didn't expect things of Amy?"

"We did, but it was different."

Erin wanted to say, "*You bet it was different. You always let Amy do anything she wanted.*" Instead, she said, "Amy used to wonder why she was short and dark-haired and I was tall and blond."

"You take after my great-grandmother, Emily Eckloe."

"I do?"

"Yes. Amy resembled your mother's side of the family—small and dark. But Emily was from Norway, and a real beauty. I think she studied classical ballet but gave up her career to marry great-granddad."

So *she* was the oddball of the family, not Amy. For some reason the information pleased her. "That sounds romantic, but I can't imagine giving up my dancing."

"Not even for love?"

Erin blushed. "Especially for love."

"I guess that love doesn't have much to recommend to you."

She knew he was alluding to his own crumbling relationship. "It's okay for other people, but I've got lots of other things I want to do first. Books and movies make it seem sort of corny, like it's nothing but butterflies in your stomach."

"That's where it usually starts, and there's no substitute for it in the world. Don't tell me you've never gone through the butterfly stage."

She thought of how simply seeing Travis used to make her feel gooey inside. "I guess I have, but I knew it wasn't the real thing."

"That's supposed to be my line," Mr. Bennett joked. "How did you come to that conclusion?"

"Probably because I was always so busy with my dancing. It's always seemed more important than guys and dating."

"I understand that. Love starts out with such enthusiasm, but somehow it gets lost between mortgage payments and kids in the right schools and jobs that pay enough money. . . ." He rubbed his eyes. "I sound cynical, don't I?"

"Just tired." He seemed defeated. "Would you rather have a job someplace besides Briarwood?"

There was a long pause between her question and his answer. "Do you know what I really wanted to be when I was in college?" Erin shrugged. "A novelist," he told her.

"A writer?"

"Not just *any* writer. I wanted to live in the East Village in New York, or maybe even Paris, and write 'meaningful' books about life and the universe."

"Why didn't you?"

Mr. Bennett gave her a poignant smile. "It wasn't very practical. Besides, I met your mother, we married, and then you came along, so starving in the Village became less appealing. I guess that's why I encouraged you and Amy when you took to dancing and acting."

Thinking back, Erin realized that it had always been her father who had favored her dance lessons and encouraged Amy's acting skills. Why hadn't she seen that before? "Remember how you used to read to us when we were little?" she asked.

"And Amy would ask a million questions about why Humpty Dumpty fell off the wall—" he said.

"And why couldn't they put him back together again."

"You used to get so exasperated, you'd clamp your hand over her mouth."

"I read that old book to her when she was in the hospital," Erin confessed, sheepishly. "I knew she couldn't hear me, because they said she was brain dead, but I read it anyway."

Her father studied her, then said, "Oh yeah? So did I."

"You did?" Goose bumps broke out on her arms. "The nurses must have thought we were crazy."

"She was my little princess."

Erin felt a surge of envy. Hadn't she always felt that Amy was 'Daddy's little girl,' and that she was just the 'responsible one'?

"Are you sorry?" she asked. "Do you wish you could do it all again and go off and write novels instead of being a teacher?"

"No. You can't trade what is for what might have been. Besides, if I had, I would never have had you or Amy, would I?"

"Sure you would have, but we would have been born in Paris."

He took her hand. "No. You would not have been born at all."

She tried to imagine nonexistence but

couldn't. "I'll go to Paris for you," she said. "I'll dance and be the hit of Europe."

"Not for me, Erin. For *you*." *And for Amy*, she thought, because her sister would never be able to realize her dreams either.

Her father reached over and clasped her hand. "And don't be so down on falling in love. Love can be very good."

"Not to worry," she said, faking enthusiasm. "I'll be on the lookout for Mr. Right." Yet she knew deep down that falling in love was the last thing she wanted to do. "Dad," she asked, choosing her words carefully. "Do you ever feel like leaving?"

"Leaving? Where would I go?"

"Off to Paris to write novels?" She said it with a smile, but her heart was hammering.

"Those were silly dreams, long ago. No, I won't go away."

She wanted desperately to believe him, because she didn't think she could stand to lose her father too. "I'll be going away in the fall," she ventured.

"You want to very much, don't you?"

She nodded vigorously. "But you and Mom seem against it. Mom more so than you."

"Letting go is hard, that's all."

"But I *have* to go. I just want . . ." Words failed her. She wanted so much to be a good daughter, but she also wanted to live her own life. "Well, you know," she finished lamely.

He picked up the check. "You want to be out on your own. It's natural. I guess we should discuss it with Dr. Richardson. I'll—uh—talk to your mother about it."

They drove home in silence, with Erin feeling detached. She was glad she'd talked to her father. It had helped for her to see him as an individual. He'd had dreams and plans for his life too, but they got changed as surely as Amy's had. Later that night she lay in her bed and wondered what kind of books he would have written. Through the darkness she heard muffled, but loud, words. Erin couldn't make them out, but she recognized their angry tone. Later she heard a door slam, and she rolled over and stared at the wall, knowing that her father had gone down the hall to sleep in another room.

"Are you *really* going to eat that?" Erin asked David the next afternoon at the mall as the clerk in the ice cream store handed him a cone heaped with three different flavors.

"Every bite," David said, taking a mouthful from the top.

Jody pulled on his arm and signed him a message. Erin watched as David signed a reply. "My sister wants the same thing," he told Erin.

"Make mine vanilla, and only one scoop," Erin insisted.

"Boring," David said, but placed the order anyway.

Erin observed David and Jody covertly, still wondering how she'd let him talk her into coming to the mall when he'd appeared on her doorstep that Saturday afternoon, uninvited. She supposed it was his little-boy charm. And his sister. Erin found the little girl adorable. Her big blue green eyes, curly blond hair, and infectious smile—so like David's—were hard to resist. Erin was also intrigued by the child's deafness. She'd never known a handicapped person, and the way Jody adapted to the regular world fascinated her.

After they'd sat down, Erin said, "Jody doesn't miss much, does she?"

"She's got a very high IQ. Once she figured out signing and broke through the communications barrier, she was off like a shot."

Jody signed something to Erin. "I don't understand," Erin told David.

"You should learn to sign," David said. "Then you can talk to Jody yourself."

"Oh, I could never learn—"

"Sure you can! It's easy. Watch." He made slow, deliberate moves with his hands and fingers.

"That's Jody's name, isn't it?"

"Very good. You remembered. Now here's yours, and here's mine." She watched, then mimicked his movements. "You're a natural," David said.

"But it doesn't seem like you spell out every word when you talk to Jody. I mean, that would take forever."

"That's the beauty of signing. Certain gestures stand for nouns and even complete phrases. For instance . . ." David drew his thumb along his cheek and down his jawbone. "This means 'girl.'" He repeated the movement, adding a circular motion with his open palm in front of his face. "That means pretty girl."

Jody tugged on Erin's arm, made similar gestures, and added the letters of Erin's name. "What do you guess she's just said to you?" David asked.

"I think she just told me that *I* was a pretty girl."

"You got it!" David smiled, and Erin dropped her eyes because it made her quivery inside. "Now try this," David said. He held up his hand and tucked his two middle fingers against his palm so that only his thumb, forefinger and pinky were extended.

"I give up," Erin said.

He repeated the move while saying the words, "I love you."

His aqua-colored eyes were so bright that they seemed to glow. Erin's stomach did a somersault, and she felt a tightness in her chest, as if her breath couldn't find a way out. She jumped to her feet. "I'm going to get a drink of water. I saw a fountain near the entrance of the food court."

"Hurry back," David called. "There's lots to learn."

She didn't want to learn anymore. David made her feel things she hadn't felt in over a year. She didn't want to care about David Devlin. She really didn't.

"Erin!" Someone called her name, and she spun.

A tall boy with black hair and chocolate-colored eyes was coming toward her through the crowd. For a heart-stopping moment Erin stared as Travis Sinclair walked her way.

Chapter Twelve

For Erin time stood still, and she saw Travis, not in the mall, but in the moonlight on the sidewalk that surrounded Tampa Bay. She could almost hear the lapping water and smell the jasmine-scented night air.

Travis approached her tentatively, his thumbs hooked on the belt loops of his jeans. "Hi," he said. "I was just coming in the door, and I thought I recognized you, so I hollered."

Erin felt her mouth settle into a grim line. "I thought you were away at college."

"It's spring break. My roommates and I are down for the week. You know, the beach and all."

She remembered last year at spring break she was supposed to go to the beach with Shara and some friends and flirt with the college guys. But Amy had been hooked to life support. "Have you seen Cindy?" She arched the words, like barbs.

Travis reddened and shifted from foot to foot. "I told you once before, Cindy's nothing to me. I never went out with her again after the dance."

Erin was angry. She wanted to hurt him; she wanted to run away. "Well, I'd like to say it was good to see you again, Travis, but why lie?"

"I was hoping you weren't still mad at me, Erin. I was hoping that you might have figured out how hard it was for me to see Amy that way—"

"Save it!" She might have said more, but David appeared and stepped between her and Travis.

"I'm David Devlin," he said. "Weren't you a senior last year at Berkshire?"

Travis nodded at David. "Yeah. I remember you. How is the old place? Is Mr. Wells still there?"

"Yep. He'll never retire. I think we're gonna cast him in bronze and set him out for the pigeons."

Erin listened while David and Travis traded school memories, and when Travis turned to leave, she refused to say good-bye. "What was that all about?" he asked.

"I don't know what you mean."

"I looked out and saw the two of you standing in the middle of the food court, and it looked like you were arguing. So don't pretend nothing was going on."

"It's not important."

He took her arm and pulled her closer. "I want to know what's between you and Travis Sinclair. Were you seeing him? I know he had plenty of girlfriends."

"Hardly," Erin said. "I hate his guts." David looked surprised. "What's wrong?" she asked. "Is it so hard to believe that every girl doesn't fall at his feet?" She played up the sarcasm because she knew deep down how much she had once cared about him, and she didn't want anyone *ever* to know.

She'd told Amy, but the truth had been buried with her.

"*Talk* to me. Tell me what's wrong."

Erin felt a tightness in her head as if a band had been clamped around it. "I need to go home. Where's Jody?"

David let go of her arm and stared at her hard. "Jody's waiting in the ice cream shop."

She felt sorry for him suddenly. David hadn't done anything wrong, and neither had Jody. They both must think she had flipped, but there was too much to tell, too much she didn't want to tell. "David, I'm not trying to hide anything from you. It's just that I'm getting this little headache, and if it gets out of control . . ."

"You do look sort of pale."

They left the mall, and Erin rested her head against the back of the seat during the drive home. By the time they arrived, she was almost blind from the pain. Her parents weren't there, so David took her to her room while Jody waited in the living room. He pulled back the covers, and she slid beneath the sheets, fully clothed. "I don't want to leave you," he said.

"Go. Please." Erin's voice was barely a whisper. She was afraid she was going to throw up, and she didn't want him to see that.

He tucked the covers around her chin and touched her cheek. "I'm gonna call and check on you later."

"Much later," she told him and groaned. After he'd gone and she was alone, Erin began to cry. The tears trickled down, and inexplicably they washed away some of the pain. "No need to wonder what set this one into motion, Dr. Richardson," Erin said aloud as if the shadows in her room would answer. Seeing Travis had triggered this headache. But knowing the cause didn't mean a cure. She longed to go to Gilead and find some magic balm. Instead, she cried herself to sleep.

"I thought you gave up cigarettes, Mom." Mrs. Bennett's back was to Erin, but she could see the thin trail of blue smoke curling upward from where her mother was sitting in the office she'd converted from Amy's old bedroom. The computer terminal on her desk blinked amber with a spreadsheet.

Mrs. Bennett stabbed out the cigarette and spun toward the doorway. "Don't sneak up on me, Erin. And I only smoke when I'm under a lot of stress. Summer's not even here, and already I've got to start buying for the store's fall line. Where have you been all afternoon anyway?"

"Tonight's Spring Fling, remember? Shara and I went to have our nails done." She held them out for her mother's inspection.

"Well, come closer. I can't see them from here."

Erin hesitated, then walked across the sun-filled room. It still made her uncomfortable, even though it looked nothing like Amy's old room. Bookshelves stood in the place of Amy's dresser, and her mother's desk took up the space where the bed once stood. The walls had been repainted a soft yellow, and the red gingham curtains replaced with decorative wooden blinds. At least the beige-colored carpet was the same. "I think the pink will go well with the blue of my dress, don't you?"

Mrs. Bennett inspected Erin's hands. "Yes, but I still wish you'd picked out your dress from stock at the boutique. You would have only paid cost for it."

"Don't you like my dress?"

"It's pretty, but it was so expensive."

Erin held her tongue and sauntered over to the bookshelves. Instead of Amy's collection of teen romances, Erin studied the bindings of books on computer software, accounting, and fashion. "Did you always want to do this, Mom? Be in fashion and own your own business?"

Mrs. Bennett leaned back in her swivel chair. "I was always interested in clothes, but I bought the store with the money your grandmother left me in her will. You and Amy were growing up, and I needed to work so that we could afford to send you both to college. It seemed like a good investment at the time."

Just one to send now, Erin thought. "Florida State shouldn't be too expensive," she said, half holding her breath because the topic usually brought on a negative comment from her mother. "I mean with in-state tuition and all. Then what will you do with the money? Dad told me he once wanted to travel—to Paris."

"Paris." Mrs. Bennett laughed. "Isn't that typical of him? I've always been the more practical of the two of us. I'll save the money, of course. It takes years of hard work to build up a nest egg. I don't imagine you'll want to take care of us in our old age."

Erin hadn't ever thought about it. When she was nine, her grandmother had lived with them until she died. She figured that she and Amy would simply help each other out with family problems after they grew up. "I'd work it out. Taking care of you and Daddy, that is."

"If my business continues to do well, you won't have to."

In other words, Erin thought, she wouldn't be needed. She wondered if her mother would still need her father if her business continued to grow. Erin retreated to the farthest corner of the room. A desktop copier stood on a short file cabinet. Once Amy's vanity table had lined the wall, and a poster of Tom Cruise had hung to one side. "I guess I should start getting ready. I wanted to take a long bath this afternoon."

"Just a minute," Mrs. Bennett said. "Have you written down exactly where you'll be tonight like I asked you to?"

Erin counted to ten under her breath. "Yes. The Columbia restaurant, the dance at the downtown Hilton, and then to Shara's parents' beach house."

"David *is* a good driver, isn't he? I wish I'd met his family. And absolutely no alcohol. Is that clear?"

"Don't you trust me?"

"I *know* what prom night is all about, Erin. Kids can get into a lot of trouble."

"Well, I'm not like other kids. I didn't even want to go at first, but Shara talked me into it."

"I'm just concerned about you. It's not like there'll be another prom night around here, you know."

Erin dropped her gaze to the carpet. A round, colorless spot stared up at her. She remembered the time when Amy had spilled nail polish and tried to take it off with acetone and had removed the color from the carpet instead. "Why are you always griping at me?" she asked her mother.

"That's ridiculous. I just want you to be extra careful tonight. You never used to care if I reminded you of things. Why can't it be like it used to between us?"

"Nothing's the same anymore." Erin's palms began to sweat.

"Are you saying that it's my fault things are different? I've done all I can to keep the lines of communication open between us."

Erin felt that Jody was better at communicating than her mother. "I need to start getting ready," she said, and started toward the doorway.

"You're all I have, Erin," her mother blurted. "I can't help but worry about you. In time I know you'll go away, and then . . ." Her sentence trailed, and Erin saw tears fill her eyes.

She wanted to cry too. "You've still got Daddy," she ventured.

Her mother looked away. "And he wants to go to Paris."

They'd come full circle in their argument, and

for an instant Erin felt as if she were on a merry-go-round. "I'll be in my room getting ready," she said. "David's supposed to be here at six, and then we're picking up Seth and Shara."

"I'll make sure there's film in the camera."

She felt like asking, "What for?" Mrs. Bennett no longer kept up the photo albums. The prints of Amy's sixteenth birthday were still in a drawer. At the doorway Erin paused. "Oh, David's sort of unconventional, so there's no telling what he'll show up wearing."

"Yes, I remember the time he came here in his clown outfit. I hope he uses better sense tonight." Her mother swiveled toward the desk and her computer terminal. "I'll be here if you need any help getting ready."

Erin realized that she couldn't begin to tell her mother what she needed from her. "What's Dad doing this afternoon?"

Mrs. Bennett shrugged. "He's at the library, I think. Safe and sound in his world of books," she added under her breath.

"Maybe he'll write one someday," Erin said.

"Don't bank on it. He talks a lot but does very little."

Erin wanted to say something to defend him but didn't know what. Wistfully she watched her mother begin to type on the computer keyboard and tune Erin out, as if she'd already left the room. Sunlight fell across her mother's shoulders and caught in her hair, which was dark, like Amy's.

Chapter Thirteen

Erin fidgeted with her hair and looked at her alarm-clock radio for the umpteenth time. She'd been ready for half an hour, and she still had time to kill before David was due to arrive. Her parents were waiting in the living room; she heard the TV playing, yet she knew that her father was reading and her mother was compiling lists of new designs and fabrics for the store. She wished they would talk to each other, like they used to do. Erin sighed, not wanting the tension in her home to spoil the excitement she felt about the night ahead of her.

She rechecked her evening bag for all the essentials, including her headache medicine. Her stomach growled, reminding her that she'd skipped dinner in anticipation of the meal at the Columbia. She went to her dresser, to the drawer where she kept an emergency cache of candy bars, and poked through her lingerie and dance leotards. At the back of the drawer, she felt a piece of paper caught between the side and a groove, buried under stuff she hadn't worn in ages. She jiggled the drawer and pulled out the paper. It was the program from the night she'd gone to a rock concert with Travis. He was supposed to take Amy, but when Amy was grounded for not finishing a history paper on time, she begged Erin to go in her place so Travis wouldn't take Cindy Pitzer. Erin opened the program. Inside was scrawled,

> *Surprise, sis! Hope this doesn't ruin your souvenir, but I couldn't pass up the temptation to sign an autograph. Someday this will be a program with MY name on it!*
>
> *Love and stuff,*
>
> *Your tragic Russian princess from the night of her term paper on the Crimean War—aka AMY!*

Erin remembered the night as if it had been last week. It had been a washout, because all Travis talked about was Amy, and Erin finally understood how hopeless her crush was. Later, on that last night with Amy in the hospital, Erin had confessed to her sister: "And I've decided that it wasn't that I really loved *Travis*. I just wanted somebody to love and somebody who loved me the way it is in the books and movies."

Well, she didn't want that anymore. In real life, people who swore to "love, honor, and cherish" each other turned into strangers who argued and shouted and spent more time apart than together. In the real world daddies went away and didn't call home. So much for commitment.

Erin traced her finger over Amy's hastily scribbled words, imagining her sister sneaking the program into the drawer as a special surprise. *Amy should be here tonight,* Erin thought. They should be getting ready together. Amy would be clowning around, and Erin would be trying to keep a straight face and ignore her antics. And then their dates would come, and Amy would do something outrageous, like pin her corsage to her hair and—

"Erin, David's here." Erin jumped at the sound of her mother's voice.

"Coming," she said, stuffing the program into the drawer.

In the hall her mother said, "If you weren't going with Shara, I'd never let you go out with this boy, Erin."

"What's the matter?"

"See for yourself."

Erin hurried into the living room. David stood facing her father but turned and flashed his high-voltage grin. He was wearing a tuxedo jacket, ruffled white shirt, paisley blue cummerbund and bow tie, and faded jeans. Down the side seams he'd sewn a blue satin ribbon. He wore red high-top sneakers and a black top hat, and a vivid red scarf poked from the upper outside pocket of his jacket. His bright red clown nose covered his real one.

Erin felt embarrassed. Couldn't David take something seriously, just once? He hastily tugged off the false nose. "Just kidding about the nose," he told her, and held out the plastic box with her corsage.

Inside lay an exquisite cluster of violets and miniature orchids. "Do they squirt water?" she asked sarcastically.

"I'm a clown, not an idiot," he said.

"Why don't I get a few photos?" Mr. Bennett said, eyeing David skeptically. For a moment Erin was afraid her mother would remind him to please drive carefully, but somehow they made it out the door without her mother hovering too much and her father asking too many dumb questions.

Outside, the moon glowed full and bright. David took her arm and turned her toward him. "You really do look beautiful," he said. "I wish I had a real coach to take you in."

Still peeved, Erin said, "Thanks." She was half-afraid to see the car he was driving, but when she looked, it was a standard station wagon.

David inserted a cassette into the tape deck and began to talk as they drove to pick up Seth and Shara at Shara's house. Erin made appropriate but nominal answers, all the while thinking how long it had been since she'd been out on a date. Not that she hadn't been asked, but she hadn't accepted any since before Amy had died. For the life of her, she couldn't recall why she'd always said no. And now that she was finally going out, it was with a guy like David, who wasn't at all her type.

Shara and Seth climbed into the backseat, chattering and teasing David about his clothes, and when they walked into the restaurant, heads turned. Erin wished again that he hadn't dressed so weird.

After dinner they arrived at the Hilton, where a valet parked the car. The grand ballroom reminded Erin of something out of Hollywood, glitzy and shimmering with crystal chandeliers and pink-linen-draped tables decorated with floral and candlelight centerpieces. She recognized friends from Briarwood, waved and smiled gaily, all the while noticing how her classmates kept eyeing David.

"Let's dance," he said, and led her to an oak parquet floor where an ensemble band played soft rock music. Erin had danced with David a hundred times in play rehearsals, but this time it wasn't the same. "You're stiff," he told her. "Come closer. I won't bite."

"Is that a promise?"

David's expression seemed puzzled and hurt. "Erin, you're supposed to be having fun."

"I am."

"How can you tell?"

Around them couples clung together, silk and taffeta rustling as they moved. Erin wanted to be like them. More than anything she wanted to be a part of the tradition of prom night. "Maybe we should sit this one out," she told David.

He caught her hand. "Maybe you should tell me what's bothering you." She said nothing. "You don't like my tux?" She felt her cheeks redden and felt petty. "This is *me*, Erin," David said earnestly. "I'm not ever going to be just like everybody else. I thought you understood that."

"Look at us, Erin," Amy said. *"You're tall,*

blond, and graceful and I'm—well, short, round, and fully packed."

"What's your point?"

"We're different, that's all. You got the looks, talent, and brains and I got—"

"Does it bother you?" David asked.

"What?"

"That I'm different from your idea of Mr. Wonderful."

"How do you know what I like or don't like?"

"I saw the way you looked at Travis Sinclair."

"I told you, I hate him."

Seth and Shara danced past. Seth leaned over and said, "You two sure have a strange way of dancing with each other. You're supposed to move like this—" He demonstrated by dipping Shara backward.

Erin was grateful for the interruption, but David said, "Buzz off, Seth."

"I can take a hint. But first, lend me your hanky. I'm dripping."

Perspiration stood out on Seth's forehead, and David reached in his outside top pocket for the red hanky and pulled. Seth took it, but it didn't stop coming. The four of them stood transfixed as the material kept sliding out of David's pocket. Around them other couples stopped dancing and closed ranks. Giggles started, then swelled into laughter, as the "hanky" looped and draped to the floor in an endless stream of multicolored cloth.

Determined, Seth kept pulling. "Trick hanky?" Seth asked with a bemused smile. Shara giggled.

"Gosh, you're quick," David told him.

"You're a real clown, Devlin."

The hanky finally pulled free, and David bowed politely from the waist. Around them, the crowd burst into applause. Erin kept wishing she could sink through the floor, unable to remember when she'd felt so embarrassed.

"*Stop being such a show-off, Amy!*"

"*Gosh, Erin, I'm sorry. Am I embarrassing you?*"

"I embarrassed you again, didn't I?" David stooped to pick up his handkerchief. The music had stopped, and couples were walking toward the tables. "I don't do it on purpose, you know. I mean, I really did want to bring this gag hanky along tonight, but I had no idea it would come out right in the middle of the dance floor."

"Let's just forget the whole thing, okay?"

"If you'll give me a smile."

Erin managed one.

"How about a kiss?"

"Don't push your luck."

Erin went to the ladies' room, where girls surrounded her. "Where did you find him?" someone asked. "He's hysterical."

"We're in the play together."

"He's adorable," another exclaimed.

"Do you think so?"

"Come on, Erin, you *know* he is."

"Yeah, better than the dud that I brought along," another girl said.

Erin toyed with tendrils of hair around her face. So the girls thought David was cool, a real find. She fumbled in her purse and dug out her headache pills and washed one down with water from the spigot. She was feeling all right, but she remembered the times David unwittingly *had* brought on a headache. *No need to take chances*, she told her reflection silently.

The evening passed, with David gathering people to him as flowers attracted honeybees. He dragged Erin to a flower-draped indoor trellis, where a photographer took a souvenir photo. And at midnight, when everyone began to leave, he stood near the door and issued "blessings" like the pope.

All the way to Shara's beach house, they laughed and joked, with Erin in the thick of the banter. Yet she felt as if she were divided into halves. Half of her acted gay and happy, while the other half seemed disengaged, like a spectator sitting on the sidelines.

At the beach house music blasted, and while David wormed his way into the kitchen for sodas, Erin slipped out the door and headed up the moon-struck beach. She welcomed the quiet and the salt air that filled her lungs and stung her eyes.

The water lapped against the shore, and moonlight flecked the caps of waves, reminding her, inexplicably, of Travis's eyes. *"I told you once that I'd*

*never met anybody like Amy. She was wild and a
little bit crazy, and we had a million laughs together. But when I walked into that hospital room,
when I saw her lying on that bed with tubes and
wires and hoses—"*

A seagull circled and called forlornly. Erin
started. She was accustomed to seeing gulls in the
daytime when they scoured the beach for food, but
here in the darkness the bird seemed out of place.

*Travis said, "See, Erin, your problem is that
everybody has to act exactly the same way for it to
be legitimate with you."*

The gull swooped lower, then hung in midair
until an updraft caught its wings and tossed it
higher. It flew away, its cry blending with the
sounds of the sea.

*"Let her go, Erin. For everybody's sake, let
Amy go."*

Erin felt moisture on her cheeks and wondered
how the salt spray could have splashed against her
face when there was hardly any breeze. Her knees
began to give way, and she sank into the warm,
gritty sand. She wrapped her arms around herself
and began to rock back and forth. The wetness on
her face tingled in the cool night air. Sobs began
deep inside her throat, little choking noises, desperate to get out.

Salt water splashed the front of her new blue
dress, but she didn't care. All she heard was the
drone of the sea that blurred with the memory of
hissing ventilators and beeping monitors. The
rhythmic litany whispered, "Alone . . . alone . . .
alone . . ."

Chapter Fourteen

"Erin, what's wrong?" David was suddenly beside her, on his knees in the sand. She shook her head, unable to speak. He pulled her up and hugged her to his chest. "It's all right," he said again and again.

She remembered the night at the pizza parlor when he'd held her while she cried. He must think her an awful baby. "I—I don't know what's the matter with me. I'm so mixed up."

"About what?"

"Sometimes I feel happy and on top of life, then other times I feel so sad. Like in the car, driving over here—wasn't I laughing and having fun?"

"It seemed like you were."

"I really *was*. And now . . . I just went out for a little walk and . . . and . . . all I want to do is cry." She pushed away from him but grabbed his lapels. "Maybe I'm going crazy. Do you think that could be it?"

"We all have our ups and downs."

She shook her head vehemently. "I hear voices too. Conversations that I had over a year ago. I'll be right in the middle of talking to somebody, and these memories come flooding into my mind. I tell you, I can *really* hear things."

"What things? Who's talking?"

"Amy, mostly." She was about to say, *Travis, too*, but decided against it. "And so many things remind me of her. A million things . . . everywhere I look."

David smoothed her hair, which had tumbled from its combs. "Come on," he urged, and led her behind a small sand berm that the wind had built up over time. He spread his jacket and sat her down on it. He sat beside her, raised his knees, and pulled her gently across his lap. "I don't think you're crazy," he said, rubbing her cheek with the back of his hand.

Erin responded as if she hadn't heard him. "But there are other times when I can't even remember what she looked like. How her face was shaped, or how her voice sounded. That seems to me like I'm going crazy." She kicked off her shoes and dug her stocking feet into the sand.

"Well, to me it seems like you're only trying to hold on to her. Life goes on, Erin. I know that sounds corny, but it's true. And what happens every day sort of shoves the past further away. It's natural."

"But I don't want to forget Amy. It's—it's disloyal."

"I don't think you'll ever forget her," David said, sifting sand through his fingers. "But you can't make a saint of her either."

For the first time Erin smiled. "Amy, a saint?

Not on a bet! Sometimes she was a real goof-up. She was always promising to do things for people—you know, help out. She meant to do them too, but she always promised more than she could deliver. I can't tell you how many times I had to bail her out, fill in for her at Mom's store and do her chores as well as mine. She could twist my parents around her little finger."

"Yeah, I know what you mean. Jody's that way. Whatever she wants, she gets. We all have to work real hard at not feeling sorry for her just because she's deaf."

The sand muffled the sound of the ocean and was making Erin feel warm and snuggly. "It used to make me mad," Erin confessed. "Amy got away with murder because she was the 'baby.'"

"Try being a guy who likes acting and clowning instead of law, like his father." David glanced away. "Sometimes my father treats me like I must have been switched at birth in the hospital."

Erin felt a jab of guilt. How little she knew about David! "Why do you suppose parents do that? Make us think we have to do all the things they didn't, or couldn't, do?"

"Don't your folks want you to have a dance career?"

"Yes, they've always supported me in my dancing, especially my dad. But now it's like I have to do things for Amy *and* me. For all the things she won't be able to do because she's gone. It kind of scares me, you know? What if I fail?"

Erin could feel David's fingers in her hair. "You can't fail at anything, Erin," he said.

A funny quiver shot through her stomach. "Why are you so nice to me, David, when I've been mean to you?"

"I like you. You're pretty. And you're a great dancer, so I respect your talent. You walk around like a princess, as if you've got everything under control." He stretched a curl, then coiled it around his finger. "But you don't, do you?"

His evaluation made her sigh. "I sure don't. My parents are hanging all over my life. If I'm even thirty minutes late, my mom is practically calling the police."

"Maybe they're scared of losing you too."

"Maybe so, but that's not fair to me. All I want to do is dance, go to school, and do things with friends. But most of my old friends pity me. Except Shara. She sort of understands."

"I hate it when people pity you. When Jody goes out in public, when people catch on to the fact that she's deaf, they either back off or start fawning over her. Both are insulting. They should just treat her like a regular kid."

Erin understood what he was saying. She'd experienced much of the same thing when people found out that Amy had died. They either avoided Erin altogether or said stupid things like, "I know exactly how you feel," or "At least she's not suffering"—as if death were preferable over suffering. "Do your parents fight a lot?" she asked.

"What do you mean?"

"Before Amy—" She stopped. "When we were all together, our family used to be happier and do stuff together. Picnics, dinner parties, my folks went out. Now everybody sort of goes separate ways. Mom used to love to cook, put together photo albums, things like that, but she doesn't anymore. She's busy with her store and all. But sometimes I wish things could be like they used to be." The warmth of David's body, the softness of the sand, and the low hum of the sea were making Erin drowsy. Her eyelids drooped.

"Are you feeling all right?" David asked.

She waved her hand. "I'm all right. I took my medicine."

"What medicine?"

Her eyes struggled open. Why had she told him? She hadn't meant to. She shifted in his arms and sat up straighter. "Sometimes I get these headaches."

"Like that day at the mall? I remember how sick you were. I was worried about you. So was Jody."

She wasn't sure she wanted him to worry about her. It meant one more person to try to please. "Why do you get them?" he asked.

"The doctors don't know." Erin paused, embarrassed to feel so exposed before him. "They've done a bunch of tests, but in the end they decided it was all in my mind. So now I'm seeing a counselor, and she's trying to figure out what's causing them." She hadn't meant to tell him about Dr. Richardson either.

"Is she helping at all?"

"I still have the headaches. I hope we have a breakthrough soon, because I've got plans to go to a special dance school this summer. I won't be able to go if I'm not well. And if I'm not well, then maybe I won't be able to go to Florida State in the fall either. I couldn't stand that, David."

"You're going away for the summer?" He sounded disappointed.

Without warning she grew agitated and struggled to her feet. "Maybe if I go away, I can get well. You know, not having to be around all the things that remind me of Amy could help me out. And being away from my parents might help too."

David rose next to her. "What does the counselor say?"

"Not much." She crossed her arms. "I'm supposed to be working through it. I sometimes don't want to go see her, but Mom freaks out if I don't."

She scrambled over the sand berm, saying, "I need to walk," and headed for the shoreline.

"Hey, wait up." In a moment David was next to her. "Slow down, this isn't a footrace."

Travis's voice said, "You know, I've suddenly got the urge to go for a run. At this hour you don't have to get out of the way for other joggers. Yeah, the world's pretty empty right now."

"Can't you keep up?" Erin asked David.

He caught her elbow. He'd rolled up the cuffs of his shirt, and his bow tie dangled around the open neck of the shirt. "Why're you running off? We were right in the middle of a discussion."

"I'm tired of talking," she said, pulling away and continuing down the beach. The tide was coming in, and waves kept lapping over her feet.

David stopped her again, taking both her elbows in his hands and drawing her close. "If you don't talk to me, how will I know what you're feeling?"

Ocean water sucked the sand away, and the sensation was one of being nibbled up by the ground. "I told you, I'm feeling all mixed up and crazy." She wasn't cold, but her teeth began to chatter. "Please let me go."

For a moment David didn't move; then slowly he released her and stepped backward. She watched him back off and felt lost. Behind her the sea pulled on the hem of her dress. "It was such a simple thing to do, you know? All she had to do was drive to the store and buy some sodas. Any moron could have done it. She knew how to drive too, you know. She told me she'd driven Travis's car, and it was a real racing machine—not like my old clunker.

"But she screwed it up. She waved good-bye, she drove off, and she never came back. I can still see the taillights of the car."

David came closer, and because the tide had eroded away so much sand from where she was standing, she was inches below him and had to look up to see his face. "She shouldn't have done that, David. I'm so *angry* at her!" Tears came, and Erin clenched her teeth. "She had no right to die. She h—had no r—right to—to—" Her voice shook, and her whole body trembled. "Why did she do it? Why did Amy go away and leave me all by myself?"

Chapter Fifteen

Erin drifted on a sea of cozy, snuggly warmth and struggled to open her eyes. Light floated around her, and slowly she came to realize that she was on a sofa cushion on the floor of Shara's beach house. She rolled over and came face-to-face with a sleeping David.

She instantly sat up, only to see that she was surrounded by many sleeping couples. They were curled and bunched next to one another on cushions and pillows spread across the floor. Crumpled taffeta and crushed satin gave the room an eerie look, as if a magic spell had been cast and people had simply dropped in their tracks.

Erin's muscles ached from sleeping on the floor. She arched her back and rubbed her arms. Carefully she studied David. How childlike he looked as the sunlight pouring in through sliding glass doors turned his hair the color of spun gold. Erin watched him, trying to remember the evening before.

It returned in snatches, like scraps of photographs tossed into the wind. Walking the beach with David and crying . . . sitting in the sand while

David rocked her . . . coming back to the house only when the music had stopped and the lights had gone out . . . stepping over bodies stretched along the floor, and David wrestling a sofa cushion from someone already asleep . . . David pulling her down next to him and holding her until the rhythmic sound of others breathing had lulled her into an exhausted sleep.

She'd made a fool of herself the night before. Why had she started talking about Amy in the first place? Why had she broken down and cried? Where had all the anger and tears come from? *Maybe it was the medication*, she told herself. Yes, that had to be it. She'd taken the pills to stave off a headache, and they must have caused her to "lose it" in front of David. How could she face him today?

Quietly Erin rose and carefully threaded her way into the bathroom. Once there, she stared at her reflection in the mirror, at her tangled hair and mascara-smudged eyes, still red and swollen. God, she looked awful! She wondered where her purse was and her hairbrush. She splashed water on her face and rinsed her mouth. She needed some orange juice and decided to go to the kitchen.

Pinky and Andy and three other couples were sitting at the pine table talking quietly.

Pinky grinned. "Did we wake you guys?" Her eyes were glassy, and Erin realized that this group hadn't slept at all.

"No. Is there any juice?"

"Help yourself." Erin took the paper cup Andy

shoved toward her. She found the juice in the refrigerator and filled the cup.

"Some party, huh?" Pinky asked. "Where'd you and David spend the evening?" There was an innuendo in Pinky's voice that Erin didn't like.

"We just walked the beach."

"Uh-huh . . ." Pinky drawled, cutting her eyes toward Andy.

Erin didn't care what they thought. She was exhausted and wanted to go home, take a shower, and sleep in her own bed. "What time is it anyway?" she asked.

"Seven o'clock."

The last time Erin remembered seeing a clock, it had been four A.M. "Short night," she said, draining the last of her juice.

"I'm glad Ms. Thornton said no play practice today," Pinky said.

The play. Inwardly Erin groaned. The performance was a week from Saturday, and suddenly she was dreading it, as if it were too big a chore to tackle.

"Hi, guys. What's for breakfast?" David stepped through the doorway.

"Whatever you want to fix," Pinky told him, and everybody laughed.

He tried to catch Erin's eye, but she refused. He'd seen her soul last night, and now, in the light of day, she felt more exposed than if she'd stood before him naked.

"You don't think I can cook?" David said, stepping around her. "What do you want? Eggs, French toast, pancakes? Just name it."

"How about cereal?" Seth said, sauntering into the room. "It's hard to screw that up."

"Ye of little faith," David said. "Watch this, hair ball." In minutes he had everyone organized, and eggs were being scrambled, toast was browning, and the aroma was bringing other sleepy kids into the kitchen.

Erin stood aside, impressed by the way David could take over a room, grateful that she didn't have to interact with anybody. Later he drove her home, but she avoided talking by feigning sleep, and at her front door he asked, "Can I call you later?"

"I'm gonna crash for the rest of the day. I'll see you at play practice Monday after school." She went inside before he could say anything else.

Her mother was waiting for her inside the door. "Did you have fun? Are you all right?" She was trying to sound pleasant, but Erin saw the circles under her eyes and realized that she'd probably been up most of the night too.

"I'm fine, Mom. I told you not to worry."

"I wasn't worrying. I was just asking. Can't I even ask if you had a good time or not?"

Erin felt guilty, but she was too tired to hassle with her mother. "Can I tell you all about it later? I'm really wiped out."

"Yes, of course. Go on to bed and we can talk tonight."

"Are you working today? Should I start dinner?"

"We'll go out for dinner."

"Where's Daddy?"

"Out. He said he'd be out tonight too. No use in cooking for just the two of us."

"No use," she agreed. "No use at all."

"Erin, it's really great to see you. I'm so glad you called and wanted to come over." Beth Wilson's eyes shone as she spoke.

Erin sat cross-legged on Beth's bed, munching popcorn. "I've been wanting to come over for ages, but with school and play practice and Spring Fling and all—"

"How was the dance? Tell me about it."

Erin still wasn't caught up on her rest, but Sunday afternoon at her house had been filled with its usual tension, so she'd called Beth and practically invited herself over. "The dance was fun, and afterward we stayed up all night at Shara's beach house. We all sort of fell asleep together on the floor."

Beth clutched her knees and giggled. "Sounds romantic."

Erin recalled how snuggly and content she'd felt in David's arms. "Hardly," she said. "My bones still hurt from the hard floor. I'd never make a camper."

"We used to camp," Beth said wistfully. "Before my mom got real sick. Before Dad left."

"How is your mom?"

Beth shrugged. "About the same. She has to go for dialysis again every other day, and they're trying to locate another donor kidney for her."

Beth's house smelled of sickness. Erin noticed it as soon as Beth opened the front door, but she smiled and came inside anyway. It reminded her too much of the hospital, of the Neuro-ICU unit, and of Amy's cubicle. "Then they'll do a second transplant?" she asked.

"Yeah, just as soon as they find a donor kidney with a good tissue match. Of course, there's no telling how long that will take, so all we can do is wait and continue the dialysis. But Mom's a priority. You know how it is."

Erin knew how it was. Somebody had to die in order that somebody else could go on living. "*You can't just turn off the machines. You can't just give Amy away in bits and pieces*," she had pleaded with her parents.

Her mother had said, "*Something has to make sense. Organ donation is our only way of making this whole thing plausible.*"

"So," Beth was saying, "how's your love life?"

Erin blushed. "What love life?"

"You know—David Devlin? Didn't you have fun with him Friday night?"

"David's all right."

"Just all right?"

Erin studied a spot on the wall, above Beth's head. "I don't know why everybody's trying to fix me up with David. It's not like that between us. He's just a guy I do things with. That's all."

"Gosh, Erin, I didn't mean to make you mad. I was only teasing."

"And I didn't mean to snap," Erin said. "It's the play and finals coming up. I don't know. I guess it's just me."

"And I'm trying to live vicariously," Beth admitted with a quick smile. "Because my life's the pits."

"Are you going to finish the school year?"

"I have to. When Mom found out I was skipping classes to help around here, she exploded. For a sick woman she really let loose. But even though I'm finishing high school, I refuse to go away to college."

"Will you go at all?"

"Just to Hillsborough Junior College. That way I can be at home, look after Mom and my brother and sisters, and still get some sort of college degree."

Erin was counting the days until she could go away and start living on her own—if only her parents would let her. She felt sorry for Beth. It didn't seem fair that she was having to give up her plans all because her father decided he couldn't cope with having a sick wife. "Has your dad ever called or written?"

Beth shook her head. "But we do have some help financially now, and I don't think Social Services is going to break up our family. A social worker with the dialysis unit figured out that things weren't going so hot for us, and she's been a big help. She checks on us every week, and so far I've been able to convince her that I'm doing a good job."

To Erin it seemed as if Beth were doing a superb job. "You are coming to the play, aren't you?"

"I'm planning on it. How's it going?"

"You know how it is toward the end of rehearsals—it seems like a disaster, but somehow it all comes together at the last minute, and you make it through. We've got dress rehearsals all this week."

Beth looked disappointed. "I was hoping that maybe we could go to a movie or something Friday night."

Erin wanted to tell Beth that the big rehearsal was all day Saturday and that she would be free Friday night. But she'd made up her mind to do something else on Friday night.

Maybe losing it in front of David on the beach was what finally pushed her into it. Maybe it was the stark, raw anguish she kept remembering from that night when she'd shouted about how angry she was at Amy for dying. Erin didn't know. She only knew she wanted to be happy again and think about dancing and college and her future. She wanted to be free of headaches and ghosts and the past.

"We'll do something as soon as this play's over, all right?"

"You're on," Beth said with a grin.

Erin had decided to attend Dr. Richardson's grief support group meeting on Friday night. She would hear what others her own age had to say who'd lost family members. For a moment she was once again tempted to tell Beth about her therapy sessions. And even though it would be nice to bring a friend along to the group meeting, Erin figured it was something she really should do on her own. Besides, Beth seemed to be doing all right now, especially because of the social worker she'd mentioned.

Debriding the wound, Dr. Richardson had called it. Erin winced, thinking of the emotional pain that lay ahead of her. Was there really no magic balm?

Chapter Sixteen

"It's good to see so many of you here tonight," Dr. Richardson said. "And a special welcome to you newcomers."

Erin looked nervously around the circle of chairs set up in Dr. Richardson's conference room. She managed a self-conscious smile, certain that she was the only newcomer there. Ten other kids nodded, waved, and said hi. They all looked normal to her. *What did you expect?* she asked herself. *Do people who've lost family members wear marks on their foreheads?*

"I've ordered pizza for everyone after tonight's session," Dr. Richardson said, and a cheer went up. "Will somebody tell me what kind of a week he or she had?"

Silence fell on the room, until an overweight boy of about twelve spoke. "My mom found the box of Twinkies I hid under my bed and blew up."

"Why'd you hide them there?" a girl asked. "That's the first place my mom always cleans."

The boy shrugged. "I shouldn't have had them, I guess."

"Then why did you?" someone asked.

"My dad and I used to sneak into the kitchen at

127

night when everybody was asleep, and sometimes we'd eat Twinkies together. I kind of feel like he's still around when I eat them."

"Sounds like an excuse to pig out to me," a girl said with disdain.

The fat boy leapt from his chair. "That's a rotten thing to say, Michelle! Take it back!"

Dr. Richardson interrupted. "But, Todd, you've been telling us for weeks that you want to lose weight. How can you if you sneak Twinkies?"

"I told you, it makes me feel like my dad's still alive."

"Well, I wish I *could* eat," another girl said. "But my stomach's upset all the time. All my mother does is try to push food on me."

"I'll trade you," Todd told her. "All my mom does is yell at me."

Erin listened as others talked, feeling close to them even though they were strangers. A thirteen-year-old boy named Benjie said, "After my baby brother died in his crib last summer, my mom sort of freaked out too. She started staying in bed all day and cried all the time. Dad always had to make supper, but we just sat looking at each other at the table. He wasn't a very good cook.

"Once I sneaked into the baby's room, but it gave me the creeps. Everything was just the same, except the baby was gone. It was like everybody kept expecting him to come home. I really wished Mom would put his things away. I stepped on one of his rattles by accident and broke it, and Mom slapped me. I cried. But I didn't want to, because I'm too old to cry."

His story sent shivers up Erin's spine as she remembered the boxes and trunk stored in the garage. And now that Amy's bedroom was her mother's office, it seemed as if Amy had hardly lived with them at all.

"You know what gets me?" Kristy, a fifteen-year-old, said. "When my mom died of cancer, people came up to me and said, 'The good die young.' Was that supposed to make me feel better? Is dying some sort of reward for being good? If so, then I'm gonna be bad!"

Erin sympathized with Kristy's anger. After Amy had died, some adults had told her, "Amy was so special that God must have wanted her with Him." Erin had held her tongue, but she'd wanted to shout, "God's got the entire world to choose from, and I've only got one sister. So why did He have to pick *her*?"

"The things people say at funerals and wakes often do sound pretty empty," Dr. Richardson said. "But expressing sympathy is an awkward thing to do, and it takes a lot of courage. At least the people who said something cared enough about you and your family to try."

Dr. Richardson looked over at one boy who had propped his booted feet on an empty chair. "What do you think about being good, Charlie?"

Erin studied Charlie's sullen expression, his black leather jacket, and his unkempt hair. "Oh, I'm real good, Doc. Just ask Terry Parker. I made it with her real good last night."

"That's disgusting," Kristy said.

"I can make it real good for you too, babe. Want to meet in my car after this is over?"

"That'll do, Charlie," Dr. Richardson said quietly.

Charlie dropped his feet with a thud and leaned forward. "Look, I'm here because the judge says I gotta be here. I don't care about this little goody-goody group."

"Good for you," Todd said. "But the rest of us want to be here."

"Butt out, Tubb-o."

Dr. Richardson calmly shook her head. "I won't allow name calling, Charlie. We're here to build one another up. If you can't be polite—"

Charlie stood abruptly and crossed to the door. "I'm out of here. Give my share of the pizza to Fatso." He left, and Dr. Richardson excused herself and followed him.

For a moment no one spoke, and Erin could hear the clock humming on the wall. "Uh—what was his problem?" she finally asked.

Kristy fiddled with her bracelets. "He was driving drunk and hit another car head-on. His cousin was killed, and the guy in the other car is crippled for life."

Erin's eyes grew wide. "That's awful."

"Yeah," Kristy agreed. "And Charlie walked away without a scratch. I guess that's why we put up with him. He's hurting like crazy. He made a bad mistake, and he can't change it. One time he sort of broke down and cried in front of us and said he wished it was him who'd died."

The boy who'd been sitting next to Charlie added, "'Course it wasn't, but Charlie keeps acting so hateful that maybe someday somebody will do him the favor of taking him out."

Erin shuddered. There was so much anger and guilt and pain in the room, and she wondered how she fit into it. She thought back to the night of Amy's accident.

"What was she doing driving in the rain at night anyway?" her mother had demanded.

"I let her take my car."

"Why? Amy's not an experienced driver. I've always counted on you, Erin, to have common sense."

The door to the conference room opened, and Dr. Richardson came back in. "Charlie's all right," she assured them. "He'll be back next week."

"Whoopie," Todd said sarcastically.

They talked some more, and the session passed quickly, and afterward, when the pizza arrived, she noticed Todd greedily grab for the first slice. Erin took a piece too, but she didn't really want it. Her appetite had fled much as Charlie had. And worse, a tightening sensation was starting up the back of her neck. It was good to be around kids her age with similar problems, but not if it brought on a headache. She'd tell Dr. Richardson at her next counseling session that it was doubtful she could ever come back.

* * *

The backstage area was in chaos. The final performance of *West Side Story* had come off beautifully, and the applause of the audience still rang in Erin's ears. "Weren't we sensational?" Shara shouted, giving her a hug.

"Next stop, Broadway," Erin called.

People swarmed around them, offering congratulations. Erin felt euphoric, but then performing always gave her a "high." The cast kept telling her how good she and David had been. Erin kept smiling, searching the crowd for Beth, who didn't seem to be there.

David nudged his way through the masses, scooped Erin up in his arms, and twirled her around. "Not too shabby, 'Maria.' So what do you say we change and head for the cast party?"

"I—uh—I'm not going."

He looked stricken. "What?"

"No . . . I can't go."

"Why?"

"My folks are sort of paranoid, and they want me to come straight home. Cast parties have a bad reputation in our family. We were having a cast party the night Amy had the accident." Erin knew she was telling a half truth. *She* was the one who didn't want to go.

"Look, Erin, this might not be the time to bring it up, but you've been dodging me ever since the Spring Fling dance."

"That's not true," she protested, but knew it was.

David pulled her to a more secluded area of the stage and took her by the shoulders. "What's wrong?"

"I told you."

"What's wrong between you and me? I mean, when we were on the beach together, you were so open and honest."

"I sort of lost it that night, David. It wasn't supposed to be that way. Too much pressure—the play and all."

"Well, the play's over."

Erin's heart thudded, and she avoided his eyes. "I know. And that means that I won't be seeing much of you anymore."

"But I want to see you."

"Look, David, think about it. School will be out in a few more weeks, and this summer I'm probably going away, and even if I don't, I *will* be going to FSU in the fall. What's the point of us seeing each other?"

"What's the point? The point is, I care about you, Erin, and I want to be with you. I thought you were beginning to care about me too."

"Oh, I do like you." She said it too quickly, and David gave her a skeptical glance. "I just don't want to start something I can't finish."

"Like dating me?"

"You'll always be a special friend." *What a stupid, juvenile remark,* she told herself as soon as the words were out. Nothing was going the way Erin had planned. She didn't want to hurt David, and she didn't want to feel about him the way she did either. She glanced around. "Everybody's starting to leave. I—uh—I'd better get going."

David took her arm. His hurt expression had been replaced with one of determination. "You need me, Erin. No matter what you say otherwise, it's as simple as that."

She blinked, speechless. *Of all the conceited, arrogant*—she jerked her arm free. "I'm getting out of this city as soon as I can. I don't need anybody." His grin started, and he backed up slowly. "You think that's *funny*?" she shouted.

"I told you once that clowns see the humor in everything. The good and the bad."

"Well then, go ahead and laugh!" Erin was furious. She watched him walk away, and the last thing she heard was his whistling.

Erin moped around the house Sunday afternoon, feeling lost. She'd done her homework, TV was boring, her father was gone for the day, and her mother was driving her crazy with dumb questions about dumb things. She still wasn't over her argument with David either. And as much as she hated to admit it, she missed him and wished she hadn't handled things so badly the night before.

She was grateful when the phone rang. "Erin? It's me, Beth." Her friend's voice sounded small and tight.

"What's wrong?"

"We got the call this morning. They have a kidney for my mother. I'm at the hospital right now, and they're prepping her for surgery. Can you please come and wait with me?"

Chapter Seventeen

For Erin, walking back into the seventh-floor waiting room at the hospital was like stepping through a time warp. Memories of the days she spent by Amy's side overwhelmed her, and she almost fled, but out of the sea of anxious faces of people waiting for news of family and friends, she heard Beth call her.

Quickly Erin swallowed her emotions and took a chair next to her friend. "Any news yet?" she asked.

"They just started the surgery. It'll take several hours."

"Last time they flew her to Gainesville. Why not this time?"

"She has another doctor. And this hospital has a transplant team now too. It's better they don't have to fly her out this time anyway so we can all be near her. Jason's at the next-door neighbor's," she explained. "He's not real aware of what's going on because he's only six. He just knows Mom's sick and the operation is supposed to make her better."

Erin was struck with the irony of the situation. Here was Beth trying to be an anchor for her family, while Erin felt more like a burden to hers. Her sister had lingered in a coma, trapped in a mysterious universe between life and death; Beth's mother was still alive, but if the transplant wasn't successful, then she would be dead too.

"I think Amy would have approved of us donating her organs," Erin said slowly, recalling how bitterly opposed she'd been to the idea at the time. But agreeing to donation meant turning off the machines and admitting that Amy was dead. Erin supposed that *that* was the part that had been the hardest for her.

"I checked the place on my driver's license to be a donor if I die in an accident," Beth said. "It seems sort of wasteful to bury a body whose organs could go to help somebody who's still alive."

The direction of the conversation was giving Erin the creeps, so she asked if anyone wanted a soda and then went to the machine. "I don't want to be here," she mumbled to herself as she opened the canned drink. There was an ache deep inside her throat she couldn't wash away with the soda. She saw a pay phone on the wall and thought about the time she'd called Travis and he'd come to the hospital to visit Amy. Of course, he couldn't deal with being in the cubicle with her comatose sister, and so he left and never visited again. Erin hadn't forgiven him for that either.

"David," she whispered, and suddenly she wanted him with her. She needed his smile and positive attitude. She dialed his number from the pay phone, and once she explained where she was and what she was doing there, he said, "I'll be right over."

He arrived within thirty minutes, and the familiar sight of him strolling into the area—hands thrust into the pockets of his baggy Bermudas, and his shirt looking as if it needed to be ironed—made her want to run up and throw her arms around him. Of course, she didn't.

"Thanks for coming," Erin said.

He flipped his blond hair off his forehead and flashed the smile she knew so well. "Thanks for asking."

In no time he'd tracked down the board game Aggravation from one of the nurses, and soon all of them were huddled around the board in a corner of the waiting area. Beth's sister Willa rolled the dice, landed on David's game piece, and sent him home to start all over again. She giggled and clapped her hands.

"I'm a terrible loser," David told the little girl, then reached over and produced her game piece magically from behind her ear.

Willa stared at the empty spot on the board where her playing piece had been. "How'd you do that?"

"You mean this?" David pulled Beth's game piece from behind her other ear. "Or this?" He opened a closed fist, and there lay Erin's and Jill's Aggravation marbles.

By now Willa's eyes were shining. "That's neat!"

David turned to Erin. "See, I told you women under the age of ten love me."

"I never doubted it," Erin said with a laugh.

"It's the ones over ten I have all my problems with." He turned back to an awestruck Willa and asked, "Would you like a dog?" He reached in his pocket and pulled out a balloon. Moments later he'd blown it up and sculpted it into a dachshund.

By now a small crowd had collected. He made other balloon animals and passed them out, and when someone handed him a deck of cards, he performed several amazing sleight-of-hand tricks.

Finally he announced, "That's about it, folks." The small gathering applauded. It surprised Erin to see that an hour had passed. He took her elbow and asked, "How about we go down to the cafeteria for some supper?"

Beth urged them to go, and once downstairs David bought their dinners and found a table near a long row of windows. Outside, twilight had fallen. "Thanks for breaking the monotony up there," Erin told him. "You really took people's minds off their worries."

"I'm a natural show-off, remember? Collecting an audience is my strong suit."

"Still, you made everybody forget their gloom and doom." She took a bite of her hamburger. "You also do a pretty good show—but don't let it go to your head."

David feigned a fainting spell. "I can't believe it! Erin thinks I'm a good act."

"Don't be a wise guy."

"Well, it so happens that I've got some news for you about my plans this summer. Since you're going off to dance school, I'm trying to get into clown school."

Erin looked blank. "'Clown school'? You can take *classes* for clowning?"

"It's part of the Ringling Circus's permanent quarters down in Sarasota, and it puts out some of the world's top clowns. I haven't been accepted yet, but since you'll be gone, why stick around here? The summer program starts in June, after the Special Olympics. You sure I can't persuade you to help out at the games?"

"Not this year. And by the way, going away to Wolftrap isn't a sure thing for me either. Dr. Richardson has to okay it and persuade my parents I'm well enough to go."

"Why wouldn't she?"

"The headaches. I'm a lot better," Erin added quickly. "But even if I was one hundred percent, my parents are dragging their feet about my going. They hate to let me out of their sight."

"Like the night of the cast party?"

Erin swallowed, remembering how she'd hurt David's feelings by not going. "They're practically smothering me to death, David. In fact, we're all supposed to meet in Dr. Richardson's office this Saturday to talk about the course of my treatment and all."

"What treatment?" Beth asked, startling them both.

"We didn't hear you come up," Erin said. "Is everything all right?"

"Mom's out of surgery, and they've taken her down to ICU. Her doctor says it went real well, and that the new kidney is functioning fine. 'Course, the next few days will tell us a lot more. Now, why are you going to a doctor? You never told me *you* were sick. I couldn't take it if you were sick too, Erin."

"No, no, it's nothing like that," Erin said.

"Here, sit down." David pulled out a chair for her.

Erin had never meant for anybody to know she was seeing a therapist, and now both David and Beth knew. She took a deep breath and told Beth about the headaches and the visits to Dr. Richardson.

Beth listened intently. "Gosh, Erin. I never would have guessed. I mean, I thought you had it all together. You seem so sure of yourself and so composed. I was the one who was falling apart."

"Well, looks can be deceiving," she confessed. David reached out and took her hand, and the simple gesture almost unraveled her. "Sometimes I guess we all need somebody to share things with."

"I know it helps me now to talk things out with the social worker," Beth admitted. "But before her, I had you to share my feelings with."

"And I never felt like I was much help to you."

"That's not true. I'll never forget the day we ended up shopping for your prom dress. It was fun, and I sure needed the break."

David's grip tightened, and he said, "Look, if everything's all right for you and your sisters now, Erin and I will go. We've both got school tomorrow."

"Oh, sure," Beth said. She hugged Erin when they all stood up. "I'll never forget the two of you being here for us."

"Call me and let me know how your mom's doing," Erin said, suddenly light-headed.

Beth promised, then hurried away. David put his arm around Erin, and she let him lead her out of the hospital and into the parking lot. Night had fallen, but the air was humid and muggy. She smelled rain. "You're not feeling good, are you?" he asked.

"How did you know?"

His arm tightened. "I'm clairvoyant. And besides, your face is the color of a sheet."

"Oh, David." She leaned against him. "I don't think I'm ever going to get well."

"I'll drive you home."

"But my car—"

"I'll get it back to you later tonight."

Thunder rumbled, and the breeze picked up. She clung to David, and when large drops of water began to spatter, she didn't even care. He pulled her under a covered walkway. "We'll have to wait until it lets up," he said. "Then we'll make a dash to my car."

She rested her cheek on his chest and listened as the drumming rain mingled with the sound of his heartbeat. The scents of wet grass and asphalt

blended with the scent of his soap and cologne.
With her arms locked around his waist, Erin looked
up into David's face. Light from the parking-lot
lamps bathed him in gold. David made a circle with
his open hand in front of her face, then ran his
thumb along her jaw. The signed gesture told her,
pretty girl. Her pulse fluttered, racing with the
rhythm of the rain. She closed her eyes as he
cupped her chin and kissed her tenderly on the
lips.

Chapter Eighteen

———⌇———

Dr. Richardson's office seemed smaller to Erin now that her mother and father were with her. They were sitting on a sofa, with Erin in a chair next to it, and Dr. Richardson in a chair in front of them.

"I don't see why we have to be here," Mrs. Bennett said.

"Because we want to help Erin," Mr. Bennett told her, as if she were a not-too-bright child.

Erin felt a tightness clamp like bands around her temples. Surely her parents wouldn't have a fight right in front of the counselor!

Dr. Richardson said, "I know you've been concerned about Erin's headaches. When one person hurts, the whole family hurts. Can you tell me how her headaches affected you?"

Mrs. Bennett said, "We've done everything we could—we've spent a fortune on tests—and frankly, I don't believe she's a whole lot better now in spite of her therapy sessions."

"But I *am* better!" Erin blurted. "They don't come on nearly as often."

"But you still have them," her mother said.

"Erin wants to take a dance scholarship this

summer," Mr. Bennett commented, as if the exchange between Erin and his wife hadn't occurred. "And she wants to go away to college in the fall, but with these headaches and all—"

Mrs. Bennett interrupted. "I don't see how that's possible. She'd be far away, and if she got sick, who would take care of her?" Erin's heart ached because she wasn't sure how she'd survive if she couldn't go away. "She's all we have you know, and—"

"You have each other," Erin exclaimed. Her parents stared directly at the counselor, as if she hadn't spoken.

"Erin doesn't understand how nervous we get over her moving away. She needs me when she's sick. . . . Why, she can barely function."

"But sometimes I feel like I'm in the way," Erin said, twisting her hands in her lap as the pressure mounted inside her head. "You have your store and all."

"My work helps me. It keeps me busy and my mind on other things."

"If you didn't have the store, and didn't have to worry about Erin's headaches, what do you think life would be like?" Dr. Richardson asked.

Mrs. Bennett toyed with an earring and stared evasively into space. "I'm sure you understand what a difficult year this has been for all of us."

"Because your daughter died?"

"Yes, because my daughter died! Whenever Erin's sick, whenever I'm busy at the store, I don't have time to—to—" She stopped, and Dr.

Richardson let the silence stretch until Erin began to perspire. She wanted someone to jump in and finish her mother's sentence for her sake. "Well, it's just easier to go on from day to day if I'm busy."

"Dad works a lot too," Erin said.

"Do you work a lot?" Dr. Richardson asked.

Mr. Bennett cleared his throat. "I've found work to be therapeutic. I keep occupied."

"He retreats," Mrs. Bennett said. "There's a difference." He glared at her, as if she'd exposed him in some way

The therapist turned to Erin. "And what do you do?"

"I've already told you—I go to school, dance, and work in Mom's store. We all keep busy."

"And what do you do together as a family?"

"Not much."

"Why?"

Erin sat on her hands. "We're not a family anymore."

Her mother gasped. "How can you say such a thing? Of course we're a family."

"When Amy was alive, we did things together. Now we don't. We don't sit around the table and eat and laugh like we used to either." Amy used to make them all laugh. Erin supposed that there was nothing left to laugh about now. She thought of David's clowning and of how he made her laugh.

"But things are different now," Dr. Richardson said. "You're all trying to find ways of dealing with the great loss you've experienced. It seems to me as though you haven't given yourselves time to grieve fully."

"We've grieved," Mrs. Bennett said, holding her head erect and blinking. "Now we're just trying to go on with life."

"Grieving is a process with many stages," Dr. Richardson said. "It's intricate and involved, and I want to help you through it. You're wise to use therapy to support the family while you work your way through the thoughts and feelings about Amy's death."

Erin squirmed in her chair. She didn't want to talk about Amy's death. She wanted Dr. Richardson to convince her parents that she was well enough to move away. "So why don't they want me to go away this summer? It's like they're punishing me."

Her father leaned toward her. "Honey, you're not being punished. You haven't done anything wrong."

"Mom said I did." Erin surprised herself with her sudden comment.

"When? I've never said such a thing!"

"Yes, I heard you. When I first came to the hospital after Amy's accident. You told me that I never should have let Amy go to the store because she'd just gotten her license and wasn't very experienced." Erin's voice sounded angry and ashamed.

"But I never—I mean, I was upset."

"It was an accident," her father added.

Erin looked at them, from one face to the other, and nodded vigorously. "But you were right. I shouldn't have let her go, but I really didn't want to go myself, and so I let her have her way. Why did I do that?"

Dr. Richardson said, "You're angry because she talked you into it."

"Yes, I let her have her way! If *I* had gone on the errand instead of Amy, then the accident never would have happened!"

"But it was raining. Could you have stopped the rain?"

Erin felt flushed all over. She twisted in her chair. "Of course I couldn't."

"So what if you had lost control of the car too? Then what would have happened?"

"I—I would have been the one who died."

"But you're a more experienced driver. You might have had better control of the skid," Dr. Richardson reasoned. "Erin, don't you see what you've done? You've built a whole case—served as judge and jury for yourself—based on 'if only.' If only *I* had driven instead. If only it hadn't been raining. If only I hadn't let her talk me into driving to the store."

"But my mother said—"

"You've beat yourself up for the last year over something you had no control over."

"But I let her drive, and she wasn't experienced," Erin insisted. Why couldn't Dr. Richardson understand that she really *was* to blame for Amy's death?

"Your sister was a sixteen-year-old licensed driver. She'd taken a driver's test and was approved for a legal license. *She* was driving the car. *She* knew how to drive. *She* lost control. It was an accident."

"But I *feel* so responsible. Because I was the 'responsible one,' and Amy was the baby. Isn't that right?" Erin couldn't help crying now as she turned to her parents. "Amy'll never get to be an actress." She looked at her father, whose eyes were brimming. "She'll never get to grow up." She looked at her mother, whose face was the color of paste.

Gently Dr. Richardson said, "Erin, this is guilt you're feeling—a natural part of grieving. It's good that you're allowing yourself to express it. It's okay to forgive yourself for something that wasn't your fault."

"Sometimes I feel so depressed." Erin blew her nose. "I feel like I'm going crazy, like I have to do it all, because Amy's gone."

"Letting these tears and feelings out will ensure that you won't go crazy. In fact, I believe that your headaches are a result of keeping these feelings bottled up inside."

Dr. Richardson faced Erin's parents. "Erin's been trying to help both of you, to distract you from your pain. She's carried on, tried to take up the slack and act as a buffer, and yet still plan for a future. The headaches are a reflection of the terrible strain she's under. It's tough being the glue that holds everybody together."

"We never meant for that to happen," Mr. Bennett said, shaking his head.

Dr. Richardson continued. "Erin's headaches have been the focus of your lives this past year. I believe that if both of you would come in for separate counseling as well as together as a family, you'll all be able to work out your grief and put the pieces back together again."

"But we're working things out," Mrs. Bennett protested, crying openly.

"As parents you're facing a double loss: Amy's death—an unnatural event—and Erin's growing up and leaving home—a natural one. It can be scary facing the unknown. Yet Erin has to feel that the two of you are going to be all right before she can afford to be well and achieve her goals."

"So you're saying that we're partly to blame for Erin's headaches," Mr. Bennett commented, shifting in his chair.

Her mother wept. "I never meant to blame you, Erin. Never!"

Erin buried her face in her hands. She felt her future and all her dreams slipping away. She felt tired and defeated. "I won't go away if you really don't want me to," she whispered.

"That's not a decision we have to make right now," Dr. Richardson said kindly. "Right now we need to focus on all of you getting your feelings out. You need to confront your anger, fear, and guilt. Then we can discuss the future."

Erin raised tearstained eyes to her parents. They were crying too, but it didn't embarrass her. She half wished she was a little girl again and could curl up in their laps and be soothed. "I want things to be like they were before Amy died," she said.

"That's impossible," her father said.

"I agree," Dr. Richardson told them. "But things can be good again. You can be a happy and unified family if we work together on your healing. Today has given you an excellent beginning."

Erin watched her parents glance at one another, then nod in agreement. She rubbed the back of her neck, but the dull ache was already starting to subside.

Chapter Nineteen

Erin watched the rain from her living-room window. The water splattered against the glass, then ran in rivulets, pooled and collected on the outside sill before running off the edges and into the shrubbery. Her insides felt as liquid as the rain. Ever since her family's session with Dr. Richardson, she'd cried off and on until she was sure that she was empty, that there couldn't possibly be one more tear left within her. And that made her task for this afternoon a little bit easier.

Erin turned and crossed to the middle of the floor where Amy's trunk sat waiting. The house was silent, because both her parents were at a counseling session, and since classes and exams were finally over, she had nothing else to do but sort through her sister's things. Dr. Richardson had told her, "I believe it will help heal you." Now she realized that more than her headaches needed healing. Her parents needed healing too.

Erin sat on the sofa, reached out, and unsnapped the catch on the trunk. She raised the lid. Clothing lay on top—Amy's favorite items. She lifted a red blouse and remembered the day Amy had bought it.

She'd said, "Erin, can you loan me the money for this. Please . . . I'll be your best friend."

Beneath the clothing she found the case Amy had received for her sixteenth birthday to hold her clown makeup. Amy had been delighted because she thought it made her look like a "real pro." Erin smiled, because on the first opportunity Amy had had to carry it—the dance recital—she'd forgotten it. Erin opened the kit and examined the tubes of greasepaint.

She unscrewed one cap, closed her eyes, and sniffed. The heavy, oily odor sent her back to the Children's Home and the day she'd filled in for Amy and had first met David.

Funny how they'd met again during the play. David had turned out to be as zany in real life as he'd been that day he'd entertained the children. So much like Amy. Erin still wondered why she never told him about their *real* first meeting. But now that they were going their separate ways for the summer, she guessed it didn't matter anymore.

Erin remembered his kiss and touched her mouth. *No use getting all sentimental*, she told herself, closing the lid of the makeup case and snapping the catch tightly. David was a part of the past now too. Time to go forward.

Inside the trunk she discovered a shoe box filled with photographs. There was a strip of her and Amy they'd taken one day at the mall in one of those "instant-photo" machines. In one frame Amy had crossed her eyes and Erin was looking exasperated. In another Amy had sneezed just as the camera had fired.

And there were photos of Amy and Travis—of the two of them beside a Christmas tree, kissing under mistletoe, and sitting in Travis's sports car.

Erin ran her fingers over the glossy surfaces, tracing her sister's smiling face locked in time, forever young. A lump swelled in her throat, so she quickly shoved the photos back into the box and put it aside.

She found a pile of gifts and keepsakes from Travis—a necklace with a single pearl, his Christmas gift to her, a football pennant, several ticket stubs, and a broken comb. "You sure kept some weird things," Erin said aloud. But then she supposed that she would have done the same thing if Travis had given them to her.

She uncovered the teddy bear Travis had given Amy in the hospital—the one Erin had tried to give back to him the night he'd dated Cindy. She'd come very close to throwing it into the bay but in the end had brought it home to Amy's room.

She hugged the tattered bear, burying her face in its fur. It smelled of Amy's perfume. She pulled the familiar bottle out of the trunk and spritzed its fragrance into the air. The scent was light and floral. She closed her eyes and inhaled.

After a few moments Erin opened her eyes again. She was alone—yet, surrounded by all of Amy's belongings, it had seemed—just for a moment—that Amy had been there too. "What do you think, Mr. Bear? What should we do with Amy's things? If we give them away, someone else will just toss them. If we keep them—" She stopped because her eyes were misting over, and her throat had clogged up again. If she kept them, someday she'd be able to tell her children all about Aunt Amy. She'd be able to let them meet Amy in a different sort of way.

Slowly she gathered up the mementos and packed them lovingly back inside the trunk. She'd save everything, and she'd have her father put the trunk in her bedroom, at the foot of her bed. And the trunk, and all it contents, would be hers for all time, and somehow that meant Amy would be too.

She closed the lid and leaned her head against the sofa. Outside, the rain had slackened, and the sun was struggling through the cloud cover. Dr. Richardson had been right. It had helped to touch her sister this way. She felt better inside. And now she had just one more thing to do. One more task before she could close this chapter on her life and begin the next one.

Erin got up and went to the kitchen and picked up the phone.

"I'd like to speak to Travis Sinclair, please."

The guy on the other end said, "Let me check his room."

The receiver clunked down, and Erin heard him yell, "Hey, Travis, some babe's on the phone!" The sounds of the college dorm, of male voices and doors slamming, filled Erin's ear. In a few minutes the receiver was picked up, and Travis's voice said, "Yeah?"

Erin almost lost her courage. Her palms began to sweat, the receiver becoming slippery in her hand. "Travis? It—it's Erin Bennett."

There was a long pause. "Where are you?"

"Tampa. Home."

"How'd you get my number?"

"I called your mom and asked her for it."

"What do you want, Erin?"

What *did* she want? "I think I want to tell you that I'm sorry."

"Sorry about what?"

"Sorry about . . . the way I treated you, you know, last year when Amy was . . . was . . ."

"It was a hard time for all of us," Travis said quickly. "It's all right, I understand."

"And then that day we met at the mall. I'm sorry about that too."

"I probably shouldn't have spoken to you. I knew how you felt. But when I saw you, I just re-membered Amy so strong. It was like she might have been there with you."

Erin leaned against the kitchen wall because her knees were trembling. "I never should have said the things I did to you that night after the dance. I know now that you were hurting too, and I never should have treated you as if you didn't care."

"I was hurting all right," he confirmed. There was a pause before he added, "Amy used to talk about you all the time, Erin. She really thought you were something special." Erin remembered the essay Amy had written for English class about sisters, and she smiled wistfully. Travis continued. "She was always telling me what a great dancer you were and how you were going to become famous."

"She had plans to be a famous actress too, and she thought we'd work together someday." Erin twisted the cord around her finger. "We probably never would have, you know. Even if she'd lived. But Amy always planned *big*."

"I was pretty mixed up when she was in the hospital. I was mad, and I didn't know who to be mad at." Travis's voice seemed to be coming through a tunnel. "Screwy, isn't it? I've had a lot of girlfriends, but the only girl I ever wanted died." Erin felt dampness on her cheeks and wiped it away furiously. "I loved Amy, Erin. I really did."

"I know," she said. "I loved her too."

"I kept some pictures of her just so I'll always remember what that feeling was like. I'll never forget her. You gotta believe that."

"I believe you." Her voice was scarcely a whisper. "And I'm just sorry I treated you so mean. I—I guess that's all I called to say, Travis."

"Look, I'll be wrapping up exams this week, then I'm coming home. Maybe we could get together and talk."

"I'd like that. It helps to talk about her." She thought of the items Amy had saved because they came from Travis. "There were some things in her stuff you might like to have. Pennants, a necklace—stuff like that."

"Sure," he said. "That would mean a lot to me.

And—uh—thanks for calling, Erin. It always bothered me that you were so angry at me. I feel better about it now."

"So do I," she said, and she meant it.

"Well, I gotta get back to the books."

"And I've got someplace I have to go."

"Good-bye," Travis said.

"Good-bye," she told him, and hung up the phone. She took a long, shuddering breath. Her head felt light, but it didn't hurt, and the tenseness along her shoulders evaporated with a few shrugs. She felt drained, but also at peace.

Still clutching the receiver, Erin rested her forehead on the wall. She closed her eyes. "Good-bye, Travis," she whispered. "Good-bye, Amy. Good-bye."

Chapter Twenty

❧

Erin stood at the chain-link fence looking over the crowded track and infield. Banners flapped in the afternoon breeze. The biggest one read: Special Olympians—You're Winners! The infield was a jumble of athletes in gleaming wheelchairs and orthopedic braces, of bright T-shirts emblazoned with the five Olympic circles, of coaches and paramedics dressed in shorts and baseball hats.

Erin scarcely saw them. She was looking for David, knowing that even if he glanced over toward the fence, he would not recognize her. After all, he'd only seen her once in her full clown makeup.

All at once she saw him. He was making balloon animals for a group of kids swarming around him near a refreshment stand. She ambled toward him, her hands deep in the pockets of her oversize, baggy pants. She asked, "Need some help?"

"I sure do, here—" He stopped midsentence and stared at her. "Hey, I've seen you before." His brow crinkled beneath his whiteface, and his orange drawn-on mouth puckered. "Last year!" He snapped his fingers. "The Children's Home."

"Someplace else too."

"Erin?" His amazed, comical expression made her laugh out loud. "But—but—who? How . . . ? *You* were the girl who worked with me that day?"

"Yes."

"But you never said anything about it all this time."

"It's a long story."

"The girl who was supposed to appear—"

"Was Amy, my sister."

David shook his head as if to clear it. "Man, am I confused."

"I'll let you buy me dinner and explain everything after the Olympics are over today."

"But I thought you weren't coming."

"I changed my mind. And besides, some clown once told me that helping out and making people laugh makes a person feel good inside."

David came closer, ignoring the kids who began to scatter as the start of various events were announced over the PA system. "I thought you were brushing me off. After the play and all, you hardly spoke to me."

"I had a lot of things to figure out. Are we still friends?"

He smiled, and she felt as if the sun had just splashed over her. "I'll be your *best* friend." He took her hand and led her over to a grassy spot, away from the bustling activity. There he stood facing her, still holding her hand. "I got accepted to clown school for the summer."

"And I'm going to Wolftrap for sure. The scholarship's for three weeks."

"So are you all right now?"

"I will be," she said. "Our whole family's going to counseling now, and I also go to the grief support group for teens. Dr. Richardson's been urging my parents to start attending a Compassionate Friends meeting—that's a support group for parents who've lost kids."

David nodded. "I guess it helps to be with people who've been through the same things you have, huh?"

"It helps a lot."

"What about FSU in the fall?" David asked. "Will you be going there?"

Erin shook her head. "I'm going to start at the junior college, and if Dr. Richardson thinks I'm ready, I'll transfer to FSU at midterm. Otherwise, I'll transfer next fall."

"I know how much you were counting on going."

Erin shrugged. "I wasn't as ready to move away as I thought I was. Beth was excited when I told her. We're going to try to take a class together."

"I guess your parents are glad too."

"Relieved, I think. We're learning a lot about our feelings. What are you going to do in the fall?"

"I'm going to FSU to major in drama. My dad's not nuts about the idea, 'cause he really wanted me to go to law school, but I can just picture myself plea bargaining—if things got tense, I'd squirt the judge in the face with a plastic flower and get thrown out of court."

Erin giggled, and David studied her. "So when

you do get up to the campus, I'll already be there. Will you look me up?"

She sought his eyes through layers of grease-paint. "You can count on it," she said. In that moment she felt as if they were the only two people in the world, and that the sunshine and the blue sky had been created just for them.

She heard the sound of running feet and glanced away from David's eyes to see Jody run up with a friend.

"Guess who this is," David signed to his sister.

Erin awkwardly spelled out her own name, and Jody's face lit up with a grin, so similar to David's. She hugged Erin's waist.

"I think she's missed you," David said with a laugh. "She's running in a race soon and wants us to come and watch."

"Tell her I wouldn't miss it."

Jody stooped down and tugged up a handful of dandelions and shoved them toward Erin. Erin felt her breath catch and her eyes fill as she took the yellow bouquet.

"Are you crying?" David asked, incredulous.

"Tell Jody that dandelions are very special to me." Erin touched the soft yellow petals, remembering seeds floating away in the breeze at Amy's funeral. She held out her hand, carefully tucking her two middle fingers against her palm and extending her thumb, forefinger, and pinky. "I love you," she whispered.

Again Jody smiled, and the smile washed over Erin like a soothing balm. The child turned, tugged on her friend's hand, and together they darted across the field toward the track.

David said, "I don't get it. Jody gives you a bunch of raggy weeds, and you start bawling. Girls are weird."

Erin poked one of the flowers into his button-hole. "Didn't you know that girls get to cry over dumb stuff for no real reason?" She reached up and placed her palm tenderly along his cheek. "And so do clowns."